To Margaret and Peter Scott-Whyte, my parents,
with whom life was never dull.

Acknowledgements

To John, Laura and Jack Horton for golden moments. Patricia and Terry Cowan and family for large whiskies, late night brainstorming and I T support. Clare Alexander and Kate Shaw of Gillon Aitken Associates for believing in me. Ben Ball and Joanna Weinberg for early encouragement that kept me going. The staff of Plymouth Hospital School and the Young People's Centre for making work a pleasure. My pupils, past and present, who have given me many challenges and much laughter. Marie Horton for restoring order from chaos. Tavistock Hockey club for keeping me sane. Pat Gigg and Poppy for long and happy walks in the park. Kate Lyall Grant, Melissa Weatherill, Nigel Stoneman and all at Simon and Schuster for making this such fun. Mr Swallow and Mr Stanley of Maidenhall School for allowing children to keep their dreams.

Like angel visits, few and far between.
T. Campbell, *Pleasures of Hope*, 1799

Prologue

Dancing Duck Lane is no longer marked on the map, perhaps it never was, but it can still be found. From the hump-backed bridge take the road to the left and keep close to the crumbling walls that enclose the charred ruins of the Big House where the roof has long fallen in and where a descendant of the Old Bugger lives now. Magpies yammer in the overgrown kitchen gardens and the statues of the white-skinned girls lie mildewing where they have fallen in the long wet grass. Follow the curve of the river away past the lonely recreation ground. There, the ghost children turn the solitary roundabout, invisible feet kicking up the black dust, their voices rising and falling on winds that still blow up the valley from the faraway sea. Climb over the rotting stile and on past the withered tree. Dancing Duck Lane is an overgrown track leading nowhere in particular.

Only the rubble remains now of Carty Annie's tumbledown house. Dandelion clocks, stinging nettles and yellow poppies grow there in wild profusion. Stoop down and run your fingers through the damp soil and there in the black coal earth you will find the splintered remnants of tiny bones and the fragments of a hundred broken jars, jars that once held so terrible and so marvellous a secret.

3

Part One

Part One

November 1962

It was a town of lopsided old houses that stretched in terraces up the steep hills towards the restless skies. Inkerman, Balaclava, Sebastopol, and Iron Row where three-legged dogs ran amok and a mad woman swallowed live fish by the bucketful.

There was a Big House hidden away behind high walls where English people had once lived and ghosts still did. It was looked after by Mr Sandicock, a gruff-voiced old misery guts who kept to himself.

In the garden there were statues of naked girls. Sometimes, when the moon was full they came alive and danced on the satin smooth lawns. Then the waters of the fishpond would begin to stir and bubble and the slimy ghost of drowned Dr Medlicott crawled out of the thick, black water and chased them round and round the garden.

The centre of the children's world was the hump-backed bridge where they had written their names in the concrete, long before they could spell them properly.

Lorence Bevan
William Jonh Edwerds

Elizabeth Gwendlin Meredith
Elibazeth Roof Tranter

It was a town of coal tips and black-faced, whistling colliers whose boots scored bright sparks in the sloping back gwlis.

There were pubs that people were chucked out of:

the Punch
the Greyhound
the Mechanics
the Black Prince

And churches and chapels they were dragged into:

Ebenezer
Carmel
Bethesda
Saint Wilfred's
the Church of the Immaculate Contraption

There was a town clock with a bong but no tock or tick.

A Penny Bazaar
The Corn Shop
Gladys's Gowns
Three Italian café's with ice cream in silver dishes with raspberry sauce and men with gold teeth serving.
A picture house called Olympia – the Limp – a fleapit where gummy old women sucked blood oranges and soppy couples kissed.

Iffy Meredith lived in Inkerman Terrace and so did Bessie Tranter.

Inkerman was one of the Three Rows. Inkerman was almost identical to Balaclava and Sebastopol. They were terraces of small whitewashed houses built for the ironworkers hundreds of years ago. They were all owned by Rabinowicz who lived with the nobs down in Cardiff. Every Thursday he sent a man called Moany Haddock to collect the rents. Moany Haddock had bright red hair and a wrinkly old arse that squeaked when he walked.

Every house had a back door and one sash window. The backs of the houses were single-storeyed, the fronts two. The fronts looked onto a small walled garden, and a gate led into the gwli. Hardly anyone ever used the front doors, only for funerals, weddings and burglary. They lived happier coming and going through the back. From the back doors they stepped onto a communal bailey that stretched from one end of the row to the other. It was where the women washed the clothes in battered tin tubs with washing boards and Sunlight or Fairy soap, where dogs and mothers fought and stray goats and chickens came for a nosy wander.

Opposite every back door was an outside lav. They were full of lurking spiders and Black Pats the size of saucers; there was newspaper on a rusty nail and icicles in winter. Next to the lavs were the coal sheds where bogeymen and rats lived side by side in the dark.

There were buckets outside all the back doors, upturned to keep the mice out. There were tin baths on nails and big stone blocks for sharpening knives. And some of the houses had old men with cloth caps and watery eyes. They sat outside in the bailey on three-legged stools. They smoked dogends and stared ahead all day long until they were taken in at night.

The Three Rows was the poorest part of town. And the night-time in that bit of town was the worst time of all. It was a time of gaslight and candle light. A mysterious world of bat shadows and owl call, of dog bark and frog song, of black, back gwlis where ghosts and blind pirates walked at midnight. It had a milky moon of its own that spun above the hill they called Blagdon's Tump, like a plate on a conjuror's stick. And beneath the moon, Jack Look Up, who wasn't all there, poor dab, flew his red kite and cried for his long-dead son all through the night.

Wandering lunatics lived there too. Loads of them. Some of them were dangerous, and some were not. But it was hard to tell the difference until it was too late. And there were secrets in the town too, well hidden secrets. But that autumn saw the beginning of change.

It was a town where mostly it rained, but all that November impudent winds flounced up the valley stirring the leaves of the trees into a bubbling broth, snatching up washing and littering the mountain with long johns and darned stockings. The winds grew more boisterous with each day until the skinny backyard dogs were whipped to a barking frenzy and the farm dogs howled and strained on their rattling chains.

The school playgrounds puffed up with whooping children, full of argument and rude, rough talk. Full to bursting with elbowing games of slap and spit and fury.

The moon blew in each night and struggled to anchor itself above Blagdon's Tump. An alien moon, waxed with blue ice, silvered with frost. Beneath her cold glare the town slept fitfully behind groaning windows and uneasy curtains.

As autumn stripped the trees and froze the wits, a little more black coal dust was blown away and slowly but inevitably secrets came towards the light. Then the winds moved on, down the valley to the faraway sea, to stir up souls in other parts and set them on a journey.

*

Iffy Meredith lay in her big bed in the downstairs bedroom in the house where she lived with her grandparents in Inkerman Terrace. Outside the winds blew roughly and made the old house groan beneath their buffeting. The curtains shivered in the draught. The candle on the ancient tallboy flickered and ghostly phantoms danced along with the hanging bat shadows on the white, cracked bedroom walls.

Down beyond the hump-backed bridge in Carmel graveyard, the owl they called the Old Bugger hooted long and low as he hunted for chapel mice. Far away, on Old Man Morgan's hill farm, Barny the bulldog rattled his chains and bawled at the melting moon.

Iffy pulled the patchwork quilt up over her head to dampen the noises. The quilt was made from snippets of dead people's clothes. It smelled of ancient candles and incense clinging to old first-communion dresses. It reeked of curdled milk sick and wet rusks on babies' rompers. The wistful perfume of love-struck war-time girls. The hard, sharp, muck sweat of a collier's shirt.

Stealthy footsteps crossed the parlour outside her room. Iffy stiffened like a corpse. She held her breath and listened. The footsteps paused outside the door.

She bit her fist beneath the covers.

The latch on the bedroom door rattled, lifted slowly.

Iffy pushed back the quilt, heart bomping against her ribs. She smiled suddenly as Nan's face appeared round the door, bright and friendly in the glow of the candle light. Tucking-in time.

The old lady's shadow wiped the hanging bats from the walls and the writhing shadows of bogeymen slunk reluctantly away into corners.

A wisp of silvery hair tickled Iffy's nose as Nan bent over

11

to kiss her. Iffy giggled. Nan kissed her softly with a toothless kiss.

Iffy breathed in deeply the comforting smells of Fairy soap and tired old lavender that were ingrained in Nan's skin.

'Goodnight. Gobless, Iffy.'

'G'night, Nan.'

She looked very old standing there in the glimmering candle light and Iffy had a thought that she'd never had before. It was a horrible thought that grew like a snowball, gathering speed beneath her ribs, pushing up hard and painfully until it felt like a punch that knocked the breath out of her.

Nan was old. She didn't know how old, but probably old enough to die. Soon. In the night. Tonight.

And Grancha was even older.

And if he died too there would be no one left for her except a few old aunties and a cousin with shell-shock from the war. And they'd put her in Bethlehem House with the nuns who smelled of strong polish and stale wee. They'd make her wear hobnailed boots and hair shirts, eat boiled cabbage with grubs in, and swede. And go to bed with the light out.

'Don't forget your prayers mind, Iffy.'

Nan turned away from her and left the room.

The shadows snook out from their hiding places.

Iffy wanted to call her back but the door closed with a soft click.

Eyes shut tight. Hands together. She prayed:

MATTHEWMARKLUKEANDJOHNBLESSTHEBEDTHATILAYON

ANDIFIDIEBEFOREIWAKE

IPRAYTHELORDMYSOULWILLTAKE.

AREMEN.

12

She listened to the soft shuffle and scuff of Nan's slippers as she went through the back parlour, past the sideboard with the withered palm crosses and the holy pictures of miserable-looking saints. She heard the latch being lifted on the kitchen door.

Iffy pulled the pillow around her face and kept it there until it was damp from her breath, until it soaked up her hot tears. She cried until her ribs stretched and ached. She cried until her eyes were swollen and itching.

She came up for air.

The sounds of the warbling kitchen wireless travelled through the dark back parlour and seeped in under the crack of the door.

In the kitchen she knew the light would be bright and the shadows friendly. Nan and Grancha would be talking quietly, the kettle would be hissing on the hob, and there would be the chesty purr of the cat and the tick tocking of the lop-sided clock that had once been pawned.

But between her and them lay the back parlour. An eternity of blackness not to be crossed on your own in the dark. The back parlour was bad enough in the daytime. But at night! At night it was thick with the dusty taste of fear, it was ghostly and terrifying.

The night noises of the house grew louder all around her. The creak of the bed beneath her, a bed where old people had lain dying in olden times. She heard spiders uncrossing their legs in dark corners. The scurry of a Black Pat hurrying across the lino.

And then she heard THEM . . . moving around furtively in the parlour. They came every night. Creeping out from the cupboard under the stairs. They were in there now.

The high-backed wooden settle creaked under their weight. The weight of resting ghosts who smelled of moth balls and Robin starch. Sitting side by side in the dark. The

13

three of them: Grancha Gallivan who only had half a face, the other half had been melted away by a splash of red-hot metal when he worked in the iron foundry; Auntie Mary Ann, light-fingered, with one leg shorter than the other and wavy red hair down to her bum, who had died in a workhouse giving birth to a dead child; William Arthur, a big-eared boy with stiff, high collars, who was a bit of a scholar. Found dead in bed. This bed. Aged twelve. RIP.

On the sideboard in the parlour there was an empty wooden biscuit barrel and Auntie Mary Meredith had told Iffy, and she wished she hadn't, that once the lid lifted off on its own and a black hand came out and grabbed her by her rude bits.

From her photo frame high on the wall, Great Granny Gallivan, the Tartar, looked down. Her beady black eyes kept guard over the family treasures: the ugly china greyhounds with dead rabbits in their mouths that stared each other out across the mantelpiece; the picture of the bleeding heart that pumped away in the blackness, splashing blood all over the chair backs.

Whenever Iffy had to go through the parlour she avoided Granny Gallivan's eyes but they followed her, scorching holes between her shoulder blades.

She tossed and turned while outside the wind blew stronger and the dogs howled in the backyards. The clink of their chains sounded like the dance of manacled ghosts. She prayed that she wouldn't have the nightmare tonight, the worst dream of them all, when an invisible ghost baby cried in a creaking crib and the smell of a foreign perfume crept out from the walls and a dark face came close to her own speaking to her urgently in a language she didn't understand.

As the town clock struck midnight she thought of Fatty Bevan. Fatty wasn't fat, just soft and round like the pictures of cherubs in old books, only dirtier. He would be out and about now in the dark on his nightly travels. He wasn't afraid of anything or anyone. He was the bravest boy in Wales and probably the whole wide world. He would be out in the cold and the winds, alone in the pitch black, there beyond the rattling window where ghosts and blind pirates would be walking the dark gwlis of the hillside.

The windows of Edwards' bakery were lightly dusted with flour and sugar that flickered like frost in the light from the street lamp. Behind the glass of an upstairs bedroom window Billy Edwards sat on the window seat looking up at the night sky, waiting for the stars to come out. Just as soon as the first star appeared he would hold his breath and, if he could, he would hold it until he had counted a hundred stars. If he could do that, then everything would be all right. The noises in his head would disappear and he would be able to sleep.

The moon was high over Blagdon's Tump. A giant, cold moon spinning in the liquorice black sky.

As he watched, a kite crossed the surface of the moon. A big red kite the colour of fresh, warm blood, and he knew that out there in the darkness Jack Look Up held the kite strings in his bony hands and would dance in the moonlight until the cock crowed and the dawn came up the river.

Behind him in the bedroom the clock ticked loudly, its doors fast shut on the long-dead cuckoo. He thought he could hear the breathing of his older brother Johnny who slept the sleep of the dead, night after night. He looked over his shoulder into the room. His own bed was unslept in. His clothes were strewn untidily across the rush-backed chair near the door. On the other bed opposite his, his brother's clothes were neatly folded ready for when he awoke. His brother's new sandals lay side by side on the floor ready for him to step into. They were brand-new brown sandals with creamy-coloured crêpe soles and the price was still written on the bottom: fourteen shillings and sixpence.

The town clock bonged the half hour after midnight.

Still no stars.

He heard the wary tread of his father's feet as he climbed the steep stairs to bed.

Billy stayed at the window. His father wouldn't come into the bedroom. He never had in the last five years. His mother was already in bed and she only ever entered the room in the daytime.

'Goodnight, lovely boys,' his father called from the landing.

It was a tired, soft voice. Billy didn't answer. He never did. There was no reply from his brother's bed.

He heard the bed creak in the next-door bedroom, as his father sat down heavily and the clatter of the fob watch as it was laid on the dressing table.

There wasn't much time left. He looked up desperately now for the stars.

One bright star splintered the darkness way above the moon.

He breathed in deeply, the icy air filling his lungs and making him shiver.

Another star lit the sky, and another, until there were five stars in the night sky. Bright as ice. Hot as molten silver.

The sobbing began in the room next door. Growing louder.

He felt his chest expand with pain.

Once again the red kite slashed the moon. Slowly the sky filled with stars, tiny pinpricks of brilliant light.

He counted them, until his pounding head seemed full of stars. His eyes ached and his chest felt as if it would burst. The sound of his brother's breathing filled his ears and the sobbing in the next room grew ever louder until his head felt as if it would explode.

Still he held his breath and counted.

Once again the red kite danced across the moon.

Eighty nine . . . ninety.

His head began to swim, hot blood pounded in his ears.

Ninety-five.

In the glass of the window he saw the reflection of his eyes, eyes full of silver fire. Multitudes of stars now where his eyes had been. The drumming in his head grew even louder.

Ninety-nine, one hundred.

He let his breath out quickly, hot breath that steamed in the freezing air of the bedroom. He drew in great aching lungfuls of frosty air.

The sounds in his head began to melt away: his brother's breathing slowed, stopped; the loud sobs became faraway laughter.

His eyelids began to droop, covering the reflected star fire. His head was full with the sound of music now. He waved to the moon, and climbed unsteadily down from the window seat. His brother's bed was empty now, the folded clothes gone. Only the sandals remained. New sandals with the price still on the bottom.

In her pink bedroom in Inkerman Terrace, Bessie Tranter slept deeply, snoring gently into the frilly gingham pillowcase. The smell of eucalyptus and disinfectant hung in the air and a candle burned softly on the mantelpiece. In a glass cabinet near the window the faces of her foreign dolls had been turned towards the wall because she disliked the feel of their cold glass eyes on her face as she slept.

The bedroom door was ajar and beyond it her mother sat

in a high-backed chair keeping guard in case Bessie had a bad dream and called out in her sleep.

Bessie slept on, dreaming her favourite dream. She had walked down the aisle of Carmel Chapel in a fairy-tale dress. The whitest lace you ever saw. White as snow, frothy as a fountain. She carried a bouquet of red roses and gypsophilia and she lost count of the bridesmaids who tripped along behind her. The congregation sang 'All Things Bright and Beautiful'. When she stepped out of the chapel, confetti fell from the blue skies onto her shiny gold ringlets, like soft rain.

She waved gaily to the urchins of the town who had lined up on the hump-backed bridge to catch sight of her. Ragged urchins with grimy faces and running noses. The strange thing was, that among these dirty children stood Iffy, Billy and Fatty and that couldn't possibly be right because they would have been grown up like her.

Later, in the kitchen of her dreams Bessie was busy making meals for her handsome new husband. She took down plates from the plate rack, dainty plates made of rice paper. From shiny saucepans that reflected her smiling face she served mint imperials for potatoes, spearmint pips for peas, chocolate slabs for meat. She sat up at the pink and white Formica-topped table, opposite her sat her husband, his face hidden by a large newspaper. And a beautiful voice on the wireless sang 'Que sera sera, whatever will be, will be'.

Fatty Bevan listened, ears cocked for any sound. He heard the sound of his father's bed groaning under his weight, a loud curse as his feet came into contact with the icy floor, the scrape of the cracked old chamber pot as it was dragged out from under the bed. His father coughed a thick, phlegmy cough. Silence. Then came the hiss as he pissed into the pot. He pissed a river, pissed as long as the Brewery horse did. Once, Fatty had looked in the pot and it had been full to the top – a brown and frothy stench. When Fatty peed it was green like cabbage water and barely covered the bottom. The stink of his father drifted across the landing. Fatty held his breath and tried not to breathe in. He waited and listened for the sound of the front door opening. Not likely. His mother wouldn't be back until she was sure the old man was flat out. She'd still be in one of the back rooms of some pub, crying into her pint pot of cider. He waited for the sounds of heavy breathing. When he knew it was safe because his father had begun to snore, he pushed back the bleached flour sacks that acted as his sheets and blankets and felt under the bed for his sandals. His feet slipped into them like old friends. He'd gone to bed in his clothes, as he always did, ready each night to make his escape. He knelt on the bed and gently pushed up the window making barely a sound. He dared not use the stairs for fear of waking his father. He didn't want another beating. He still had wheals on his back from the last one.

He eased his small body out onto the window sill, swivelled round with the dexterity of a monkey and lay, belly down, across the sill. He manoeuvred himself until he hung from the sill by his elbows, his bare knees grazed by the rough stone walls.

He gathered his strength. This was the tricky bit. He had to heave himself up on an elbow, and pull down the window so the draught from it would not wake the old man.

One, two, three. Yes! The window slid shut without too much noise.

He took a deep breath, let go of the window sill and dropped towards the ground, pushing himself out from the wall with his feet. He turned in mid air and landed on all fours in the frost-stiffened, clumpy grass of the yard.

19

A sharp stone grazed the palm of his hand. He licked the wound and it left a smear of blood on his chin. Then he was up and away hot-footing it off down the lane.

He kept close to the high walls that surrounded the Big House and when he heard the rumble of wheels coming over the hump-backed bridge he stepped into the overgrown gateway to the gardens of the house and pressed his body deep into the shadows.

The sound of the wheels came closer and he could hear Carty Annie cursing loudly to herself.

Carty Annie fascinated Fatty. She was mad, but only with grief; she wasn't a dangerous lunatic. She was ancient, over a hundred years old people said. She was Irish and years ago she lost all her babies in one go. They got drowned in a storm in a lake in Ireland.

She had arrived in their town one day, pulling the same old cart she had now, trundling up the road that led from the faraway sea. She had moved into a tumbledown house in a place called Dancing Duck Lane and had stopped there ever since. They called her Carty Annie because she never went out without her cart. It was a wooden cart with buckled wheels and a piece of old rope for pulling. It was always full of queer old stuff that was no use to anyone: empty tin cans; clods of earth cut from the mountain; dead rabbits; jam jars; an old stone covered in green moss and slime; a cracked piss pot; a rusty tin bucket with no handle and a picture of the Pope with faded pink tinsel round the frame.

Sometimes, when the wind was in the right direction, she set up shop on the Dentist's Stone. In the olden days the dentist came on a horse and people sat on the stone to get their teeth pulled out with pliers. No gas or nothing. There were still bloodstains on the stone and marks on the ground where they'd dug their heels in deep. She told fortunes.

Free if she liked you, a tanner a go if she didn't. The queue often went right down over the hump-backed bridge almost as far as Carmel graveyard. Someone always kept an eye out for Father Flaherty and everyone scattered if he came on the scene.

Fatty never called her Carty Annie to her face, none of them did, just Old Missus. He didn't know anyone who knew her real name.

He peeped through the bushes that wrapped him round and caught a quick glimpse of her as she passed. She walked with her head bent low and as she came level with the Big House she walked in a wide arc into the road, just the way all the kids did who believed it was haunted.

He'd watched her before as she wound her way towards her cottage. He knew her habits now. If he gave it ten minutes she would be back home, she'd park the cart in the lane and would head straight to her pile of sacking in the bare back bedroom. Another five minutes and she'd be fast asleep and when she was, he was going to peer through the windows and take a good look at whatever it was she kept in there.

The moon was high over Blagdon's Tump and a candle still burned in the Old Bake House where the Tudges lived. There wasn't a Mr Tudge because he'd run away with a fancy woman from over the mountain. Lally Tudge was fat. Her sister Dylis was fatter. Mrs Tudge was the fattest. That was the rule they learned in school.

Fat. Fatter. Fattest.
Daft. Dafter. Daftest.

They didn't use the word daft much. Twp was the word they used. Twp meant not right in the head, but not dangerous. Lally Tudge was twp. Two splashes short of a birdbath. Ninepence to the shilling. No lights on upstairs. That made him smile. It was probably Lally who had the candle still burning now, too afraid to blow out the flame for fear of goblins and the sandman. He wasn't afraid of anything like that. It was the living he was afraid of: he had reason to be.

The wind was icy now and blowing much stronger. He shivered in his thin clothes and hugged himself. He waited. The Old Bugger hooted down in the chapel graveyard and the dogs in the Three Rows began to yelp and howl.

He slipped out of the shadows and walked on past the Big House. Over to his right on the lonely piece of ground they called the rec the roundabout turned slowly in the wind. He climbed the stile. No sign of Carty Annie anywhere up ahead.

The twisted branches of the withered tree were black against the sky and their shadows dripped onto the path. Once an old man had hanged himself there by his boot-laces. They had found him on Christmas morning, his arms and legs splayed out as though he were doing a star jump the way they did in games lessons at school. They had to cut him down and defrost him with a blowtorch so they could fit him in a coffin.

Fatty reached the house, which had grass and moss growing from cracks in the walls and an old bird's nest sitting on the crooked chimney pot. He stepped stealthily up to the darkened windows and pressed his small nose up against the dirt-streaked glass. His hot, loud breath made rivulets in the grime on the cracked panes as he strained to see inside.

It was too dark to see much, moonlight barely reached through the filthy windows, ice was beginning to form on the cobwebbed curtains. He took the cheap torch from his pocket, turned it on, and pointed it into the room. Its weak yellow light picked out an old table that looked as though it had a tablecloth made from clods of earth.

He jumped and nearly dropped the torch. A huge pair of glassy green and yellow eyes glared back at him from within. He steadied the torch and focussed it towards the startled eyes.

He smiled.

A scrawny tabby cat sat on the kitchen dresser, head tilted to one side looking at him curiously.

Curiosity killed the cat.

Miss Riley told them that in school. He didn't believe it. Curiosity made you learn, made you wary.

He moved the beam of the torch round the room. The cat put up its paw and tried to catch the little arc of moving light. For a few moments Fatty continued with the game, then he shone the beam higher, out of the cat's reach.

He sucked in his breath. The torch wobbled, and he had to use both hands to steady it.

A large pickling jar stood on the dresser between filthy cracked cups and leery-eyed Toby jugs. Inside the jar was the strangest sight he had ever seen.

'Fuckin' Ada!' he yelped.

He switched off the torch and fled, racing down past the withered tree, over the stile and away past the Big House without stopping once.

Spain, 1962

Agnes Medlicott woke from a deep sleep and realised that she was smiling. She lay quite still in the blissful aftermath of a lovely dream, listening to the distant chiming of the clock on the church of Santa Maria Magdalena.

She had rarely dreamed in the past ten years but tonight

she had dreamed that she was back in the Big House in Wales where she had lived for many years.

In the dream she had been standing at the window in the upstairs drawing room looking down towards the hump-backed bridge that spanned the river. It was high summer and bright sunlight came in through the open window and wrapped her in its warmth. Sunlight glinted on the white statues in the garden below and the perfume from the flowers was heady, a glorious fusion of sweet peas, stocks and roses. There were other familiar smells too, the bitter-sweet aroma of the dark coal-rich soil, the smell of the nettles down near the river.

She could hear the sound of water gurgling lazily in the river; the humming of contented bees and the querulous call of a magpie in the kitchen gardens. Most delightfully she heard the carefree shouts of her girls calling to each other playfully somewhere in the gardens below.

Now, sitting up in bed and fully awake, she thought how happy she had been to dream of the past, how enchanted she had been to find that nothing seemed to have changed about the old house. She thought sadly that she was disappointed to be awake, to find herself in her own bed in her small house in Spain where she had moved after her husband's death.

All around her the room exhaled the familiar fusty night smells that had long been her own: ancient lavender and camphor; beeswax polish and worn linen.

The window shutters were open to the night as they always were in her bedroom. Through the window she could see, above the huddled roofs of the clustered houses that a candle was alight in a window of the Convent of Santa Engracia. A wakeful nun was praying in the darkest hours. She could hear the gentle swish of the waves on the seashore and a soft breeze rattled the window. Moonlight bathed the room in a peaceful light.

Eager to return to her dreams of the past, Agnes slipped back down between the bed covers and closed her eyes, drifting easily and hopefully into sleep.

She awoke a little later in a state of absolute panic from a nightmare. Her whole body was trembling violently and her night clothes clung to her body with perspiration. Her heart was hammering painfully, every sinew in her body was taut with anxiety.

Slowly reality dawned. She told herself that it had just been a dream, a pleasant dream that had somehow evolved into a terrifying nightmare. She reached out a trembling hand for the candle on the bedside table but only succeeded in knocking it to the floor. With increasing panic she pulled back the covers and rose from the bed.

She picked up the fallen candlestick and found the matchbox. Her hands fumbled in an effort to light a match. Candle light pushed at the darkness of the room, shadows leapt, then fell, until the room was washed with an eerie light.

She felt for her spectacles on the bedside table. Hastily, she put them on.

The familiarity of the room soothed her momentarily. It was just as it always was. The rush-backed chair, the small washstand, the blue and yellow jug and bowl, the large crucifix on the flaking, whitewashed wall which loomed black as gangrene.

Her legs shook and the bones between her knees grated as she crossed the worm-chewed floorboards. When she reached the window she saw the reflection of her eyes and their intensity and brightness made her start.

Somewhere outside a dog howled, then another, until all the dogs in the village were joined in a cacophony of primeval yowling.

She heard the cock crow in the gardens of Senor Garcia's villa and the convent bell calling the nuns to prayer. The wind banged a loose shutter in a nearby house. She tried desperately to banish the memory of the nightmare, but to no avail.

She had slipped back into the first dream and found herself again in the Big House, looking out of the window down towards the river. She had stood there for a long time, so happy to be back. It was all just as she remembered it.

Then, she had turned away from the window and with absolute dismay, saw that the walls of the drawing room were charred and blackened by fire. As she looked upwards she saw that the roof was gone, there remained only fire-ravaged beams exposed to the blue summer sky.

She had turned back again to the window. Outside the sun had disappeared behind darkening clouds. The beautiful garden had, in the space of a few seconds, been transformed into a wilderness and the statues that had stood so proudly and looked so beautiful lay fallen in the overgrown grass.

She had been startled then by the sound of someone digging in the garden. She heard the harsh noise of a spade catching against stones. A figure was over near the lilac bush.

Agnes watched, transfixed with horror. Suddenly, the figure stooped towards the ground and gave a shout of alarm.

She held her breath, her heart hammering painfully. Slowly the figure stood up, turned around and looked up towards the window where she stood. It was a man, his face partially hidden by shadow, a man staring up at her with dark, accusing eyes.

She had wanted to turn away from him but she couldn't: she was numb with fear, hypnotised by his expression.

Slowly, the man looked back down towards the ground. Agnes followed his gaze.

At his feet in the damp black soil lay a broken skull. A tiny white skull. A long-buried, long-forgotten secret, or so she had thought.

Oh God! Wide awake now she began to sway backwards and forwards, clutching at the window sill for support. Outside the window, the wind had grown wild and the sound of the sea was alarming in its fury.

She knew with a terrible certainty that it was time to return and face up to the truth.

November 1962

Winter came to the town. It was the coldest winter they had known. The snow came one November night, billowing up the steep-sided valley in a freezing white mist.

Iffy woke early. She opened her eyes just a crack, then closed them quickly against the myriad coloured lights that seeped through the worn patchwork quilt: rosy pink; blue; bright gingham and dowdy Paisley; polka-dot and check.

Beyond the kaleidoscope of the quilt, the room was still and strangely silent.

Iffy sniffed the world outside the quilt. The air was sharp, freezing on her nose. She burrowed back into the warmth of the bed. Then put one ear out. It buzzed with cold. She tunnelled back into the warm again. Out again, nose first sniffing like a dog.

The smell of bacon fat slipped through the parlour and under the bedroom door, making her mouth water.

One cheek and an ear out now.

Out in the parlour the clock whirred and tinked seven tinks.

A subtle shift of the early morning light pricked at her eyes and she felt at once that somehow the world was different. An intangible difference. A faint fizzing of unexplained excitement stirred in her belly.

She left the comfort of the bed, hop-footed it across the ancient green lino that splintered beneath her small feet like thin ice. She stood shivering by the washstand. In the blue and white striped washbowl a spider was spread-eagled in ice. Milky light seeped mysteriously through the curtains. Jack Frost had worked a doubler during the night.

She pulled back the curtains. They were stiff as boards, pleated with frost, freezing to the touch. The window was frosted with diamonds and doily patterns.

She breathed hard and hot on the thickened glass and scraped furiously with her nails until her fingers turned to indigo and pink and hummed with the cold.

She saw the world through a jagged peephole. A world that had tilted overnight towards the North Pole. It was a soft smudged town now, with no hard black edges, reshaped in the dark secret hours of the night. The roofs of the houses slumbered beneath billowing snow quilts. Soft and smooth and spotless.

The rutted road was gone. In its place an ivory highway led down to the now invisible hump-backed bridge. Crystal spears dripped from the trees and the groaning guttering of the houses. Below in the valley the river was a twist of frosted glass.

She wondered if polar bears and penguins would come sliding over the Sirhowy Mountain and would there be Eskimos walking on snowshoes like tennis racquets, slipping down to the Cop to buy candles for their dinner?

She flew through the lightening parlour and into the kitchen where Nan was stoking the fire as if it were an engine on an uphill climb.

Iffy danced up and down in front of the fire.

'You'll have to hang on,' Nan said. 'You can't get out to the lav. It'll be frozen over.'

But she didn't need to wee. It was excitement that made her hop up and down. A buzzing of excitement that fizzed over the tendons at the back of her knees, like telephone messages on wires.

She drew back the bolts and opened the back door. An eye-aching white bank of snow, reaching up past her head, way up past the latch . . .

'Shut that bloody door, Iffy. You'll have the knackers off the cat.'

Sometimes Nan could be very vulgar.

No way out of the back door. There was no going anywhere. Not even to Bessie's.

No point anyway. Bessie's mam would keep her indoors for days in case she got lost forever under a snowdrift.

Billy would be snowed up in the baker's shop where even the huge red-hot ovens would fail to thaw a way out of there.

There was a scrabbling noise outside the back door, then someone cursing loudly. A fist battering at the door.

'Suffering Angels!' Nan said. 'Who in God's name would be out and about on a morning like this!'

Fatty heard his father calling out from his bedroom across the landing. 'Give us a hand with these bastard trousers.'

Fatty played with the thought of ignoring the voice and legging it out of bed and away down the stairs and out of the house.

'I know you're in there. Shift your fuckin' arse in here, boy.'

Fatty sighed, got up, slipped on his red sandals and crossed the freezing landing. He peeped through the crack

29

in the door. His father, half sat, half lay across the bed, his trousers twisted about his bloated legs. Fatty looked round the room for the belt. It was way over by the window out of harm's way. A large, brown leather belt with a spiteful buckle. He'd felt the cut of it on his skin many times.

He crept towards the bed, nerves raw. His father opened one red-rimmed eye and glared at him.

'About bastard time too.'

In a flash he'd helped the trousers up over the blue-veined legs, over the stained baggy underwear. He'd held his breath against the stink, piss and worse, beery sweat and stiffened socks.

His father coughed, spluttered, struggled to sitting.

'Give us a fag.'

Fatty picked up the packet of Players from the floor. He slipped one out. His father took it between his wet lips. Fatty flicked back the lighter's lid. He ran his thumb down the wheel, the wick lit and a warm paraffin smell filled his nostrils. The cigarette glowed in the gloomy room and his father set to with a racking cough, unable to speak.

Fatty flew while the going was good. Down the stairs and out of the door, except that when he opened the door his way was barred by a wall of white snow.

In the living room his mother was sleeping. She was still dressed in last night's clothes, her green tweed coat and a battered old fur hat. He stood looking down at her. Sleep had softened her face making it almost pretty again, like it used to be when he was little. In the good days when the old man had been away in the army. Away for so long they were able to forget he even existed. Before she drank. He touched her hand gently. It was freezing. For a second, even though she slept, she squeezed his hand, a warm little touch that reminded him of how it had once been. She was a wreck now, but he loved her, couldn't imagine how life would ever be bearable without her. He took down the heavy old army greatcoat that hung on the back of the scullery door and draped it across her, tucking it in around her body. He couldn't light a fire because the coal shed had been empty for weeks. Underneath the kitchen sink he found a box full of old clothes. He dressed as best he could and then launched himself into the drift of snow outside the door.

He grew scarlet in the face with the effort of moving through the deep snow from Coronation Row down to the road that led past the Big House. No one else was about. Despite the cold, his body was hot. He felt more alive than ever before.

He was out of the house. He'd escaped! He felt full to his skin with bursting. It was pure pleasure.

He'd seen snow before but not like this. It was bloody magic. The slag tips had been transformed into undulating hills, the rutted road was a fairy-tale highway and the tumbledown houses with missing slates and crooked chimneys were winter grottoes with pointed icicles and patterned windows.

A robin perched on the wall of the Big House. Its red breast was the only colour in the whole of the world at that moment. This new white world crackled with freshness, it smelled sweet and strange and exciting.

Smoke spiralled up from the enormous chimneys of the Big House. The smell of sausages cooking drifted over the walls and made his belly ache. It was almost a day since he'd last eaten anything. There was nothing in the pantry at home except a brown paper bag of split peas and a jar of dried-up Bovril.

It took him a good twenty minutes to climb the hill that ran alongside Inkerman and Balaclava. When he reached the steps that led down into the bailey of Inkerman he turned to look back down the valley.

The snowdrifts rolled way down past all the lonely farms and the abandoned village, probably all the way down to the sea. One day he was going to reach the sea. He was going to escape for good. He was going to stow away on a boat, travel to faraway places, and come back for his mam when he was rich. And if he could get his hands on what Carty Annie had hidden in her house he'd go as soon as possible and p'raps, if she'd come with him, he'd take Iffy Meredith too.

Iffy jumped in fright, stepped backwards in alarm and trod on the cat as a snowman came clambering over the step and into the kitchen.

The cat yowled, hissed and slunk away under the table.

'Morning, Mrs Meredith!' said the snowman.

'Suffering Jesus!' shrieked the old woman and dropped the poker with a clang.

The snowman shivered and shook until he became a mini blizzard in the doorway.

'Hiya, Iffy! Mrs Meredith!'

Fatty Bevan stepping out from the flurry. Mrs Meredith laughing. Iffy staring.

'Good God! You gave me a right turn then. You're like a bloody Egyptian mummy only more colourful. Get by the fire and warm up, you must be perished,' Mrs Meredith said.

Iffy couldn't take her eyes off Fatty. He was wrapped from head to foot in frosted bundles of woollen scraps . . . like Joseph in his coat of many colours. He wore his father's holey brown working socks pulled on over his sandals, and a pair of odd socks for gloves, one green, one maroon, both holey. His head was wrapped in an ancient flannel vest, his blue black eyes glistened through slits cut into the cloth.

He stood quivering on the coconut matting and began to

unwrap himself, layer by layer, a pass the parcel game with clothes.

Iffy watched, mesmerised. It took him ages, until at last, he stood in his khaki shorts and faded blue T-shirt, grinning at them cheerfully.

He got close to the range and soon steam oozed out from his clothes and joined up with his warm breath, hot cumulus clouds drifting up towards the ceiling.

'It took me nearly an hour to get up here. I had to dig myself out of home.'

'Why didn't you stay in the warm like normal people?' said Mrs Meredith.

'Cos it wasn't warm and I needed a pi— a pee.'

'Mind your tongue, Mr Bevan!' said Nan, but Iffy could tell she wasn't really cross which Iffy thought wasn't fair. She would have killed Iffy if she'd nearly said pee i double ess.

'See anyone else about on your travels?'

'Ay, Mrs Tudge going down the hill on skis.'

'You lying little monkey!' Mrs Meredith said laughing.

'No. Didn't see no one. You can't get up the road from town. The drifts are too big. Old Man Morgan can't get out of the farm with the milk cart and the town clock has seized up.'

'Ay, I wondered what was missing. It was the sound of the chimes. Well you'd better stay and have a bite to eat now you're here.'

Soon he was sitting in the grandfather chair, in the cosy kitchen, wrapped in one of Mr Meredith's old grey working jumpers that came down almost over his blue knees.

At the kitchen table Mrs Meredith cut thick doorsteps of bread from a Swansea batch, jabbed them on the end of the blackened toasting fork and held them close to the roaring fire. The smell of toasting bread and wetted tea filled the kitchen and mingled with the smell of dog and horse and bubble gum that steamed out of Fatty's drying clothes.

Fatty, half hidden by a mountain of toast, munched away happily, his face red and shining, his knees turning slowly from blue to pink, yellow butter running down over his chin.

'Damn!' said Mrs Meredith. 'It's a pleasure to see you eat, boy! Our Iffy eats like a bloody sparrow!'

Iffy nibbled toast and pulled a face behind her nan's back.

Fatty wolfed down four pieces of toast on the trot before he spoke.

'The drifts outside the Big House are up to the top of the gates. It'll take that Mrs Medlicott a week to shovel her way out.'

The toasting fork dropped from Mrs Meredith's hand and clattered to the stone floor. 'Mrs Medlicott! What do you mean Mrs Medlicott?' she said.

'The woman from the Big House,' said Fatty through a mouthful of toast.

'But Lawrence, Mrs Medlicott moved away years ago. Abroad somewhere. She's probably been dead this long time!'

'Well, then she was a healthy-looking ghost when I seen her.'

'Seen her? Don't be so daft, boy!'

'I'm not being daft. I seen her. Honest to God.'

'Where?' Her voice was a breathy whisper.

'Last night.'

'Last night!' She echoed his words.

'Ay, old Gravelwilly, sorry, Mr Sandicock brought her in a big black car.'

'What time was this?' Mrs Meredith asked and sat down suddenly with a sound like the air rushing out of water wings.

''Bout five o'clock yesterday.'

She wiped her eyes on the skirt of her faded old pinafore.

'It couldn't have been her, she wouldn't come back here.'

'Are you crying, Nan?' Iffy asked staring at the old woman's face.

'Don't be so soft, Iffy. Crying! Just the heat from the fire making my eyes run, that's all. What did she look like, Lawrence?'

'Old. Oh and posh. She had a hat, a black hat with net on the front of it. She was wearing a big fur coat. And she had a big hooky nose like a witch.'

Mrs Meredith stared at Fatty but didn't speak. She closed her eyes, the veins on her eyelids were pale lavender. Her knuckles whitened as she pushed down hard on the wooden arms of the chair as though she were about to stand up.

Fatty helped himself to another piece of toast.

Iffy kept count. Five.

Mrs Meredith stayed sitting, rocking backwards and forwards in the chair.

The gaslight popped. The fire roared up the chimney.

Beneath the table the cat rasped and purred.

'They say she's come back to live here,' said Fatty, licking butter from his grubby fingers.

Mrs Meredith stopped rocking and opened her eyes. Blue eyes swimming beneath a cloudy film of water.

'Who says?'

Her voice sounded as if it came from somewhere far away.

'I can't remember who told me.'

Iffy watched her nan's face with interest. It was as though someone had dipped a paintbrush in water and diluted the deep pink of her cheeks and the dark blue of her eyes, until she was a faded picture of her real self. Mrs Meredith coughed, stood up and poured herself more tea. Her hand shook and the cup rattled against the saucer. She spooned three spoons of sugar into her cup, which Iffy thought was strange as she normally took none.

'I wouldn't like to live in the Big House,' Iffy said. 'It's haunted!'

'Don't talk so daft, Iffy!'

Iffy wrinkled her nose and thought better of arguing for once. It *was* haunted though. All the kids knew that. When it was dark they never walked past the gates in case long hairy arms came out and grabbed them. They stepped out into the road and walked in a wide half circle. Except for Fatty of course who wasn't afraid of anything.

'The ghost of old Dr Medlicott comes out of the pond when the moon is full,' said Fatty.

'Don't be so silly!' Mrs Meredith banged down her cup and went into the pantry.

She stood in the icy room and leant her back against the wall trying to get her breathing under control and stop her heart from beating so fast. She felt in the pocket of her pinny for the bottle of pills. With fumbling fingers she opened the top and tipped out a small pink pill. She popped it in her mouth and swallowed. He must have got it wrong. He could be a fanciful little fellow. He'd say anything bar his prayers would Lawrence Bevan. Agnes Medlicott would never have come back after all this time. She took down the medicinal whisky from the shelf, filled the cap and drank it down. Beyond the door she could hear the children talking.

'They say he chopped a girl's head off and she comes back to look for it,' said Fatty.

'Don't, Fatty! It gives me the shivers just thinking about it. He kilt himself, didn't he?'

Fatty nodded and grinned. 'Yep. Drowned himself in the fishpond!'

Mrs Meredith came back into the kitchen and sat down at the table.

Fatty glanced up at her. Her eyes were red as though she'd rubbed them too hard, or had been cutting up onions.

'Why did he drown himself?' Iffy asked.

'Because the girl he loved, loved someone else.'

'Who was she?' said Iffy her eyes bright in the glow of the firelight.

'A foreign girl. She had a baby in the home for bad girls. She gave it away.'

Mrs Meredith banged her cup down hard on the table and tea slopped over the side into the saucer, strong dark tea made with Fussell's milk.

'Whoever told you that! That's a load of old nonsense. Nobody had a baby! Nobody! That's just nasty old gossip.'

'Sorry, Mrs Meredith. I was only saying what I heard.'

'Oh forget it . . . that's enough talk of ghosts and daft old stuff. Who's for a game of cards? Go and fetch them, Iffy.'

The playing cards were kept in the right-hand drawer of the sideboard in the back parlour. Iffy hated going into the back parlour on her own so she dragged Fatty with her.

Together they stepped from the warm glow of the kitchen into the gloom and fustiness of the parlour.

'Who's that?' Fatty said.

Iffy jumped.

'Where!'

He pointed up at an enormous sepia photograph of an old woman that hung on the wall.

Iffy breathed with relief.

'Oh, it's only my nan's mam's mam.'

'Ugly old cow, ent she?' said Fatty.

'Shhh!' Iffy giggled, and put her finger to her lips. 'She swam all the way over from Ireland.'

'Why?'

'They ran out of potatoes.'

'By the size of her she probably ate them all.'

'Hush up! My nan'll hear you.'

'What's that, Iffy?'

Fatty pointed at an old green glass bottle at the back of the sideboard.

'Holy water,' she said.

'Oh.' He sounded bored.

'It can do miracles though.'

'Don't be daft!'

'It can. Come on, let's go.'

She didn't want to hang around in the parlour a minute longer than she had to. She pulled open the drawer in the sideboard, snatched up a packet of cards and dragged Fatty back into the kitchen.

'It can, can't it, Nan?' she said.

'It can what?'

'Your bottle of holy water can do miracles.'

'Well, it cured Mrs Bunting's warts when nothing else would shift them . . . she'd tried everything. And Auntie Blod down the valley's shingles . . . And Auntie Mary Johanna had the baby she'd always wanted.'

Fatty winked at Iffy over his seventh piece of toast.

She knew what he was thinking. She shook her head.

'My dad brought it back from abroad, didn't he, Nan?'

'Ay, he did, Iffy, God rest his soul . . . that bottle is all that we have left of him. Now who's going to shuffle?'

Spain, 2003

The clock on the ancient church of Santa Maria Magdalena clattered out the hour, and the dusty pigeons perched between the sleepy gargoyles woke from their early siesta and flew in disarray above the square.

Will Sloane crossed the baked dust of the road, on his way to the clinic on the Avenida de Los Angeles for his appointment with the heart specialist.

The air was still, the heat overwhelming. For months now there had been no respite from the sun. He wiped the sweat from his brow and winced as the pulse in his head hammered into a headache.

Then, far away, thunder rolled over the mountains and a cool wind stirred the plane trees above his head and suddenly the rain came. A delightful, torrential cloudburst turning the walls of the church to the colour of dried blood. The gargoyles began spurting cascades of frothy water onto the scurrying people below.

He would have liked to stand beneath the downpour, enjoying the feel of cool rain on his face but, not wishing to arrive for his appointment soaked to the skin, he hurried into the nearest small café for shelter, where the rain was diluting glasses of red wine left on the outdoor tables to pink.

He ordered a hot chocolate and a sugary *churros* ignoring the fact that he was meant to be on a strict low-fat diet. Somehow he knew that whatever he ate now wasn't going to make a lot of difference. Seeing an abandoned newspaper on the next table and catching a glimpse of the headlines, he gave up on his dietary thoughts, leant across, picked up the newspaper and unfolded it. The headline read:

SKELETON OF A YOUNG CHILD FOUND.

His attention was immediately aroused. Old policemen never die, he thought with a smile, and read on with growing interest.

> Builders renovating an old villa
> yesterday discovered a skeleton thought
> to be that of a child aged between eight
> and ten years old. Francisco Martinez,

aged eighty-nine, who has lived in the village all his life recalled that a child went missing when he was himself a young boy. A lad called Pedro . . . The search had lasted for weeks but the body was never discovered. At the time it was presumed that the boy had drowned as there had been several days of heavy rain and the local river was swollen. There were tales too that gypsies had kidnapped the child . . .

Will sighed. Weren't there always such stories when children went missing? Gypsies came in for a lot of unwarranted stick and from what he'd seen they always had enough kids of their own, no need to steal any.

He read on avidly,

The small skeleton had been buried beneath the kitchen floor of the villa. Senor Martinez went on to say that many of the villagers thought the disappearance suspicious at the time, and now more than eighty years later they had been proved right. 'Even though the murderer can't be brought to justice, it shows the truth can't be buried forever.'

Will drained his cup of chocolate, ate the last morsel of *churros*, licked his fingers and garnered the last grains of sugar from the plate. He folded the newspaper in half and slipped it in his pocket.

Outside the rain had stopped. The dark clouds had moved on and the sun burned fitfully above the church. His mind, abandoning the newspaper story of the skeleton, was roving back over events that had happened nearly forty years ago. He was thinking of a case that he'd been involved in back in the Welsh valleys, the only major case which he'd been unable to solve. And after all these years he realised that it still rankled with him that they'd never had a definite suspect, never been able to bring anyone to book. They had never found the missing child, alive or dead.

He supposed that nowadays it would have been different, with all the DNA tests and scientific methods they might have made more headway. But even then without a body it would have been nigh on impossible to prove anything substantial.

It must have been murder of course. Kids didn't just disappear off the face of the earth.

Will stepped out of the café and turned into a narrow alleyway, a short cut he'd taken many times since he'd lived in this northern Spanish town.

The dreary houses on either side of the dark alley were crushed up too tightly together. They had blistered paintwork, crumbling masonry and splintered shutters. And yet, as he looked upwards towards the crack of blue sky above, he was taken aback. He'd never really taken much notice of the place before, now he was amazed by the beauty of it.

Despite the fact that sunlight would hardly ever penetrate this dark backwater, high above his head there were glorious splashes of colour everywhere, the rusting balconies were bedecked with vivid scarlet and orange flowers. Startling hues in the dusky gloom. Burgeoning clusters of the deepest purple bougainvillaea, the agonising beauty of damp violets, trailing from pots and jars of all shapes and sizes.

He stood pondering the extraordinary sight for several moments. He'd always considered himself an observant man and yet somehow he'd walked through the alley with tunnel vision, never paused before or looked skywards. It just showed

41

that you could miss things under your nose, or in this case above it. He walked on, stopping in front of a small dusty-windowed junk shop optimistically bearing a faded sign in Spanish, ANTIGUEDAD.

A faded notice on the door read *Cerrado*. Shut.

He'd often walked past this shop, too, without ever giving it a second thought. Now, however, he peered curiously through the bleary window. The shop held little in the way of antique treasures, it was full of worthless old junk, cluttered with piles of rubbish festooned with cobwebs and dead flies. There was a pair of rusted, dented candlesticks, with thick wax encrusted on the twisted stems. Wicker baskets held an assortment of chipped crockery and yellowing table linen, nothing of any historical or aesthetic interest at all.

Except for one thing. Will's eyes were drawn to something at the back of the haphazard display. He stared in fascination at the statue of a young child. Beneath years of dust and grime the young face stared fearlessly out at the world. The immense skill of the sculptor had imparted a glimpse of unbridled glee about the partly opened lips, an undiminished optimism in the tilt of the head. The dimpled arms were outstretched, palms turned upwards. It was a child with the chubby limbs of a Renaissance cherub. The tiny toes, one of which was broken off, were curled in an ecstasy of delight.

It was the only treasure among the rest of the dross, and whoever had made it had worked with tremendous skill and devotion, with an absolute love of their craft.

Intrigued and wanting to get a closer look, Will tried the handle of the door but it was locked, indeed it looked as though it hadn't been opened in a very long time. He stared at the statue again, mesmerised. It was quite remarkable! How it came to be among all this rubbish he couldn't imagine. Then something stirred in his mind. His thoughts were drawn back for the second time that morning to the past. Dear God! It seemed that everything he saw today reminded him of that bloody case!

For a moment he was transported back to the Welsh valleys. A hot afternoon when he'd gone to visit one of the witnesses, one of the last people to see the child alive. She was an elderly woman who had lived in a big house overlooking the river. He'd sat talking to her in the garden, a most beautiful garden. The lawns had been mown to perfection; all around them had been the soothing sound of falling water from a hidden fountain. The humming of contented bees, the sharp heady smell of nettles, and the bitter-sweet smell of the black coal earth. And there in that garden there had been a collection of the most delightful statues, each as breathtakingly beautiful as the one in this dirty old shop.

In his mind's eye he could picture the old woman quite clearly, but as much as he racked his brains he couldn't for the life of him remember her name. Damn it! He hated it when his memory failed him. He knew it would plague him all day and probably half the night too. If her name didn't come to him eventually, he'd have to dig out his old police notebooks and look it up.

The hand of a master had sculpted the statues in that garden, like the one before him now. He remembered that he'd been flabbergasted when she'd told him that she was the artist, the sculptor of all those wonderful figures. She'd told him too, that she'd lived for many years in Spain. And that must be the answer to this mystery before him now. He knew that this statue was without a doubt one of hers. He'd put money on it.

Will checked his watch, he'd have to step on it a bit to get to the clinic on time. He took a last look at the statue and smiled sadly to himself. He would have loved a child of his own. It was the greatest sadness of his life that he and his wife had not been blessed with children, but fate had decided otherwise and nothing could change that.

As he walked on his way to the appointment, his thoughts turned again to home. Home! It was funny how he still thought of it as home even after all these years.

He'd moved away from Wales after he'd retired from the police force. He'd sold his house in Cardiff and travelled around Spain and France for almost a year. Eventually he'd found this town and decided it was a place where he could spend the rest of his days. He'd settled down in a waterfront apartment, learned Spanish, made a few acquaintances and he had never had the urge to go back. Until now. Looking at that chipped statue had for some reason disturbed him. It had evoked such vivid memories of his homeland. For the first time in all the long years away he felt an inexplicable and immense feeling of homesickness.

He couldn't get the statue out of his mind. Something about it had unnerved him. It had stirred up all kinds of long-buried memories, fragments of half memories, but for the life of him he couldn't think what significance they held.

After the excitement of the first days of snow, things went downhill fast. Mrs Tudge came out of the Old Bake House and took a tumble.

'Apex over base,' said Bessie Tranter.

'Arse over tit,' said Fatty.

She slid on her big fat bum all the way to the bottom of the hill and knocked over Moany Haddock.

'Sent him flying,' said Bessie.

'Came a right fuckin' cropper,' said Fatty.

It took two big men and the Brewery horse to get her on her feet and a half pint of brandy to get her moving again. Moany Haddock had to get himself up. Nobody would help the rent man.

The town set to with a vengeance and dug its way out of the snow and struggled to get back to normal. The steps and paths lost their beautiful whiteness, they were spoiled, blackened with warm fire ashes to stop people slipping.

The shops opened again for trade. The smell of hot new bread, doughnuts and custard tarts wafted up from Billy Edwards' dad's shop. The caretaker stoked up the school boilers, cleared the playground of ice, and defrosted the bell and the teachers, and the doors, to the children's dismay, reopened for learning.

Bessie was kept at home for two whole weeks with her chest being bad. They only got to see her through the window. They took turns standing on a bucket mouthing and waving. Mrs Tranter wouldn't have anyone in giving her germs, especially that filthy Bevan boy.

Behind the window Bessie was like the Queen of Sheba, propped up with fluffy pillows, drowning under comics and colouring books, chocolate and Lucozade.

Each morning Iffy was pushed out of the back door, muffled up against the biting cold. She met up with the boys down at the hump-backed bridge. Iffy and Billy wore balaclavas and itchy woollen mittens, mufflers and horse liniment. Their chapped lips were glued together with Vaseline. Goosefat stuck their vests fast to their aching ribs. Fatty still wore his khaki shorts and sandals, topped off with an old army jacket. The icy winds whipped up the valley and tore at Iffy's and Billy's school macs until their bare knees were chapped and sore and tingled all day long in the chalky sour-milk heat of the schoolroom. Chilblains hammered at all their toes and their ears were furnaces of icy pain.

The snow quilts slid down the roofs and were never again as beautiful as they had been that first morning.

The town clock stayed stubbornly silent.

Fatty was right about Mrs Medlicott coming back to the Big House. At night, from the upstairs bedroom window

Iffy watched the smoke spiral up from the long-disused chimneys and saw the electric lights burning behind the big arched windows. And Nan, catching her looking, told her to stay right away from there because Mrs Medlicott was a dangerous old woman who couldn't be trusted where babies and young children were concerned.

The town tipped towards Christmas.

The shops filled up with mountains of sultry tangerines and polished chestnuts, dusty brazil nuts, cob nuts, wrinkled walnuts, almonds, sticky dates, boxes of cheese footballs and Pompadour fans. Selection boxes and comic annuals tantalised them from the newsagents' windows. The lights in the butcher's blazed until late into the night. Bleary-eyed rabbits dangled on cold hooks. Goose-pimpled turkeys hung head down in the windows.

In the Penny Bazaar battered boxes of tired-looking crackers were stacked from floor to ceiling. Paper snowmen with concertina'd legs danced in the icy draughts when the door was opened.

The town clock sprouted holly and behind the back of the Mechanics, Dai Full Pelt sold turkeys with three legs.

Georgie Fingers built a grotto in his house and dressed up as Father Christmas. There was no charge to sit on his knee under the mistletoe and take a present from his sack, but no one did. Except Lally Tudge.

Every year Jack Look Up was the first person to put a Christmas tree in the window of his house at the end of Inkerman Terrace.

'God love him,' said Mrs Meredith as she and Iffy passed the house. 'I can see him now, as if it was yesterday, lifting up his boy . . . beautiful little fellow, only a nipper then he was – no mother, she died giving birth to him – his little hand stretching up to put the fairy on the top.'

And every year since Jack had buried his son, he had decorated the tree the same as he'd always done.

After school Iffy and Fatty stood outside his house for ages looking at the tree. It was the most beautiful tree they had ever seen. It was darkly green and mystical. There were tiny red candles in silver holders that Jack lit with a shaking taper as the day turned to dusk.

They watched the bright dancing flames, flickering in the twilight, lighting up the gloom of the damp bailey. Each branch of the tree was draped with tinsel, shimmering silver and gold. There were shiny baubles that reflected their wide-eyed faces. There were lanterns and chocolate decorations wrapped in foil paper. And a fairy on the top with a sparkling wand and no knickers. A fairy whose eyes shone and winked wickedly in the twinkling light of the candles.

It was magic that tree. A wishing tree.

Time after time they stood together on the bailey looking up at Jack's tree, stamping their feet to keep warm.

'I wish,' Iffy said, 'I wish I wasn't a norfan.'

'I wish I was,' said Fatty.

Iffy stared at him with disbelief. 'Fancy saying a thing like that!'

'Well, just half an orphan then.'

'You can't be half an orphan, Fatty.'

'I'd like it to be just me and my mam . . .'

He never talked much about his dad. Iffy knew that his dad beat him with a stick, so bad once that his T-shirt stuck to his back with dried blood. She'd seen the marks. Red and purple wheals.

Mrs Bevan was famous for being about the pubs all hours of the day and night. She drank like a fish, only cider not water. Fatty's dad had never done a full day's work in his life since he'd left the army.

47

'Make another wish, Iffy.'

'It's the same. I just wish I had a mam and dad. I've never even seen them only in photographs.'

There wasn't even a proper photograph of her mother, just a cutting from the newspaper with a blurry picture of a woman who looked as though she's been startled by the flash of the camera.

'If I can't wish to be an orphan, then I wish I had a dog,' said Fatty longingly.

'Wishes don't come true though,' she said.

'They might,' said Fatty, and winked.

The fairy on the tree winked wickedly back.

Will Sloane was dying. Time was running out fast, of that there was no uncertainty, uncertainty lay only in knowing how long he had left. At his appointment at the clinic, the solemn-faced specialist had confirmed what deep down Will had known for many months.

Dr Garcia had shrugged uncomfortably when Will had asked him how long he might expect to live. 'Days? Weeks?' Will had asked.

'A twelvemonth at the most,' Dr Garcia had replied quietly, avoiding Will's eyes.

Will needed to get his life, what was left of his life in order. He had always been an extremely practical man, a logical man with a dislike for disorder of any sort. After seventy-odd years he had little to show in the way of possessions. He was not a sentimental man and he had kept few reminders of the past. He acted swiftly. He put his apartment up for sale. The proceeds would go to his favourite charities for he had no living family.

Looking round the comfortable apartment he decided that the furniture could be easily disposed of. There were a few good-quality pieces that he would offer to neighbours. The rest, along with his clothes, he would leave at the local animal charity shop run by two retired English schoolteachers. His few personal effects he would sort through and dispose of. And then he was going back home to die.

He had always planned to live out his days in Spain but now that he knew those days were numbered, that time was ticking away too quickly, he made other plans. The feeling of homesickness he had experienced that day outside the junk shop had grown and he knew that he had to go back. He had a terrible yearning to see his homeland for the last time, to smell the sweet smell of coal, to feel the incessant soft rain on his skin. To stand in the twilight and watch the green hills turn to violet, to watch the big cold moon rise over those darkened hills.

As Will busied himself with sorting and clearing, despite his efforts to put it from him, the memory of the statue in the dusty antique shop would not leave him. Disconcerting thoughts about the unsolved case were never far from his mind and kept intruding upon his daytime reveries.

The guest bedroom was the last room in the apartment that he had to clear. He found his collection of old case notebooks in a cupboard. He had always been a meticulous taker of notes. These would be of no use to anyone else so he set them aside on the bedside table ready for disposal. On the top shelf of the cupboard, pushed to the back he found an old chocolate box. He lifted it down, sat on the bed and prised open the lid.

He had forgotten all about the box, it must have been years since he'd last opened it. An envelope lay on the top. It had once been dark brown but was faded now with age; there were a couple of photographs inside. He slid them out carefully. A black and white picture of him and his wife taken on their wedding day. Two hopeful young faces looking at the camera. She was laughing, holding tightly onto his arm, a horseshoe on a ribbon dangling from her small hand . . .

Christ! Within five years of this photograph being taken

she was dead and buried. And soon, soon he would be joining her . . .

The second photograph was one of his wife, taken standing alone on a beach. In the background he could see children playing down at the water's edge, the funnel of a ship in the distance. At her feet lay an overturned bucket, a spade and a crushed sandcastle. He turned the photograph over. She had written, 'Alone again. Barry Island 19—' The date had been erased by time. No doubt he'd been too busy on a case to go with her, he'd been busy on too many cases as far as his marriage was concerned. He'd been on a case the night she'd been taken ill.

He threw the photograph down with a violence that surprised him. That was the official line. He'd said it so many times he'd almost come to believe it. He'd been on a case the night she'd been taken ill. It was a lie! A lie he'd grown to believe. He hadn't been on a case, he'd been with another woman, a woman he hardly knew, and he still hadn't forgiven himself. And soon, soon he would be laid to rest, if that were the right word, in the black soil on a windy Welsh hillside.

Next he picked up a moth-eaten, faded velvet pouch that his mother had given to him on his tenth birthday. It had once been a glorious scarlet colour. He pulled apart the shrivelled strings that drew it together and tipped it up. Five alley bompers clattered into the palm of his hand.

Alley bompers! These had once been his pride and joy. Five large silver metal marbles, the king of marbles in his youth.

He lifted a sheet of yellowed tissue paper that disintegrated at his touch. Underneath it lay a battered book, the faint gold writing on the spine almost obliterated. He opened it up and the musty smell of bygone years pervaded the room. It was a copy of *Hamlet*. He was quite sure it wasn't one of his own books. He had boxed those up and they were ready to go to the charity shop. He couldn't work out how this book had got into the box or where it had come from. He turned a yellowing page. It was a library book and the date stamp declared it to be nearly fifty years overdue. He made a rough mental calculation of the fines due. Well, he made his mind up that as he was going back to Wales, he'd return the book!

He turned it over in his hands. Something was niggling him about it. He closed his eyes for a moment and let his mind wander. He had a vague recollection of standing in a bedroom opening a box. He'd been with Sergeant Rodwell. That was it! They'd been searching the missing child's bedroom. He'd stood looking down at this book for a long time and wondering, then he'd slipped it into his jacket pocket thinking that it must have some significance, some bearing on the case, only he hadn't been able to work out what it was.

He laid the book down and lifted out a card. It was a funeral card, the type mourners attached to wreaths and flowers. His hands began to shake as he turned it over and read the smudged words written on it in a childish hand.

Then he picked up another photograph. Four faces looked out at him from across the chasm of many years. Four young faces captured for posterity in a black and white photograph.

He picked up the rolled-up poster from the box. He slid his finger inside the rubber band that held it together and it perished beneath his touch. He unrolled the poster carefully; it had been made by enlarging the original photograph. Thousands of posters like this one had been pinned on lamp posts and in shop windows from Land's End to John o' Groats. Three of the faces in the photograph had been deliberately blurred, but the fourth face was ringed in black. Beneath the photograph, the faded writing read, HAVE YOU SEEN THIS CHILD?

And in almost forty years no one ever had . . .

Over the past days he had become fixated with this case. He supposed it was because he was a rational man and his mind was trying to tidy up unfinished business before he died.

It was pointless though even thinking about it. It had all happened such a long time ago. It was ancient history. An unsolved crime like hundreds of other unsolved crimes. Dead and buried. Yet he knew he had never really let it go. He supposed he had kept all these things, these sad mementoes of a lost life because it was the one mystery that still intrigued him. He knew – he'd always known – that there was something that he had overlooked. Something that had probably been staring him in the face.

He was going back to Wales, going back to die but, before he did so, he had to go over everything about this case. He was determined that at long last he would try to lay this mystery to rest. He replaced everything carefully in the box, stood up wearily from the bed and picked up his old notebooks from the table.

As the sun went down and coloured the room with an eerie orange light, he sat back on the bed and slowly turned the pages of one of the notebooks, pages that were as thin and crisp as onion skins. Sitting in the growing darkness he became immersed again in the past, a past he couldn't let go of.

The moon was high and full above Blagdon's Tump, the air was spiked with danger. Far away Iffy heard the clop of horse's hooves somewhere on a lonely road. She looked around fearfully but the road was empty, glistening with powdered ice. Behind the high forbidding walls the Big House was a moving shadow, with smoke drifting up from the chimneys.

The smoke was different to their smoke. Wood smoke. Apple and pine. The chimneys of the town breathed coal. Fossil and dinosaur.

She thought of the pond in the garden. She hoped the ice was thick. A thick stopper of ice keeping the lid on him. The twisted old body of dead Dr Medlicott beginning to stir as the moonlight filtered through the black oily waters of the fishpond.

She climbed carefully down over the river bank. The ground was rutted and frozen beneath her wellingtons and the stiffened clumps of grass crunched noisily. She stepped warily into the blackness under the hump-backed bridge.

Silence.

Her heart was loud in her ears and she felt it battering through her skin against her vest.

'Pssst!'

'Shit!'

She jumped in fright. Torchlight hit her in the eyes. She put up her hands against yellow glare.

'Bloody hell, Fatty! You frightened the life out of me! I could have peed myself.'

Fatty's laughter echoed eerily underneath the bridge.

'Have you brought it with you?'

'Yep.'

'Gis a look then.'

Carefully, she pulled the green glass bottle out of the pocket in the lining of her gabardine mac.

Fatty shone the torchlight on the bottle. The green glass glowed in the circle of yellow light.

'It doesn't say holy water on it.'

'No, but it says Lords, only the French can't spell. See. L O U R D E S.'

She knew all about Lords. It was a place you could go to play cricket or else get cured.

'Go on then, I dare you to use some, Iffy!'

'No! I only said you could look at it.'

'If you did, miracles might happen, your wish might come true.'

'You can't wish dead people alive again, Fatty.'

'Well, wish for something else then.'

'But you've got to have something wrong with you for it to work.'

'No you haven't. That woman . . . Auntie Mary Johanna, the one who wanted a baby . . . she got what she wanted.'

'I don't want a baby.'

'You don't have to have a baby. If it can magic up babies it can probably do puppies and monkeys and other stuff too.'

'No!'

'You just drink a bit and wish for something . . . like a wishing well.'

'Drink it! You don't drink holy water.'

'But it'd probably work quicker if you drank it, like syrup of figs.'

'No, Fatty!'

It was freezing under the bridge. Icy air oozed out from the old stones and damp cold seeped up through her wellies, on up her legs right up to her ears. Goose-pimples erupted like volcanoes on her flesh. She shivered, her knees knocked with cold and fright.

'Go on, Iffy.'

She shook her head. She couldn't drink holy water. It was a sin. A huge one.

'No, my nan will kill me,' she said through chattering teeth.

'How will she know? You can fill it up with river water and put it back.'

'Not on your nelly! Anyway, the river's all froze up.'

'Double dare you, Iffy Meredith.'

Her heart was a battering ram against her ribs.

'We can't, Fatty! We'll get into trouble.'

'No one will know.'

'*No!* God'll know.'

'What's he going to do? Drop a rock out of the sky and flatten us?'

'He might!'

'Double, double dare!'

'No! Just a smell that's all you're getting.'

The sound of the ancient cork popping out of the bottle echoed loudly under the arch of the bridge.

Iffy looked round, fear shooting up her backbone like pins. 'Fatty, I can hear someone. Listen.'

But there was no sound except her breathing, fast and heavy, making smoky clouds. Fatty swung the torchlight around in the darkness. Iffy was sure she saw a hunch-backed shadow moving across the arch of the bridge.

'There's nobody here, only us. Go on, Iffy, just have a sip.'

'No.'

'Cowardy, cowardy custard. Dip your teeth in mustard,' sang Fatty.

She glared at him and shook her head angrily.

'Just a smell, then,' he said.

'Nope.'

'Yellow belly. Yellow belly.'

'I am not!'

'You are too!'

'Not!'

'You're like Bessie . . . she's afraid of everything.'

'I am not!'

'Prove it then.'

'Why should I?'

'No reason. See you, then.'

He moved away towards the far end of the bridge taking the torchlight with him.

The Old Bugger hooted in Carmel graveyard.

'Fatty! Don't go. Look!'

She swigged from the bottle and choked. The holy water tasted stale and salty on her tongue, not how she imagined holy water would taste.

It'd be Fatty's fault if she started growing wings or horns. Then her nan would guess what she'd done and she'd kill her . . . what if a baby came out of her bum?

She wiped her mouth angrily with the back of her hand and glared at him.

'Quick. Make a wish,' said Fatty.

She closed her eyes and wished. A very secret wish. A scary wish. Once she'd made it, she wasn't so sure she wanted it to come true.

Fatty grinned at her, his eyes shining in the torchlight.

She passed the bottle to him and he handed her the torch.

He raised the bottle to his lips, tilted back his head and swigged long and hard. The precious water glugged down his throat.

'That's enough, Fatty!'

Then he did something worse than swallowing it: he spat. He spat out a stream of holy water! An arc of bottled holiness rose in the air and splashed down all over his holey sandals.

'Bloody hell!' he yelled. 'It's horrible! It tastes like . . . tastes like . . .'

'Tastes like what?'

'Like . . . like Father Flaherty's piss.'

Iffy gasped. She was too shocked to laugh. Hearing Father Flaherty's name said in the same breath as the filthy word piss made her head spin. She stared at him. She couldn't believe he'd said such a thing about a priest. He was mad. Dangerous. A bloody lunatic.

He began to dance round and round in the flickering light.

'Stop it, Fatty!'

But he wouldn't stop.

'Father Flaherty's wee wee . . . Father Flaherty's piss piss,' he sang.

'Pack it in, Fatty!'

He was making her afraid, but there was no stopping him. On and on he sang until the air underneath the bridge was a mangled echo of his filthiness.

He handed the half-empty bottle back, took the torch from her and tucked it into the side of his balaclava.

He held out his hands for Iffy's. She shook her head and held them tight behind her back. Daft as a bloody brush he was, but it was hard to ignore his laughter. It was catching.

She gave her hands to him, together they danced round and round and the torchlight bobbed up and down.

The soft patter of Fatty's crêpe-soled sandals was like rain on the smooth worn stone. Iffy's wellies were noisier, slip-slap slopping.

And as they danced she played silently with the word piss in her head. From a wicked thought the word grew until it was vibrating on her lips. Slowly she formed it into a whisper. 'Ppppppppp . . .' Louder. 'Pi pi pi . . .' A whispering hiss, slipping over her warm tongue, buzzing on her hot lips, a burning, fizzing rapture of filthiness. 'PISS PISS PISS PISS PISS PISS PISS PISSSSSS.' Her ears hummed and scorched with the sound of her daring.

Fatty's hands were sizzling in hers. His fingers were soft as warm toffee. Wicked as worms.

The bridge echoed and reverberated with the terrifying awfulness of their words.

Over in the Big House a dog began to bark.

From above their heads there came a loud crack, a splintering sound.

God! Paying them back. They stood quite still, their breath coming hot and fast.

Blood raced round and round Iffy's body, her head swam with giddiness.

The echoes died away.

Fatty let go of her hands. She felt the warmth in them die. He shone the torchlight on the roof of the bridge.

GEORGE LOVES BRIDGET

CM LOVES EVO

EVO LOVES CM

LB 4 eGM

MERVYN PROSSER IS A FAT BAS . . .

The torchlight flickered and died.

Their hands joined again in the blackness. There was silence except the sound of their breathing.

Then there was another loud crack. They clutched at each other. An icicle broke away above their heads. It fell from the roof, missing them by inches. Splintered shards of ice exploded around their feet.

The torch stuttered back to life.

They laughed with relief, roared until the bridge was filled with the sound of their laughter. All around, the icicles began to drip, faster and faster, as if their wickedness had started a thaw.

The river of ice below them splintered and cracked. The water beneath the thick ice gurgled lazily . . . Then came a rushing sound, slow at first, growing louder. Large slabs of ice floated away down the river.

The torchlight played on the water. Iffy looked down and stared in disbelief. A skull was stuck fast in the ice – mouth gaping, front teeth missing. She saw it for a split second, then it was gone.

Fatty turned his back towards her taking the torchlight with him. There was a hissing sound in the darkness.

He turned around and shone his torch – steam billowed from the bottle from Lords.

Iffy gasped. 'You dirty, filthy pig!'

Fatty rammed the steam into the neck of the bottle with the cork.

Iffy knew they were done for. She made the sign of the cross: ace, jack, king, queen.

Ace on the forehead
Jack – just above the belly button
King on the left nipple
Queen on the right nipple.

'Shit! What was that!'

The town clock bonged for the first time in weeks.

Then Fatty kissed her. Hard and soft right on the lips. Just the once.

And then they were away out of the shadowy, dripping darkness. Up over the river bank, slipping and sliding as they went. They stood together on the hump-backed bridge. The moon was spinning fast. The sky an uncharted map of glimmering stars.

A red kite crossed the moon. Jack Look Up. Alone on Blagdon's Tump trying to reach the stars for his long-dead son.

Agnes Medlicott stood alone in the upstairs drawing room of the Big House. She stood quite still looking down towards the bridge that spanned the river.

In all the years she'd been away the view from this window had stayed the same. She'd stood there so many times as a young woman, newly married, watching the road for her husband's car when he'd been out on a call. The years had passed and she'd grown tired, tired of waiting, tired of the same old excuses. A call to a difficult labour over in another valley, a child taken to hospital. All lies. It was always another woman somewhere. Another brief liaison which wouldn't last. They never did. When she'd fallen with child she'd thought things might improve, that love for his child, if not for her, would keep him closer to home, but she'd lost the baby at eight months. A little boy. She still kept a tiny shoebox containing the clothes she had knitted. Tiny matinee jackets and hats, mittens and booties wrapped in tissue paper. Stillborn. She hadn't even seen him or held him in her arms, the nurses had whisked him away. On the anniversary of his birth and death she updated him in her head, a new image of him every year. From the dark-eyed baby through to the chubby toddler, a bright-eyed child, then a teenager. Now, if he'd lived, he would be a man of fifty, a father, a grandfather even.

There hadn't been any more children, much to her regret. She could have stood her husband's infidelity if she'd had a child of her own. All those years she'd grieved for the lost child, grieved for all the children she'd never have.

The pain of it had been barely tolerable. The ache she felt when she saw a baby in a pram, a mother holding the hand of a toddler, wiping a tear away from an eye. Until in the end the pain had made her afraid, and for a long time she had barely left the house for fear of what she might do.

1963

Christmas came and went. The wishes that Fatty and Iffy had made beneath Jack Look Up's tree and under the bridge didn't come true. Neither were there any thunderbolts sent from God as a punishment for drinking the holy water.

Spring eventually came slowly up the valley. First came the call of early lambs born on the hill farms. The mountain ponds filled up with murky clouds of frogspawn. Then the apple trees in the Big House exploded into dusky pink clouds and sent showers of petal confetti over into the lane. Ragged daffodils pierced the black soil on the hillsides and Barny the bulldog broke his chains and rampaged through the town in search of love.

It was dusk. Darkness drifted up the river like bonfire smoke.

The four of them, Iffy, Fatty, Billy and Bessie, were sitting on the Dentist's Stone. Midges hung in a shifting cloud over the hump-backed bridge. The long grass down by the river was alive with the sound of frog song and the sly rustle of bright-eyed cats out on the razzle. Far down the valley the bell of Zeraldo's ice-cream van clanked out its tired old tune.

Behind the high walls, the Big House turned from dusky grey to a menacing black.

The moon was coming up fast, spinning dizzily over Blagdon's Tump. The Old Bugger hooted down in Carmel graveyard.

A light came on in an upstairs room of the Big House. Electric light. Quick and yellow and sore on the eye. No soft build up like gaslight.

They watched the big arched window, eager as moths for its glowing light. A snapshot into that other world. Just a peep to whet the appetite.

The walls surrounding the house were too high to climb and creepers and bushes overgrew the big wrought-iron gates set into the walls, so this was the closest they ever got.

They were fascinated and terrified by the place.

No one had clapped eyes on Mrs Medlicott since that night in the winter when Fatty had seen her getting out of the car. She hadn't stepped outside the door once. Old Sandicock, who had lived alone in the house since Dr Medlicott had died, did all the shopping. He was a bad-tempered old man, he never spoke, and he kept a shotgun for apple thieves.

At night Iffy, Fatty, Billy and Bessie hung around on the stone, waiting for the off-chance of a look: pianos and diamond chandeliers; decanters with silver labels; aspidistra and waxy lilies. There was talk of a greenhouse with grapes. And inside lavvies where a hand came out to wipe your bum when you'd finished, like the Queen of England.

Iffy grabbed Fatty's arm and pointed. 'There she is!'

A shadow crossed the arched window.

'Spooky,' said Bessie, pulling her bunny-wool cardie closer round her body.

The light was extinguished as quickly as it had come on.

'Now you see it. Now you don't,' said Fatty.

It reminded Iffy of a curtain closing on a stage set, like the plays she'd seen once or twice in the Welfare Hall.

'Hey, look!' Fatty said pointing down towards the bridge.

Reluctantly they took their eyes from the window. Carty Annie came over the hump-backed bridge dragging her wooden cart behind her.

Iffy waved. Carty Annie was nearly as fascinating as Mrs Medlicott. She was a lunatic, quite mad but not dangerous.

Carty Annie stopped when she reached them and stared at the four of them as if she had never seen them before. Then she smiled a warm, wrinkly, smile.

Bessie looked away quickly.

Iffy smiled back and peeped slyly into the cart. Just empty jam jars and the usual pile of old junk.

'Couldn't ketch any of them little feckers today! Too bloody quick by half so they were . . . but I'll have the little bastards. I'll get the devious little wasters.'

Bessie sniffed with disgust and pressed her hands tight over her ears.

'What you trying to catch, Old Missus?' said Fatty innocently.

'Aha, wouldn't you like to know!' said Carty Annie tapping her nose with her finger, her eyes twinkling wickedly in the moonlight. 'This time o' night's a good time . . . when the moon is rising. Moonlight's a good time. They get drowsy see. Aha! Early or late I'll nab the feckin' little eejits!'

Iffy snorted.

Bessie nudged Iffy hard in the ribs and then pulled her cardie up over her head to keep the filth out.

Iffy loved the way Carty Annie swore. It made her shiver with pleasure.

A dog barked over in the Big House. It was a pedigree, Fatty had told Iffy. Pedigrees knew more about their families than most people did.

Carty Annie sidled up closer to them and whispered, 'You keep away from there, mind,' and she pointed towards the shadowy house.

'Why's that then?' asked Fatty.

'Bad things happened in there. Very bad things.'

She looked at Iffy. Iffy stared back into the old woman's shining eyes, she could see herself reflected in them, her own eyes huge with interest and fear.

'Things that should never have happened.'

'What sort of things?'

'Lies and secrets. They sent her away,' said Carty Annie, shaking her head from side to side. 'Sent her away and she never knew the truth. And worse things besides happened in there. Babies buried, then not buried. Disgraceful what they done to that cat!'

'What sort of things?'

'You just keep away. I seen him, see.'

'Who?'

'That old fellow, the old doctor what killed himself. Didn't kill himself because he was sorry, not at all. Killed himself so's he wouldn't swing on the rope.'

'What rope?' said Fatty.

'If they'd found a body they would have had him.'

'When did you see him?' asked Fatty, his eyes bright with excitement.

'One night last November, the Feast of all Saints. I followed one of them little bastards in there through the secret way, then I lost it . . . and then I seen him.'

'Where was he?'

'I heard this glugging sound.' She made choking noises in her throat. 'Then bubbling and a slappy slopping sound and there he was . . .'

Iffy shivered.

'He come up out of the pond . . . dripping with weeds.'

Iffy's eyes were stretching so much they ached.

Bessie turned her back on Carty Annie. She didn't believe her. It wasn't true.

'He was soaked to the skin, covered all over in slime . . .'

Bessie wanted her to stop.

'He opened his mouth and a goldfish popped out . . .'

Bessie began to wheeze.

The Old Bugger hooted again.

'And the statues started to dance, round and round, and the one, the one with no head, was searching all over for something.'

Fatty wondered how it could search with no head.

'Then he started to walk round the garden – slip slop

slip – like he was looking for something.'

Then Carty Annie stopped. She looked Bessie up and down. Got up close and stared right into Bessie's face.

'Jesus!' she said. 'You're as ugly as a feckin' gargoyle with your jaw hanging open like that. Well, see you then.' And Carty Annie trundled away up the road, muttering to herself. When she came to the gates of the Big House she stepped out into the road and took the same half circle that the chidren always did. On she went, away past the Big House and on towards Dancing Duck Lane.

'She's horrible,' said Bessie. 'What's a gargoyle?'

None of them knew.

'I don't believe her anyway, about ghosts and things. She's mad. And she smells,' said Bessie.

'That's just because you don't want to believe her,' said Fatty.

'I don't believe in ghosts.'

They knew she did though. Bessie was afeared of her own shadow.

They all believed in ghosts. They wanted to see one and they didn't at the same time.

'Have you ever seen where she lives?' said Bessie.

Fatty shook his head. He didn't want anyone to know he'd been poking about in Dancing Duck Lane, didn't want them to know what he'd found there, especially Bessie, she could never keep her trap shut about anything.

'No,' said Iffy, 'but it's supposed to be haunted.'

Bessie shivered.

'Where is it?' she said.

'Up past the Big House, over the stile and on down a lonely spooky lane where once a man hanged himself from a tree by his bootlaces.'

'I wonder what it is she catches,' said Bessie.

'Probably butterflies,' Iffy guessed.

'Moths,' said Fatty. 'Big hairy ones with teeth!'

'Ugh! I hate moths!' Bessie said.

'Spiders and poisonous snakes!' Fatty said.

Bessie screwed up her face with horror.

'Look! There she is again.' Iffy pointed.

The light had come on again in the Big House. The dark shadow of old Mrs Medlicott moved again across the archway of light. They caught a fleeting glimpse of the silhouette of a stout woman, with a big hook nose and tight-coiled plaits arranged on the side of her head like earmuffs.

Iffy shuddered and pulled down the cuffs of her jersey over her hands.

'She looks horrible,' said Bessie.

'Like a witch!'

'No such thing as witches,' Bessie stammered, but she didn't sound too sure.

Somewhere nearby a bat squeaked. So did Bessie. She held on tight to her ringlets, she was terrified in case a bat got caught in her hair and she had to have it all cut off into a crew cut. There were foreign bats that sucked your blood . . . Iffy imagined Bessie sucked dry until she was just a pile of loose skin and ringlets.

The shadow crossed the lighted window again. The old woman paced back and forth like a soldier on guard.

'Looks like she's reading a book,' Bessie said.

'The Bible,' said Fatty. 'They say she reads it all the time. To make up for all the bad things she's done.'

They counted: one, two, three, four, five. The old woman crossed the archway of light. One, two, three, four, five. And again. Like clockwork.

'Did you hear what Carty Annie said, that she got in there through a secret way . . . One day I'm gonna find it and have a look at all them dirty statues in there.'

'Fatty, don't be so rude!'

'They say they're all naked girls.'

'That's not very nice.'

'I wouldn't go in there if you paid me. Anyway my nan said I'm not allowed near there because she's not safe with children.'

'My mam said she's all right,' said Fatty.

'Does she know her?'

'Not now, but she used to work for old Dr Medlicott.'

'What do you mean she's not safe with children?' Bessie asked. Her eyes were shifting puddles of muddy blue.

'I dunno. My nan doesn't like her. She won't talk about it.'

'P'raps she's a murderer just let out of jail!'

'Stop it, Fatty!'

'I bet she cuts off babies' arms with a bread knife and sucks up the blood for her breakfast.'

'Fatty!'

It was nearly calling in time.

'Hey,' Fatty said. 'You hear about that ghost?'

'What ghost?' Bessie and Iffy spoke together in a nervous chorus.

'The one up in Inkerman.'

Iffy stared at him. Bessie gawped.

'Get lost, Fatty, you're making it up.'

'Honest to God! Cross my heart. Bridgie Thomas seen it, didn't she, Billy?'

Billy nodded seriously.

Iffy looked across at Bessie. Bessie's lips were trembling, her eyes wide and glossy in the moonlight. Iffy looked down towards the graveyard, to the crooked old gravestones. Her own legs were trembling, a soft, sure hum of fear behind her knees.

Bridgie Thomas wouldn't lie about seeing a ghost. She was holy. She went to church every day, twice on Sundays. She had visions and saw saints. She'd seen Mary

Magdalene over in the rec, crying her eyes out on the roundabout, and John the Baptist sitting on top of her wardrobe, eating bananas and stark staring naked.

Bessie checked Fatty's face for signs of a smile. Nothing.

'What did she say it was like, this ghost?' Iffy asked, trying to sound unafraid.

'It was wrapped up in white sheets, it was carrying its head under its arm and its eyes were red as blood.'

'Don't mess about!'

Iffy remembered the skull she'd seen that night under the bridge. Fatty hadn't believed her but it had been true.

A chalky-white skull with two teeth missing.

'Honest, didn't she say so, Billy?'

Billy nodded solemnly.

'And it was carrying a chopper.'

'Where was it by?'

Bessie was trembling, her ringlets bouncing up and down on her shoulders, her chin wobbling.

'Halfway along Inkerman, in between Bessie's house and yours. It stopped there and twisted its head back on.'

Bessie made a whimpering noise and her chest set up its rattling.

'Bridgie said it stood there for ages moaning and sobbing as though it was looking for someone and then . . . and then it vanished into thin air . . .'

Bessie twisted up her dress into a knot just below her fanny. She bit her lips tight together to stop the wobble. She wanted to cry.

A bat swooped down low out of the trees. It squeaked. So did Bessie. She let go of her skirt, crossed her legs and held on to her ringlets.

'Ghosts can't hurt you anyway,' said Fatty.

Billy nodded in agreement.

'Why's it carrying a chopper then?'

'I dunno.'

The shadow crossed the window of the Big House again.

'Unless it's old Medlicott out looking for girls' heads to chop off.'

A cool wind came up the valley, rustling the leaves into a bubbling black broth above their heads. Up on the Black Band a fox barked. The Black Band was reached by climbing up a steep slope from the road. No one knew why it was called the Black Band, it was just a part of the mountain. There were chicken coops up there, a few pigeon lofts, it led away up towards the shale tips and the top ponds.

An owl flew down low across the Black Band. It flew just above their heads and its bright eyes took them all in. Iffy heard the sound of its wings batting the air. She shivered again.

'Iffy!'

Calling in time.

'Bessie!'

Cats chorused on the doorsteps of Inkerman. The town clock rattled, clattered, bonged, once, twice.

'Billy!' Mrs Edwards on the steps of the bakery. 'Billy-O!'

The callers always added an 'O' on the second time of calling.

Billy's mam called again, her voice more insistent now.

'See you, girls!'

'Fatty, don't go!'

But he was already lolloping off, his arm around Billy's small shoulders, walking him home through the dark to his waiting mam.

No one ever called Fatty in.

Billy turned and waved.

'Mind how you go, girls!' Fatty called over his shoulder. 'Don't go losing your heads now!'

Bessie put her hands to her neck.

Iffy watched the boys as they walked away down past the bridge and were swallowed up by the dark night. She and Bessie had been left, two small figures standing close together, shivering with fear and cold in the weak circle of wavering light from the street lamp.

Iffy looked up at the lighted window of the Big House. The old woman was standing quite still staring down at them.

Iffy pulled Bessie's arm. 'Look, Bessie!'

The old woman waved to them from the window, a soft sad wave.

Iffy lifted her hand to wave back. Then she remembered her nan's words. 'Not safe to be around little children.'

'Bessie-O!'

'Iffy-O!'

Second time of calling. There'd be trouble if they didn't shift themselves. Five minutes grace and then they'd be out looking for them, and then watch out.

But home was in Inkerman Terrace where Bridgie Thomas had seen a red-eyed ghost with a chopper. They were too afraid to move.

Suddenly the light went off in the Big House. Iffy grabbed Bessie's arm.

'Ouch! Iffy, you're hurting me.'

'Bessie, look, over there by the gates!'

'What is it?'

'There's somebody there.'

A cigarette butt glowed in the blackness.

'Who is it?'

'I dunno. I can't see in the dark.'

'Hello, girls. How about a nice sweet from my pocket?'

It wasn't much of a choice. Georgie Fingers or the ghost. They flew. All the way up the hill without stopping. Iffy in front, Bessie behind, puffing and squeaking like a squeezebox. Iffy stopped at the steps leading down to Inkerman and waited for Bessie. She didn't want to go down into the darkness of the bailey alone. They stood side by side. They didn't want to stay where they were, didn't want to step down into the bailey. Iffy wanted more than anything to be in the house, safe in the light, cosy in the warm kitchen.

Mrs Meredith and Mrs Tranter had gone back inside. The back doors seemed a million miles away through the dark, stirring shadows . . . All sorts of terrors could be lurking there in the bailey. Lav doors that might swing open, bogeymen's hands pulling them in, ghosts hiding in the cobwebby coal sheds. Ghosts could hide anywhere. They could melt away behind doors, slide under buckets, skulk unseen in quiet, dark corners.

A cat wailed nearby. Bessie grabbed Iffy's hand. Iffy let her hold it.

An owl toowhit toowooed on Blagdon's Tump. The Old Bugger called back from among the crooked graves.

Washing danced eerily on the clothes lines that were strung across the bailey. A figure loomed out from the gyrating washing.

Bessie yelped. Her fingernails dug into Iffy's hand.

'It's only a mop, you fool!'

'Sorry, Iffy.'

'God, you frightened me then!'

Nearly there. A lav door creaked, opened a crack. They stopped still, clinging to each other for grim death.

Bessie was holding Iffy's hand so tightly she was getting pins and needles. Bessie's breathing was as loud as a train. Iffy's heart was doing roly-polies, tight ones that hurt.

They heard a noise.

'Oh frig!'

Then they giggled.

It was only someone widdling. Mrs Evans from number four.

71

'Ghosts can't widdle,' Iffy whispered. 'They're all air.'

They went slowly on their way, huddling close together through the darkness. They took pigeon steps, though they wanted to run. Their heads revolved as if on swivel sticks.

They reached Bessie's back door.

'Wait by there, Bessie, and keep an eye out till I get to my door.'

Bessie was safe. The light from the doorway of the Tranters' house was warm and friendly.

'G'night, Iffy!'

'Bessie! Wait!'

But she pulled her hand away from Iffy and shot in through the back door. Iffy tried to follow her, but the door slammed shut and the bolts were pulled noisily across.

A cat wailed up in the gwli.

'Moly Hairy Mother of God!' Iffy crossed herself.

Just a few more steps then in through the back door. Nearly there. Nearly there.

A mouse ran out from under a bucket.

Iffy squeaked. Fear shot up her backbone and splintered into her shoulders and head.

'Oooooooooo.'

Shitty Nora! It was the ghost come for her. Mad Dr Medlicott fresh from the fishpond.

'Ooooooooooo.' Dripping with slime, belching out goldfish, holding a sharpened chopper.

Chip Chop Chip Chop
The last man's dead.

Any second now he would appear. The chopper would slice through the air. She'd be dead without ever seeing a willy. Without learning all the filthy swear words that Fatty already knew. Without becoming famous. Her head would roll across the bailey, eyes bulging, tongue hanging out. She wondered if she'd run around headless like chickens were supposed to.

'Ooooooooooo.'

Iffy screeched like a banshee. Her bladder squeezed tight with fright. Warm wee dropped fresh into her pants. More on the way.

A shriek from somewhere above. There was laughter up in the gwli. Screaming and roaring. Mad men. Lunatics.

Fatty's head popped up above the roof of the Merediths' outside lav, followed by Billy's.

Fatty, laughing like a fool; Billy, grinning with a face full of dimples.

'You should have seen your face, Iffy!' yelled Fatty.

'Very funny I don't think!'

'Had you there!'

'Buggers. Bloody shitty buggers,' she said it under her breath. She was too close to home to swear.

Nan came out onto the step.

'Iffy, stop that bloody screeching, it's enough to wake the dead!'

Iffy raced over the step and into the light of the kitchen. From the doorway she gave the boys the two-finger sign behind Nan's back. Not Churchill's victory sign. The other way around. Shag off.

'Go on, you boys . . . off home. Billy's mam will be hoarse with calling him.'

'G'night, Mrs Meredith.'

'Good night, boys.'

'Night, Iffy.'

Arseholes.

Hairy ones.

With pwp on.

PART TWO

PART TWO

July 1963

It was a town where mostly it rained. If it didn't rain it tamped down. But all of that strange July it boiled until the tar on the roads bubbled and sucked and got all over Bessie Tranter's new cotton socks and made her cry buckets. It stewed and simmered until the silver fish gasped in the black mud trickle of the river that led down the valley to the faraway sea the children had never seen.

The children turned from khaki to burned umber with freckles, except for Bessie who went pillar-box red and then peeled over and over.

Mr Morrissey the sweet shop owner dripped sweat from under his curly black wig until his eyebrows were waterfalls. He drew down the brown paper blinds on his shop windows, but still the aniseed balls paled to pink and the coconut ice thawed.

Up in the long grass of Blagdon's Tump grasshoppers lit fires with their rubstick legs and blacked Mrs Tudge's smalls that were really bigs.

Fat bees, drunk on the heat, bumbled their way across the Black Band and crashed into late dandelion clocks.

Mrs Bunting walked across the bailey of Inkerman

without her wooden leg squeaking once. Ruby Gittins lay out in her bit of back garden and said it was 'Fan tas tick' and wore a yellow bri-nylon bikini that melted into the crack of her rude wobbly bum.

Outside the Old Bake House the Brewery horse fainted with the heat and had to have buckets of snuff and whisky to get it going again.

Winston the cockerel refused to crow at dawn. Mr Meredith's chickens laid hard-boiled eggs.

And Bridgie Thomas went daft with the heat.

It was the last day of July. The town was steaming.

The sun, a giant Catherine wheel, was spinning away high above the town clock.

The four of them, Iffy, Fatty, Billy and Bessie, were sitting on the bottom step outside the Limp in a patch of sticky shade, taking a five-minute whiff before they headed on up the weary road through town towards home.

They were worn to a frazzle with the heat, too tired to move, too hot to talk, staring down at the ground.

Fatty counted feet. Four pairs: four times two, eight. Toes: eight times five, forty. No. Forty-one toes.

Left to right. One pair of new black lace-up daps – Billy's. Fatty's own ancient red sandals two sizes too small. The stitching long since rotted, the uppers gaping away from the soles. One of his toes peeped out of the front. Iffy thought it looked like a friendly grub. Black daps. Iffy's. Slip-ons with scorch marks on the toes from sitting too close to the fire. Bessie's small feet tucked into brand-new white summer sandals. Pigskin sandals she said they were. Iffy and Fatty didn't believe her. Fatty had said all the pigs he'd ever seen were pink or blotchy grey. Iffy'd said that if hairs started to grow on the pigskin sandals she'd pinch one of her grancha's razors and shave them off.

Billy stared intently at the ground. Beneath his feet the pavement was a desert of black dust: Sahara, Kalahari, Gobi. Ants were tired-looking camels, trailing over the parched mountainous dunes in search of water, coming to sticky ends in black oases of bubbling tar.

'Smile, please!'

They looked up lazily and were caught on film by a shifty-looking man from the *Argus* newspaper.

The four of them. The only picture of them ever taken together. Four kids squinting in the white, hot heat, captured in black and white.

Three scruffy kids and a fourth one done up like a dog's dinner.

Iffy always thought it was a shame that it was a black and white photograph. Colour would have shown Bessie's new pink and white gingham dress with bows and her white ankle socks with pink frills, and her shocking-pink bunny-wool bolero. And beneath her bleached-white sun hat a face to match her dress: pink and peeling. It would have shown the dark chocolate-coloured beauty spots on Billy's tiny face, and Fatty's eyes, which were the deep blue and black of wet mussel shells, the most beautiful eyes she'd ever seen. You'd have seen that his hair was the colour of warm syrup; his face, the hue of a toasted teacake, and the little red scar above his lip where a fox bit him, or so he said.

The man with the camera limped away and climbed into a shiny red Vauxhall Victor that was parked outside the Corn Shop. He drove away raising a billowing cloud of coal dust.

Next to Iffy, Bessie breathed heavily in the heat and the settling dust. Wheezy, whistling noises came from deep down under her vest. Her ringlets were oily with sweat and hung limply around her heaving shoulders. The smell of calamine lotion and coal-tar soap oozed out from her hot skin.

Bessie always sat next to Iffy and as far away from the boys as possible, especially Fatty. She wasn't supposed to bother with him because he came from a family of rotters and Mrs Tranter thought Bessie might catch something: nits, fleas, worms or bad language. So she was perched next to Iffy, sitting tidily on a clean starched handkerchief to keep her frock clean.

Bessie smoothed down her frock over her pink knees. She had a million frocks: good frocks, best frocks, very best frocks. Not like Iffy. Iffy hardly had any frocks and she didn't even seem to care.

Fatty sat on the other side of Iffy, their brown knees touching. Bessie gave him a sly look up and down. He wore the same old clothes day in and day out: a pair of men's khaki shorts he'd had since the infants, which were still too big for him, bunched up round his waist, kept up with a frayed red and white cricket belt; a faded blue T-shirt, with a rip that showed the silky brown skin of his belly underneath.

Billy sat on the other side of Fatty with Fatty's arm resting over his shoulder. A chick under a hen's wing.

The town was hushed and still.

The orange cellophane blinds were pulled down tight on the windows of Gladys's Gowns to stop the chalk-faced dummies from burning.

A crow tap-danced on the crooked chimney of the Corn Shop, too hot to keep both its feet still at the same time.

Outside the pub called the Punch, drunken flies reeled on a current of rancid beer fumes that wafted up through the trap doors of the cellar. The pungent reek of stale blood and sawdust seeped out through the plastic strip blinds of Tommy Sackful's butcher's shop.

The town clock rattled, and bonged out the first lazy stroke of noon.

The dusty crow lifted off the chimney of the Corn Shop and flapped silently away over the baked rooftops.

In the doorway of the Corn Shop a skinny cat stretched and yawned, its gums as pink and shiny as seaside rock. Lazily it crossed the road, its paws raising tiny clouds of hot dust.

On the twelfth exhausted, rackety bong of the clock Mrs Tudge and Lally Tudge came waddling around the corner in a shimmer of striped heat. The sharp, sour smell of the sweat from their hairy armpits reached even to where the children were sitting. The bell rang over the door of the Penny Bazaar as they squeezed through the doorway.

Bridgie Thomas followed behind the Tudges. Bridgie Thomas lived in Sebastopol Terrace in a house filled with boxes of sacred old bones, and scrapbooks that contained the yellowing toenails of long-dead saints.

She was a thin, poker-legged old woman. She kept her head bent low as she walked and the pleats of her long shiny grey skirt were hot blades in the heat.

She was a maniac, but not a dangerous one as far as they knew.

She wore a huge black crucifix around her neck, it was big enough to hang on a church wall. The weight of lugging it around had curled her bony back into a grey, darned, woollen hump. Under her clothes they said she wore vests that she knitted from stinging nettles and thistles. She put tin-tacks in her shoes to please God.

She had quick darting eyes the colour of boiled goosegogs. Hairs grew from her sharp, pointy chin, as white and wispy as spring onion roots.

She was in the wrong part of town. Usually she only walked from her house in Sebastopol Terrace to the

Catholic church and back; once a fortnight to the Cop for brown bread and prunes.

They watched her through eyes narrowed against the bright, hot light. She carried a Fyffes banana box that she set down very carefully in front of the town clock. From a pocket of her skirt she took a pair of black thick-lensed spectacles and put them on. They magnified her eyes: huge, green and mad.

She stepped up on top of the rickety box, and swayed dangerously. But didn't fall off.

Pity.

The crucifix swung across her chest like a giant pendulum. Beneath her grey cardigan her titties were the shape of tinned tomatoes.

Fatty stared at them in tired fascination.

'What's she doing?' Iffy asked.

'She's going to make a speech by the look of it,' said Bessie.

'Who to? There's nobody here, only us,' Fatty said.

Bessie was right though for once.

Bridgie cleared her throat and thrust her hairy chin skywards. Her neck was as wrinkled as a dead tortoise.

'Hark unto me. I call upon the people of this town, I, the handmaid of Christ. I come to warn you. For I tell you that God the Father is sorely tried by your ungodliness. He is sending a warning to the sinners of this valley . . .'

'She's bloody crackers,' Fatty said, screwing a grubby finger into the side of his head.

'Haisht!' Bessie said, and sniffed.

Billy peeped around the front of Fatty and rolled his big brown eyes at Iffy, who giggled. Billy liked Iffy. She was always kind to him and didn't mind about him not speaking at all. Bessie gave him queer looks sometimes, slant-eyed looks that made him feel uncomfortable. He would have liked Iffy for a sister.

He watched her face as she looked at Bridgie. Her dark curls hung down almost over her eyebrows. Smooth black curls with a sheen of deep blue. Her upturned nose made him smile. It was a nosy nose, a cheeky, question mark of a nose. She wrinkled it when she was puzzled and screwed up her deep-blue eyes. She never wore dresses like Bessie. She wore clothes more like a boy's: shorts and T-shirts. She looked across at Billy then, and grinned. He grinned back, and blushed.

'All this sun we've been having is a sign from Him,' Bridgie croaked, pointing up towards the cloudless sky.

Iffy looked up. The sky was an empty blue dome, aching for clouds. No sign of Him anywhere.

'To punish all the wickedness and filthy goings on hereabouts . . .'

Fatty sniggered, and elbowed Iffy. Bessie told him to hush up.

Bridgie wobbled dangerously on top of the banana box.

Billy had a wooden, toy giraffe at home which stood on a round box. When you pressed the bottom of the box the giraffe bent his long neck this way and that, his head wobbled, his knees knocked, and his legs buckled beneath him. Bridgie reminded him of the giraffe as she struggled to balance on her skinny legs.

Bridgie waved her bony fist at no one in particular and called out again to the silent town.

Somewhere a window slammed shut.

A bee fizzed loudly overhead. It flew away, higher and higher until it was a small, agitated grain of black against the hot blue sky.

A drunk stumbled down the steps of the Punch and staggered away up the road.

A bow-legged old woman wearing ripped daps came out

through the park gates. A rheumaticky dog followed on her grubby heels. The woman stopped in front of Bridgie and squinted up at her.

'Dirtiness and smutty carryings on, adultery and f-f-f-or-nication . . .'

The old woman shook her head, turned to look at them, grinned a toothless grin, shrugged her shoulders and walked on. The dog stopped, cocked a bloodshot eye at Bridgie, then cocked its crooked leg against the banana box. A stream of yellow, steaming piss splashed down over Bridgie's hard black shoes and dried almost as it hit the ground.

The three of them giggled and elbowed each other in the ribs.

Bessie edged away from them.

'Ay, you can grin and pull your daft faces, but soon there will be plagues of locusts raining down on this town . . .'

'What's a locust?' said Bessie, edging back towards the three of them.

They ignored her.

'She's bloody cracked,' said Fatty.

Bessie sniffed again, loudly, as a warning. She didn't like bad language. She couldn't even say words like knickers or underpants without blushing.

'The graves will break open and the dead will walk the hillsides and come looking for those who have done them wrong.'

Iffy shivered and sweated at the same time.

'Secrets will out and the sinful keepers of those terrible secrets will blister and singe in the flames of hell. Burn and scorch until their skin peels away from their bones.'

'A bloody singed fanny might wake you up, old gel.'

They jumped in alarm. Bessie gasped and began to cough. Iffy banged her hard on the back.

While they'd been watching Bridgie, Georgie Fingers had crept up quietly behind them. Soft-shoe shuffle. Brothel creepers. Crêpe soles and black suede uppers.

No one was allowed to go anywhere near him, not even Fatty. Georgie was a lunatic, a dangerous one. He pretended he was a pastor and had made his own church in a shed. He tried to get girls to go in there, but they wouldn't unless they were half soaked.

Every day he stood on the corner and called out to the girls from the big school, 'Come to me, my lovelies, and be saved, let me help you find salvation . . . come to terms with all those lovely wicked thoughts.'

The big girls laughed and shouted back, 'Bugger off, Georgie, else I'll tell my father. Dirty old get that you are. Save yourself you want to!' And they laughed and sang:

Georgie Fingers pudding and pie
Kissed the girls and made them cry
When the boys came out to play
He kissed them too
Cos he's funny that way!

'Babies born out of wedlock will die of thirst at the dried-up breasts of the wicked women,' screeched Bridgie.

'Fine pair of perky tits on her, mind, when she was a girl,' said Georgie Fingers, pointing at Bridgie.

Fatty doubled up laughing and held onto Billy.

Bessie gulped and started a fit of the hiccups. She got up stiffly, folded her hankie carefully and walked away, trying to swallow the hiccups as she went. The rest of them followed her quickly. Further up the road they sat down on the scrubbed steps of Gladys's Gowns. Gladys Baker who owned the shop never minded them sitting on her step. She was nice to kids especially Fatty. She always gave him chocolate when she saw him, sometimes a bag of cakes.

Mrs Tudge and Lally came out of the Penny Bazaar. Lally waddling behind her mam like a giant duckling. She was holding a red and yellow windmill on a stick.

She smiled at them. Her teeth were as brown and holey as sucked honeycomb. They smiled back shyly, except Bessie who looked away quickly.

Lally waved a pudgy hand at them. She puckered her thick pale lips and blew hot air through them until the sails of the windmill turned stubbornly round. She got bored with the windmill and stuffed it crossly into the pocket of her stripey skirt. Then she stuck her finger into her nostril and began to pick her nose.

They watched her, enthralled and disgusted.

Then she wiped her finger on the sleeve of her blouse.

'Once I saw her eat it,' said Fatty.

'Urgh!'

'And the men who scatter their wanton seed will shrivel and droop,' yelled Bridgie and shook her bony old finger at the Tudges. 'And the swollen bellies of the bad girls will burst open and spill out dwarves!'

'Ugh!'

One dwarf. Two dwarves. Another rule, thought Fatty.

Once Iffy and Bessie had seen a dwarf. He was coming out of the toilets in the park carrying a tin bucket.

'Hello,' Bessie had called out in her best bit of posh.

'Fuck off, dirt box!' the dwarf had said.

And they had. Hell for leather, flying up through the park without looking back once.

'They will give birth to monsters and cripples, demons and goblins . . .'

Mrs Tudge stopped dead in her tracks. Beneath the

stripey frock her body wobbled and shook dangerously.

Jelly on the plate.
Jelly on the plate.
Wibble wobble, wibble wobble.
Jelly on the plate.

She turned around slowly and stared at Bridgie. Mrs Tudge was huge, the fattest woman in Wales and probably in the whole wide world.

'You want sodding looking at!' said Mrs Tudge. 'You dried-up barren old bitch! Come on, Lally. Stop dawdling and pick your bloody feet up.'

And she pulled daft Lally roughly by the arm and they waddled off together, away past the Punch, scattering a cloud of drunken flies.

'And the eyes of the keepers of secrets will drip out of their skulls and their lying tongues will frazzle . . .'

The children grinned and giggled, except for Bessie who looked afraid.

Bridgie stared at them long and hard with her boiled goosegog eyes. 'Ay, you can laugh! But I know what you've been up to, Lawrence Bevan!'

'I haven't done nuthin!' Fatty called back.

'Ay, I've seen you hanging about the Big House peeping into the garden, trying to look upon the statues of the filthy women.'

'No harm in looking is there! The cat can look at the queen you know!'

'Keep away from there! Mark my words. Evil deeds were done in that place!'

'Let's go,' said Bessie. She didn't like trouble.

'I've seen you talking to that heathen old woman with her cart full of mucky things. I've seen you up Dancing Duck

Lane. Up to no good! Looking for trouble if you hang around with the likes of her, boy!'

Bridgie turned her gaze on Iffy. 'Ay, and you Iffy Meredith. Remember, my girl, there are no secrets from God!'

'I've never been near the Big House!'

'I've seen you under the bridge, my girl, up to no good . . . defiling the Lord's name!'

'What were you doing under the bridge, Iffy?' Bessie hissed.

'Nuthin.'

Iffy looked sideways at Fatty. He looked away quickly.

'The guilty will be punished, mark my words, and that means you two.'

But no one wanted to hear any more.

Bridgie waved her fist and they closed their ears to her ranting and ran away up through the deserted town.

Fatty looked over his shoulder and dived for the shadow of the bridge. He had an eerie feeling that someone was watching him. He peered out of the archway of the bridge. No, he was just imagining it. There was not a soul around. He was worried though. If Bridgie Thomas had seen him hanging about in Dancing Duck Lane then she must have followed him. But he'd been careful and was sure no one had followed him. Besides, he'd nearly always been to Carty Annie's at night except for a couple of times. Bridgie would hardly be following him around in the middle of the night. He wasn't worried about her telling Carty Annie that he'd been snooping around because they never spoke to each other. Carty Annie had nothing to do with the church and Bridgie was hardly ever out of it. But what if Bridgie had looked inside the house herself and seen what Carty Annie had hidden there? She couldn't have though. If Bridgie knew what was inside that jar she'd have run for Father Flaherty and probably the Pope himself. He'd have to be careful now though, keep his eyes peeled next time he went. And he'd been loads of times since that first night when he'd hardly been able to believe his eyes.

For a second, he thought he saw the glow of a cigarette in the darkness, a fleeting glimpse of a shadow crossing the far end of the bridge. He pressed himself back against the wall and waited.

That night in the winter when he and Iffy had drunk the holy water, Iffy had said she thought someone was there. He'd better watch his step. He didn't want anyone snooping on him and spoiling all his plans.

He waited for a few minutes, clambered up over the river bank and went hot-foot through the gulleys and legged it over a garden wall.

It was the last night of July. Iffy lay in her big bed thinking of what Bridgie Thomas had said that afternoon about there being secrets in the town and that God would punish people.

That afternoon, when Bridgie had stared at them with her green, mad eyes, Iffy had felt sure that Bridgie knew about what she and Fatty had done that night under the bridge.

She heard the stealthy sound of footsteps crossing the parlour outside her door.

Nan came into the room, her smiling face illuminated by the candle light.

She kissed Iffy softly and Iffy felt deeply ashamed of what she and Fatty had done. She wanted to tell Nan, to say sorry about drinking the holy water which was all she had left of her son.

'Nan . . .'

'Yes, my angel?'

She didn't though. Nan would go mad if she knew what was in the bottle now.

Iffy listened to the soft shuffle and scuff of Nan's slippers as she went back through the back parlour, back past the sideboard where the bottle of Fatty's cold pee stood beneath the withered palm crosses and the holy pictures of miserable-looking saints. She heard the latch lifting on the kitchen door.

Whenever she had to go through the parlour she avoided Granny Gallivan's eyes. She, like Bridgie Thomas, knew what they'd done. Iffy could tell from the way her sharp eyes followed her, scorching holes between her shoulder blades.

Iffy tossed and turned, sticky with sweat and guilt. She heard the town clock strike midnight and then she slept. And while she slept July boiled over into August and things were never the same again.

Will took the train to Cardiff, then boarded a bus and began the slow journey up the steep-sided valley and wondered whether he would live long enough to make the same journey back.

He rubbed a clear patch in the steamy window and peered out into the already darkening day. The rain was torrential, hitting the tarmac of the road and bouncing back up. Rivulets of black water travelled down from the mountains, coursing across the road and on down the steep-sided valley to the river which was a turbulent stream of fast-moving foam.

The dark mountains on either side of the road had blurred into forbidding clouds. The bus travelled long stretches of lonely winding roads where sheep huddled against stone walls. A sheep dog barked lethargically at the bus from the gateway of a tumbledown farm.

It was a helter-skelter ride occasionally punctuated by their passing through small deserted towns with their streets of dark-grey terraced houses. The doors of the houses were closed against the driving rain, weak light filtering through faded curtains. Smoke curled up miserably from chimneys. A group of ponies stood forlornly in a silent square.

Turning a steep bend, Will gasped at the sight of the house. Of course, he should have realised it would still be there. He supposed that it had for so long been a part of his dreams that he no longer thought of it as a real house of bricks and mortar.

There it was, a lone house perched halfway up the mountain reached by a narrow stony track. A board proclaimed it to be a bed and breakfast. Sunny Views.

Dear God! He couldn't imagine a worse place to spend the night!

He had visited it many times on his rounds as a young constable. It had been as desolate a place as he had ever been in. A dank and dismal house, the brown distempered walls running with condensation, a place of ill-lit corridors, the air redolent with the smell of drying nappies and cloying baby milk. From behind closed doors came the sounds of muffled sobs and anguished partings. It was a house awash with the reek of shame, a veritable hell-hole.

He thought now of all those young girls and their babies. Babies crying. Babies soon to be separated from their young mothers. It should have been a house full of joy at the absolute miracle of birth. Instead it had been a house where you could almost taste the shame. He wondered if all those young girls, middle-aged women now, still thought about the last look they ever took of their babies. He sighed. Lost babies. Lost girls.

Did those girls still dream of this house? Still wake in the night filled with terror? He had dreamed about it many times, it was the nightmare he dreaded above all others. He turned his eyes away, he didn't want to dwell on memories that were too painful. Memories that racked him with guilt and blemished the love he had felt for his wife, Rhiannon. The house hadn't had a board proclaiming its name in the old days, but everyone for miles around had called it the home for bad girls.

August 1st

Still boiling.

The Merediths' back door was open on to the bailey. It was always open even when it rained.

At four o'clock it was as hot as ever.

Three doors away, the Tranters' door was shut tight. It was always shut even when it was hot. The Tranters only pulled back the bolts when someone wanted to leave or get back into the house.

Iffy crossed the bailey, ducking and diving between the washing on the lines. She knocked hard on Bessie's door until her knuckles hurt. The Tranters' door was painted with thick green paint, the colour of shiny cucumbers.

She hoped Bessie would answer and not her mam or dad. She never knew what to say to them. Bessie's mam and dad were really old, nearly as old as her nan and grancha.

Mrs Tranter cleaned the doctor's surgery and the doctor's house. She made felt toys and crocheted and knitted patchwork blankets for black babies. She never smiled.

The Tranters were chapel. Carmel.

The Merediths were Catholic.

Mrs Tranter played the organ and the harmonium.

In the infants, Fatty had made up a dirty song about organ players.

Fanny Morgan plays the organ and she plays it very
   well
But her sisters all have blisters in the middle of their
   Fanny
Morgan plays the organ and she plays it very well . . .

Bessie had got mad, had her hair off as they said. She had
sobbed and stamped her shiny patent shoes up and down
on the playground floor.

Chapel people were different to Catholics. They didn't
drink or bet on the horses but they ate meat on Fridays and
God didn't give them so many babies.

Bessie grunted noisily as she pulled back the bolts. Bessie
was famous for her grunting. The door was dragged open
and the smell of polish and disinfectant came over the step
in a rush that brought tears to Iffy's eyes.

Bessie blinked her small eyes in the bright sunlight.

Iffy thought that Bessie had eyes like a pig but not so
intelligent.

Her cheeks had been scrubbed until they shone, and
below her hemline her bony pink knees were polished to
shining. Her fat, glossy ringlets dripped down onto her
shoulders. She smelled of talcum powder and the cod liver
oil that she took for her chest. Bessie had a chest that rattled
like an abacus when she wasn't rattling from all the pills
she took. Her mam gave her medicine for everything.

Medicine to make her pwp regular.
To get the wax out of her ears.
And the badness from her blood.
The worms from her bum.

But she never looked healthy.

'Hello, Iffy,' Bessie said, in a voice that sounded as

though it had been washed in vinegar and put through the mangle twice.

'Hiya, Bessie.'

Bessie closed the door carefully behind her and the bolts were drawn back across from the inside. They walked across the bailey of Inkerman towards the broken steps at the end of the row that led up to the rutted road. Bessie walked carefully so as not to stand on any cracked stones and get mud all up her socks, even though it hadn't rained for weeks. She hated having dirty socks.

Bessie was Iffy's best friend but only because she couldn't find a better one. Bessie was spoilt rotten. She was the youngest. She had two brothers who were in the army. Derek and Brian. There were framed photographs of them on the harmonium in the parlour. Mrs Tranter polished them every day, twice. They had heads the shape of swedes and were dead ugly. When they came home on leave they brought Bessie dolls in foreign costumes: Dutch, French, Spanish, Irish. Iffy liked the French one the best. It had red lipstick and no knickers. Just like Bessie's sister. Dolores.

Dolores had white hair and two babies who ran about half naked, but no husband. Bessie's mam had no truck with Dolores.

Iffy liked the name Dolores, just saying it made her shiver.

Dolores's real name was Hilary and they called her Lurry for short. She changed it when she ran away from home.

DOLOREZ.

Bessie said her hair was really ginger but she put peroxide and toilet cleaner on it. One day it would all fall out, or, if she was lucky, it would just turn green.

Mrs Meredith told Mrs Bunting that Hilary Lurry Dolores was hot in the knickers, but Iffy couldn't ask what she meant because she was hiding under the kitchen table and shouldn't have been.

Fatty was waiting for them down by the Dentist's Stone at the bottom of the hill.

Fatty sat cross-legged, busily shaving a lolly stick into an arrowhead with a penknife. He was dead lucky! Gladys Baker who kept the gown shop in town had given it to him as a present. Iffy was dying for a penknife. She wasn't allowed one in case she had her bloody fingers off.

Fatty looked up as the girls approached. 'Wotcha, girls!'

Bessie checked over her shoulder in case her mam or dad were anywhere about. She'd have a lambasting if she got seen with Fatty, but she never did because her mam and dad hardly ever came out, only to shop or go to chapel.

Bessie's mam had said that the last time Fatty had had a wash was off the midwife. Iffy didn't like her for saying that.

Fatty's mam used to be a midwife but she got drunk and dropped a baby head first into a bucket. Probably Bessie, thought Iffy. Midwifes caught babies in buckets when they shot out of women's bums. They washed the pwp off and wrapped them in shawls. If they didn't breathe they smacked their arses, or their faces by mistake if they were ugly. Midwifes made tea and sent someone to get the dads from the pub.

'Where's Billy?' Iffy asked Fatty.

'Down under the bridge. I'll call him in a minute. There's hardly any river left.'

'P'raps it's a sign from God like Bridgie said,' said Bessie.

'Bridgie Thomas is bloody twp,' said Fatty.

Bessie sniffed and looked down at her feet.

The three of them walked down towards the hump-backed bridge. A pile of horse manure steamed in the middle of the road. Bessie wrinkled up her nose and looked the other way in disgust. They clambered up onto the bridge and sat dangling their feet over the edge.

Billy came scrabbling over the bank.

'Hiya, Billy.'

Fatty gave Billy a leg up onto the bridge. Billy was the same age as the rest of them but he was little for his age. Too short to cut cabbage, Fatty said.

Billy never said a word. Not a peep. Not even when Mervyn Prosser got him behind the sheds and jabbed him in the dicky with a cocktail stick.

His mam had taken him to see doctors up near England and a woman in Cardiff who heard voices from under her armpit, but still he never said a word.

No one ever talked about what had happened to Billy's brother in case they had nightmares and peed the bed leaking. It had happened in another valley before Billy moved to their town. Over the hills and far away in a place they had never been to and couldn't yet spell the name of.

And Billy never spoke after. Not once. Not a boo, bah, kiss your arse or nothing.

'What's he been doing under the bridge?' Bessie said.

'He's been looking for fairies,' said Fatty.

Bessie rolled her eyes up towards the sky.

'Speaking of fairies,' hissed Fatty, 'look who's coming.'

Dai Full Pelt came towards them on his way home from the Mechanics. He was a lunatic. A dangerous one.

'Let's go,' Bessie whimpered.

'Stay put,' Fatty said. 'Don't run away from the likes of him. Don't let him see you're afraid.'

Dai staggered up the lane towards them.

They got down off the bridge in case he pushed one of them over the edge and into the river. Lunatics did things like that for no reason.

Bessie kept her head well down. She was terrified of Dai.

They all were, even Fatty a bit, only he wouldn't show it.

Dai Full Pelt was really Dai Gittins. He was called Dai Full Pelt because he worked on the buses and drove them too fast – full pelt, hell for leather, breaking the bones and teeth of his passengers as he went. Dai was horrible. He was a monster of a man, with the ugliest mug on him you ever saw.

He had a huge head as big as a pumpkin. His hair was like the tumbleweed that blew down the streets in cowboy films: Roy Rogers, Tonto, the Lone Ranger. He had ears big as saucers and pale-blue bulgy eyes the colour of sucked gobstoppers. A nose, red and swollen and pitted with blackheads. Black bristly hairs stuck out of his nostrils, nostrils as wide as arches. His mouth was the very worst bit of him. It was a great black dirty hole where one yellow fang hung by a sticky thread.

He was married to Ruby Gittins who had been married before. And before that. She was as rough as a badger's arse. The children weren't allowed to go near the Gittins's house. Except Fatty. Fatty could go where he liked.

Ruby Gittins only changed her knickers when the moon was full. They weren't the sensible type of knickers that mams and nans wore. Not cotton double gusset, white aertex and room to breathe. They were red and black with frills on. Some had no gusset at all and needed darning.

She hung them on the washing line for all the valley to see.

'No shame at all,' said Bridgie Thomas.

'Dis bloody gustin',' said Iffy's nan.

'Dirty stinking old cow,' said Mrs Bunting.

They watched Dai out of the sides of their eyes. He stopped quite close to them, poked a fat slug of a finger against one hairy nostril and blew out a stringy ribbon of green snot from the other.

'Ugh!' said Bessie.

Dai changed nostrils and blew more snot.

Bessie held onto her dinner but only just.

Fatty leant close to Iffy and whispered, 'Once he had a cat and it stole his dinner so he cooked it alive in the oven and then ate it. It was called Lucky.'

'Shut up, Fatty.'

'He did. Honest! He peeled off the fur and ate it with brown sauce and pickled eggs.'

'Stop it, Fatty.'

'He's nothing but a big fat gobby git,' Fatty muttered under his breath.

'Hush up!' Bessie said. 'He might hear you.'

Dai staggered on towards them until he was close enough for them to smell the beer on his breath. There was a wet patch of wee on the front of his trousers.

He glared at Bessie first. She squeaked with fright and Fatty swore he heard her tonsils hit her ribs and bounce back up.

'What you bloody gawking at, Bessie Big Drawers?'

Bessie gasped, and pulled her bunny-wool bolero up over her head.

'What you staring at?' he asked the headless Bessie.

Silence.

'What you staring at, eh?'

No answer from Bessie, just wheezing rasping noises that came from the depths of the bolero.

Dai turned on Billy. 'Cat got your tongue, eh?'

Billy looked up at Dai, his eyes wide with fear, softly damp round the lashes. A lump moved up and down in his neck.

Fatty stiffened next to Iffy. She felt for his hand and took hold of it tightly.

'Just ignore him,' she said through clenched teeth.

It was her turn next.

'Got something to say have you, Sambo?'

Iffy looked down at her daps.

Sambo wasn't a nice thing to say. He said it because she was dark. The sun never burned her no matter how hot it was.

'Damn, you're an ugly-looking little bugger, Iffy Meredith. Can't blame your mam for taking one look at you and running.'

Hot tears pricked at the back of her eyes, and her heart rattled in the space behind her heaving ribs. A wobble started in her lips, her throat grew tight.

It wasn't true. Her mammy died when she was born. Nan said. Everybody knew that.

Fatty squeezed her hand tightly.

She bit her tongue, kept her trap shut.

Dai turned to Fatty. 'Who are you looking at, fat guts?'

Iffy held her breath and squeezed Fatty's sticky fingers. She prayed. Hard. Please God, don't let him say anything.

'Don't know. A pile of shit, I think,' Fatty muttered.

Iffy jabbed him hard with her elbow. Dai wasn't safe to give cheek to.

'What you say?' Dai growled.

There was brown spit in both corners of his mouth and yellow crystallised bogies in his left nostril.

'I said it's a nice day, Mr Gittins,' Fatty said, dead cool.

'Ay, well, I don't take no bloody lip off the likes of you, Fatty Bevan. I could paste the living daylights out of you.'

'Go on then.'

Iffy held on to him like grim death.

Dai stumbled, belched loudly and the stink of rotten teeth, slimy gums, beer and tobacco wafted over them. He glared at them with his gobstopper eyes, lost interest, spat a big glob of frothy spit over the bridge and then reeled off up the hill.

'Fat-faced fart!' Fatty shouted out loud to his back.

'Haisht!' said Bessie coming up for air. She was scared he'd come back and belt them. So were they all.

Dai swayed and staggered away up the hill. If their eyes had been bullets he would have been a dead man.

The sun disappeared behind a cloud for the first time in weeks. The sky grew dark. They heard the first bashing together of thunderclouds away in the next valley, where all the men had one extra long finger so that they could pick pockets dead easy.

The mountains went from green to plum to damson. Growling clouds rolled above the valley. Lightning forked over Old Man Morgan's hill farm.

Barny the bulldog howled. Thunder clapped and shook the valley, rattling the stones in the river bed.

Then the rain came. Fat warm splodges of rain at first. Then thinner, faster and cooler. Until down it came. Bucketing. Tamping.

Shrieking, they raced for the cover of the tree that overhung the Dentist's Stone. Standing beneath it and watching the rain bounce off the road, they listened as it made tunes on the tin roofs of sheds and on all the upturned buckets.

Water gushed down the hill until the gutters were torrents of liquorice-black water. Lollipop sticks, sheep shit and dog ends rode the rapids until the drains were spouts and the wonky steps that led to the terraced houses were waterfalls.

And then it happened. Just like Bridgie Thomas had said it would.

It was magic. It was a curse, or a miracle. It was great. It was terrifying. They came dropping out of the dark August sky. Raindrops with legs on. Raindrops with eyes. Mad eyes, bright in the sudden afternoon gloom. Millions of them.

Bessie screamed and grabbed hold of Iffy's arm. Iffy pushed her away.

Billy pointed. His eyes were as shiny as alley bompers.

They stared and gawped, goggle-eyed.

A cloudburst of frogs. Tiny frogs raining from the sky. Falling and falling until there were puddles of green, puddles of eyes, hopping puddles. Their eyes were puddles.

'Fuckin' Ada!' said Fatty hopping from one foot to the other, water squeaking through his holey sandals.

Bessie screamed fit to bust.

Water dripped from the tree and soaked them.

They were mesmerised. Except for Bessie, who leapt up and down like a chicken with an egg up its arse. She held down her gingham skirts in case the frogs took it into their heads to leap into her knickers.

There was no one else about, only the four of them to see it. But Iffy and Fatty knew it was God and he must have been dead mad to send plagues of frogs to their little town.

The thunder rolled away over the Sirhowy Mountain.

Up on the mountain the dried-up ponds would be full again and watery-eyed rats would be flushed from the overflow pipes.

Bessie wailed on and on.

'Shut your trap, Bessie, you're like a bloody banshee. They're only frogs,' said Fatty but his voice for once, sounded a little bit scared.

'Waaargh!' wailed Bessie.

They ignored her, standing there sopping wet and staring. Bessie's ringlets unringled, like fat sausages split into limp skins.

Fatty hopped up and down, yelped, swore some more, 'Bugger bugger bugger shit shit damn! It's bloody great!'

101

Billy held on to Iffy's arm tightly and the two of them shivered together in alarm and excitement.

The road was a moving carpet of tiny frogs. The frogs blinked, winked, grinned stupidly up at their stupefied audience.

Bessie screamed till her tonsils went red.

Then the frogs fled, hopping and leaping away down the hill and over the ragged bank to the river. Like bloody magic they were.

Bessie took off. She went flying up the hill, clutching at her skirts, screeching for her mam, splashing through the water on her skinny white legs. Lucky legs; lucky they didn't snap. Belloching all the way home.

The three of them stood transfixed. Raindrops splashing on them from the tree. The watery sun peeped out from the dark sky, and they steamed in the wobbling rainbow light.

In the distance Bessie was still wailing for her mam. They listened to the slip-slapping of her pigskin sandals as she shot up the hill. They grinned with glee because they knew that as she ran across the bailey of Inkerman the black mud would slop up over her white sandals and all over her ever-so white socks.

They stayed put for ages afterwards just watching the empty puddles. Puddles still rippling in the wake of a million frogs.

The black frog clouds had emptied over their town and rolled away over the mountain to the valley of pickpockets.

They were afraid.

All around them the air was a fading croak.

Then the town clock bonged out. Five bongs. Billy's and Iffy's tea time.

Fatty walked away down towards the bridge holding Billy's hand.

Iffy wished there was someone left to hold hers. It felt

strange standing there all alone after the frogs had gone.

The world around her had changed. The colours were brighter. A golden glow outlined the trees, the wonky bridge and the wings of a bird flying high above. The air smelled of weed and nettles, electricity and wet coal dust.

Iffy looked round fearfully for stray frogs.

For a moment she felt as though she was standing in a different town. A town of magic, of spells and miracles and secrets. A town touched by God.

It made her afraid. And glad. And even more afraid.

Fear got the better of her and she raced up the hill in the echo of Bessie's roaring wash. She leapt down the steps to Inkerman, splashing through the deep black puddles on the bailey. As she passed Bessie's closed door she heard her blubbing in the kitchen. Bloody big babby. She ran past all the back doors. Black mud splashed up from loose stones and splattered her legs, her back and her neck, it felt great.

Someone was piddling in an outside lav. She laughed rudely out loud.

She flew in through the back door. The kitchen was a cloud. A white cloud with her nan somewhere in the middle of it singing.

'Oh, Danny Boy . . . the pipes the pipes are calling . . .' She clanked the battered lids on bubbling saucepans. 'From glen to glen, and down the mountainside . . .' The cloud lifted. 'The summer's gone . . .'

Nan grew from a spectre in the fog to a red-cheeked granny, pushing back silvery wisps of damp hair that had escaped from her bun.

The salty smell of boiling ham and cooking lentils filled the room.

Iffy told her about the frogs.

'The trouble with you, Iffy, is you're a bloody Tom Pepper.'

Iffy stood by the sink dripping with indignation.

Nan lifted a saucepan lid and poked boiled potatoes with a wonky fork without looking at her once.

'Honest to God, Nan, it rained frogs!'

'Don't tell lies, Iffy.'

'I'm not! I'm not! Cross my heart and swear to die, stick a needle in my eye. Honest to God, Nan, it rained frogs.'

'Frogs my arse!'

'There was lightning and a bloody big crack of thunder and—'

'Watch your tongue, my girl, or I'll give you a bloody crack round the ear if you carry on.'

'On my life, Nan, hundreds of them.'

'Ay, and I'm a monkey's uncle. Pass me that salt.'

Iffy passed the salt.

A blue tub of salt, sweaty with steam.

'Green ones, thousands, millions, hopping all over the place. Laughing they were . . . It's a plague from God. Just like Bridgie Thomas said, to punish us for all the bad things we've done.'

'Bad things! Bridgie Thomas! Bridgie Thomas is soft in the head. Rained frogs be buggered! Get them wet clothes off and put them to air on the fender.'

Iffy stood by the fire steaming in her vest and pants.

It was boiling in the kitchen. There was always a fire even on scorching hot days. The fire was the only way to cook and boil water for tea.

'Fatty'll tell you.'

'Fatty? Fatty'll say anything bar his prayers.'

'It's true! And Bessie and Billy seen them. They was swimming in the puddles and then they all hopped away down to the river. Nan, Nan honest . . .'

'Raining frogs! Laughing frogs!'

'But Nan . . . Bridgie Thomas said it would happen. That

the graves would crack open and dead people would be walking about all over the place!'

'Dead people walking! How the hell can dead people walk! I have enough trouble and I'm alive!'

'That's what she said! What if it happens, Nan? What if my mam and dad come alive and come after me!'

'Don't be so dopey, Iffy. Your dad is up in heaven.'

'And my mam?'

Mrs Meredith poked the bubbling potatoes and didn't say anything.

'And my mam, Nan?'

She coughed, lifted a lid, and poked the ham with a vengeance.

'Ay, and your mam, God forgive—'

'But what if dead people do come after me when I'm in bed?'

'Iffy! Dead people can't hurt you! It's the living you want to be afraid of.'

'Why do I have to be afraid of the living?'

'You don't.'

'You just said I did.'

'Well, you don't! There's nobody you have to be afraid of.'

'What about Georgie Fingers and Dai Full Pelt and old Mrs Medlicott?'

'You keep well away from that lot.'

'Why, if they're not going to hurt me?'

'Just keep well away and don't even speak to them if you can help it.'

'But you said they wouldn't hurt me.'

'Go anywhere near them and *I'll* bloody hurt you!'

'Dai Full Pelt called me Sambo.'

'What were you doing talking to him?'

'I didn't.'

'Ay, well, Dai Full Pelt doesn't know what he's talking about. Tell him to go and scratch.'

'How can I if I'm not allowed to talk to him, Nan? How can I, Nan?'

'Oh Iffy, Nan's arse for a bloody raffle! Don't Nan me . . . go and get some dry clothes on before you catch your death – and mind out the way or you'll have that pan over . . . Rained frogs, be buggered!'

Iffy thought grown-ups believed in lots of things but they never wanted to believe in miracles.

But it was true. Bridgie Thomas was right! There were secrets in the valley that they were being paid back for. She and Fatty had drunk the holy water. Fatty had peed in the bottle! A skull had sailed away down the river. And God had made it rain frogs. She knew without a doubt that anything might happen now.

Iffy was afraid. Nan had been to tuck her in and now she lay looking up at the hook in the ceiling that had been used in ancient times to hang meat on. Grancha had told her that in the olden days the houses had been shared by two families. The poorer family had the back of the house, the kitchen and a loft above it for sleeping. The posh family had the front, the parlour, this room of hers as a kitchen, bedrooms upstairs and they came in and out through the front garden. Iffy hated that hook. It reminded her of the hooks that pirates had in the ends of their arms in story books. She was terrified of pirates even though she'd never seen one or even been to the seaside.

One night when she was little the hook had started turning round and round and she had screamed until she was sick.

She sniffed the air. Sometimes she thought she could smell the perfume from her nightmare. No smells tonight.

She prayed not to have the nightmare when the smell of the strange perfume crept out from the cracks in the walls. And she heard the cry of a ghost baby in a creaking crib. Or, worst of all, when a dark face grew out of the writhing shadows and got close to hers, whispering frantic words she couldn't understand.

Every time she had the dream she peed the bed leaking.

On windy nights when the branches of the bushes tapped against the window she thought it was the tap tap tapping of Blind Pugh escaped from the pages of *Treasure Island* and come to get her. Tap tap tapping with his stick along the hillside gwlis, his blind eyes glowing in the moonlight.

She thought of all the lunatics who lived in the town, they could be outside the window now, prowling around in the dark. She counted them up.

Three harmless ones: Auntie Mary Meredith who was family, mad but not dangerous, three splashes short of a birdbath; Lally Tudge, no lights on upstairs; Jack Look Up, daft as arseholes but nice.

Then Dulcie Davies who lived down Iron Row and ate live fish made four. Mrs Dwyer who slept with pigs in her bed made five.

Dangerous lunatics were the worst sort. Two of them for definite: Dai Full Pelt for a start, and Georgie Fingers, then old Mrs Medlicott according to Nan.

The candle on the tallboy flickered, then hissed and the light in the bedroom grew dim then bright again. Long-legged shadows ran over the bed and scurried away into dark corners.

The tapping started on the window pane.

Iffy closed her eyes tightly, held her breath and pulled the patchwork quilt up over her head, tight against her face until she could hardly breathe. Her heart beat like a Sally Army tambourine.

The tapping got quicker, and quicker. Tap tap tap. A hard insistent tapping on the window pane.

Blind Pugh!

Bugger!

Tap tap tap!

Ghosts from the cracked open graves. Just like Bridgie Thomas had said. It could be her mam. Got up from her grave. Or her dad risen from the bottom of the sea. Both of them walking hand in hand through the gwlis looking for her. Bones rattling. Ribs white as chalk in the moonlight. Teeth grinning in gumless mouths with no lips. Smelling of fish, of coal earth, of dead flowers and rotten wood.

TAP TAP TAP

Worms wriggling out of their earholes.

TAP TAP TAP

Slugs peeping from their eye sockets.

'Iffy!'

She shot out of bed, over the cracked lino and pulled back the thin curtains.

The moon hung high and full above Blagdon's Tump. Far away the town clock bonged and the Old Bugger hooted long and low in the graveyard.

'Hiya, Iffy.'

It wasn't her mam or her dad! Or Blind Pugh! It was Fatty Bevan.

'Oh, it's you.'

'Did I frighten you?'

'No!' she lied.

Her toes were banging up and down on the lino like piano keys.

'Sorry, Iffy.'

Fatty smiled. His eyes gleamed wickedly.

She forgave him instantly.

'Anyway, what you doin' out in the dark all by yourself?'

It was pitch black outside the window. Black as a collier's nose.

Fatty was like a bloody tom-cat, out all hours, running ragged. He wasn't a bit afraid of the dark or ghosts or anything.

'Listen, Iffy, I reckon Bridgie Thomas was right.'

'What do you mean?'

Cold fingers ran up her spine and across her shoulders.

'About the Big House. About keeping away.'

'Why?'

'I was coming past the gates and I heard something.'

'What?'

'Someone in the garden crying.'

'Honest?'

'Honest to God. I got up close as I could. I think it was old Mrs Medlicott.'

'What did you do?'

'I called out.'

'You didn't!'

'I did. And she whispered back.'

'What did she say?'

'She said, "Is that you, cat?"'

'What?'

'"Is that you, cat?" Whispering she was that they didn't bury the baby cat . . . Then she said, "I'm sorry, cat. I'm so sorry I thought bad of you" . . . Something like that.'

'Why was she talking to a cat?'

'I dunno. I fancy she's a bit simple or else . . .'

'Or else what?'

'Remember what your nan said about her not being safe . . . Well, what if she's right? P'raps she kills things . . . anything. Kittens. Babies. Grown-ups even.'

'You want to keep away from there, Fatty!'

'Not likely! P'raps there's bodies buried in the garden.

Skeletons in the cellars . . . Remember that skull you said you saw? To be honest, I didn't believe you at first, Iffy, but I reckon that's what you did see. It probably came from the grounds. It got washed down into the river.'

'Pack it in, Fatty!'

'Strange things have happened since she came back.'

'Like what?'

'Them frogs, for a start. When was the last time you seen it rain frogs?'

Iffy shook her head. 'My nan didn't believe me about the frogs,' she said.

'That's the funny bit, Iffy. I don't think anyone else saw them, only us.'

'I was worried it was because we drank the holy water. That God was paying us back.'

'No. He wouldn't send frogs, would he? I mean it'd be a lightning bolt or leprosy or something.'

Iffy shivered.

'I think it was a sign,' said Fatty.

'What for?'

'To warn us.'

'What about?'

'To be on our guard. Remember what Bridgie said about there being secrets in our town?' Iffy nodded. 'Well, there are.'

'Are what?'

'Secrets, Iffy!'

'How do you know?'

'I just do.'

'What sort of secrets?'

'I can't tell you.'

Iffy screwed up her nose. She hated secrets.

'I don't believe you!'

'Honest Injun.'

'How do I know you're telling the truth?'

'I am. Cross my heart.'

'You could just be saying that.'

'I'm not.'

'Prove it then!'

He looked over his shoulder into the darkness of the garden.

'What's the matter?'

'Just making sure there's no one there.'

He made her swear to secrecy. Standing on the lino, the moon picking up the blue-black glint of her curls, she crossed her heart.

'Say it, Iffy,' he said.

'Cross my heart and hope to die stick a needle in my eye!'

'Promise?'

'Double promise.'

And then Fatty told Iffy about what he'd seen. About the terrible things in the jar on Carty Annie's dresser.

She didn't believe him.

Then he said, 'I'm bloody boiling. You fancy coming for a swim?'

'A swim! In the pitch black! Where?'

'Up the top pond. It's lovely up there. Cool you down a treat. You want to come?'

She shook her head. She wasn't allowed to swim in the mountain ponds. Drunk men and wild boys had drowned there and sometimes the bodies were never found.

'I'll see you in the morning, then. Remember your promise.'

'Good night, Fatty.'

'Night, Iffy.'

He winked at her in the flickering light. His eyes shone, underwater eyes, the blue and black of mussel shells. And then he was off.

She watched him amble down the little bit of garden, leg it over the wall like a monkey and drop down into the darkness of the gwli where ghosts and dead people walked at midnight.

He was the bravest kid she knew. The bravest in the whole of Wales and probably the whole wide world. She listened to him as he went whistling along the gwli and then she pulled the window down quick, yanked the curtains together and shot back across the lino. She leapt under the covers. She didn't want any walking skeletons or mental old women getting hold of her.

The town clock clattered out eleven o'clock. She thought of the secret that Fatty had told her and even though she didn't believe him, she wished he hadn't told her.

She slept then and dreamed. She dreamed of her mam whom she'd never seen. Not a skeleton, bone-rattling mam, but a mam with soft satin skin, who tucked her up tight in bed and stroked her face with her dainty wedding-ring hands, kissing her with her warm silky lips. The bed rocked with her soft songs and Iffy felt her mam's heart beating against her own through the starchy sheets.

She dreamed of dead men floating up from the bottom of black ponds, their mouths opening and closing and spewing out live fish. She dreamed of a pirate ship with a skull and crossbones sailing up their little river. She dreamed of blind eyes staring and dead men's tongues hanging out.

She woke up with a jump. The hook in the ceiling was turning round and round, faster and faster.

She screamed the place down.

Footsteps came rushing through the black back parlour, the latch on the door lifted.

Grancha came round the door waving a poker, his eyebrows like birds flying. Her nan came behind him, eyes wide in the candle light.

Then she was safe in Grancha arms, he was cwtching her tightly and her nan hushing and blowing soft kisses. Grancha cradled her in his arms like a baby, carried her out of the room and up the worn-down stairs, kissing her with his sandpaper whiskers.

'Come on, little gel. Nothing to be scared of,' he said, and laid her down gently on the big high bed in the upstairs bedroom.

'It's that bloody Bridgie Thomas and all her half-cocked tales frightening the kids to death!' said Nan.

'You don't want to take no notice of her, mun. She's cracked.'

Nan tucked her up in the big high bed, tight up against the wall, safe from the long arms of bogeymen and the walking dead. Grancha went back down the stairs to lock up for the night.

She watched her nan undress through half-closed eyes. Nan pulled her nightie down over her head. It was as big and white as the tents that posh people had weddings in. She undid her bun and her hair slipped from the hairnet and as she climbed into bed it slid over the pillow towards Iffy, a silver river of sweet-smelling hair.

She was safe, lying beside her nan, smelling the warm, soft smells of Fairy soap on her wrinkly old skin and the pear-drop smell of her breath.

She lay quite still, listening. Downstairs she heard the ghosts whispering softly from their seat on the settle.

Her nan's breathing slowed until a soft whistling sound came from her chest and her arm felt heavy and cosy over Iffy's body.

Later, she heard her grancha climb up the stone stairs that they called the wooden hill, the soft pad of his slippers on the worn-down stone. She heard his knees creak as he bent down to pray. He stayed on his knees for a long time.

She tried to hear the words but they were just a whisper. She could smell the coal on him even though he bathed after every shift down the pit. He smelled of lots of things all mixed together: of snuff and warm corduroy, of damp wool and sticky toffee papers. The smells tickled her nose. She closed her eyes and listened to his bare feet squeaking as he crossed the lino to snuff out the candle.

The only light was warm moonlight.

He climbed into bed and soon he was snoring and whistling in his sleep as if to farm dogs in his dreams.

Far away the town clock bonged midnight.

The Old Bugger hooted amongst the crooked graves.

Iffy thought of the statues in the grounds of the Big House and Dr Medlicott sleeping at the bottom of the fishpond, of the horrible things in Carty Annie's house, of Fatty swimming alone in the black pond.

Bessie and Iffy looked all over the place for Fatty and Billy, but they were nowhere to be found.

They checked under the bridge. Walked down to Gladys's Gowns in case Fatty'd gone on the scrounge for food. No good. They even trailed over to Shanto's shop, which was out of bounds.

Willy Shanto's shop was over near the Catholic church. It wasn't so much a shop as a tin hut, a rusty tip of a place with cracked dusty windows and higgledy-piggledy shelving that bore everything from candles to nails, hairnets to gripe water. Shanto had only one eye. He had lost the other one in France in the war. The false eye was made of glass.

Shanto sold fireworks all year round, squibs and bangers, jumping jacks and Catherine wheels that hardly ever worked. He sold them cheap and never asked anyone's age.

Iffy was banned from Shanto's for life. Her nan would skin

her alive if she ever bought bangers again because someone somewhere that somebody knew had had their leg blown off by a firework. And there was the matter of the twenty bangers they'd put under a bucket on the top of Winnie Jones's lav. There was a bang! And a pasting to go with it!

Bessie wouldn't go anywhere near Shanto's. She said Shanto was a filthy discustin' pig and waited for Iffy further along the road.

The day they'd bought the bangers, Bessie had gone into the shop and up to the counter because she was the only one with any money. Shopkeepers were always nice to her because she spent a bomb. They always kept an eye on the rest of them, especially Fatty, though he never pinched from a shop. Only apples and stuff off trees.

'Twenty bangers and four bars of Fry's Five Boys,' Bessie had said, dead sweet.

Willy Shanto had put the chocolate bars down on the counter and then counted out the bangers.

'Close your eyes,' he had said to Bessie, 'I've got a present for you.'

Bessie had shut her eyes tight, grinning like a fool.

Shanto had winked at the others with his good eye, turned around then back again. He put something into Bessie's hand, and closed her fingers round it tightly.

'Something to see you through the week,' he'd said.

Bessie had opened her eyes first and then her hand. Shanto's glass eye had looked up at her. It was all blue, shining and staring.

Iffy had seen it wink at Bessie.

'Waargh!'

The eye had shot up in the air, landed by Bessie's feet and rolled across the wooden boards. Bessie had shot out of the door roaring.

They'd had to go after her because she had the money to

pay for everything, but she wouldn't go back in the shop again. Fatty had to go back for the chocolate and the bangers.

And she had cried and cried and ran all the way home.

So Bessie kept a lookout further down the lane while Iffy went up to the shop and peeped in through the dusty windows. It was empty. No customers. No Shanto. No Billy or Fatty.

They had no luck at the rec, either. No sign of them at all.

Iffy and Bessie stood together on the hump-backed bridge and called out their names but there was no answer. Sometimes Fatty took off like that, away down the river on the scent of foxes or badgers . . . going where none of them dared to go. He slept out in broken-down barns or in abandoned cars in quiet fields. They'd always said that one day they were all going to run away for an adventure, like Fatty. They'd follow the river right down the valley till it came to the sea. They were going to wear wellies and take sandwiches and fishing nets to catch their supper. They were going to sleep under the bridges at night, for a month at least. They were just waiting for the right day, that was all.

They never, ever, called at Fatty's house to see where he was. They were too afraid. Mr Bevan was huge and red, hairy and bad-tempered. Mrs Bevan was always drunk. It was a place to keep away from.

Iffy and Bessie walked down past Armoury Terrace and along to the bakery to see if Billy was there.

Bessie went into the shop first. The bell above the door tinkled merrily, and the smell was mouth-wateringly lovely: caramel and custard; flaky sausage rolls and juicy steak puddings; icing sugar and raspberry jam; Swansea batch and red-hot bloomers; coconut and almond; marzipan. The air was sweet to breathe, gritty with sugar. The floor was a carpet of flour and crumbs.

Billy's dad, Mr Edwards, stood behind the counter, his clean, pink hands clasped over his rounded white belly.

He smiled down at them. 'Good morning, ladies.'

'Morning, Mr Edwards.'

'Is Billy coming out to play?' said Bessie.

'Billy's not here, my lovelies . . . he's away with his mam for a few days.'

'Oh. Sorry.'

They turned to leave.

'Don't rush off, girls. I don't suppose you'd like to join me in a little something special . . . a spot of tea to keep you going?'

They turned slowly back towards him. They never ever got asked to tea.

'You're Billy's friends, aren't you?'

They nodded shyly. They didn't really know Billy's mam and dad, just enough to nod to, not to talk.

He beckoned to them and the girls went behind the counter, and followed him through a velvet-curtained archway into a cosy little parlour at the back of the shop. It was a very pretty little room. There was a squidgy green sofa over which a creamy lace cloth had been draped. There was a small table with a blue gingham tablecloth that was laid all ready for tea. In the middle of the table stood a silver vase with six deep-pink tulips. There were four dainty china plates with shiny gold rims and tiny pink roses, and matching cups and saucers.

'Come in. Come in. I won't bite!'

Iffy and Bessie giggled and looked nervously at each other.

'Take a seat, ladies, take a seat.'

They stepped gingerly towards the table.

'Now, what are your names, girls?'

'I'm Elizabeth Tranter. Only everybody calls me Bessie.'

'Iffy Meredith.'

'That's an unusual name.'

Iffy smiled and began to explain, 'Really it's Elizabeth Gwendoline. But I'm always called Iffy. When I was little I used to say if all the time: if I was bigger, if I was rich. So my nan said they ought to call me Iffy. So they did, and it stuck.'

She didn't tell him that her nan had said, 'If, if, if . . . if Granny had balls we'd call her grandad,' in case he thought she was a rough girl from a filthy family.

Mr Edwards laughed. He had a nice laugh and a kind face, plumply pink, with tightly rounded cheeks, teeth as white as wedding-cake icing.

'Well, Bessie, sit down do.'

Bessie sat down very daintily on a high-backed chair.

'And you, Iffy.'

Iffy pulled out the chair opposite Bessie.

Mr Edwards jumped nervously.

'Oh, not that seat, Iffy, that's our Johnny's chair. We lay a place for him every day just in case he comes in through the door.'

Iffy looked across at Bessie, but Bessie looked away quickly.

Johnny was Billy's dead brother. They knew that.

Out in the shop the bell rang.

'Make yourselves comfortable. I won't be a moment.'

Mr Edwards went back through the curtained archway into the shop.

Iffy and Bessie sat in stiff-backed awkwardness, afraid to speak and break the humming silence.

Iffy gazed warily around the room, there was a painting on the wall of some dried-up sunflowers in a vase, and a photograph of two small boys holding hands – Billy when he was about five and his dead brother – both smiling shyly at the camera.

The clock on the mantelpiece ticked loudly, a kettle hissed in a room that led off the parlour.

Mr Edwards's voice drifted in from the shop, 'Good day to you, Mrs Titley . . . well we were glad of that drop of rain. Right, one cob and four custard tarts . . . there you are, that'll be—'

The sound of the till ringing cut off his words.

'Let's go!' Bessie whispered. 'I don't like it.'

'We can't, it would be rude.'

'He might be funny. We're not supposed to talk to strangers.'

'He's not a stranger, he's Billy's dad.'

'Yes, but we don't know him.'

The clock chimed the hour and they both leapt in alarm.

Iffy looked at the empty chair next to her. A chair waiting for a dead boy to take his place at the table. She trembled.

Bessie was biting her lip, her eyes wide and anxious. The velvet curtain jingled on its gold rings. Iffy held her breath. The air in the room was stiff with fear. She breathed out as Mr Edwards stepped back into the parlour.

'Well now, Bessie, as you're in my wife's seat perhaps you could be mother. Just a second while I fetch the tea.'

Iffy looked again at the place next to her and thought of Billy sitting up to every meal next to the empty seat, waiting in case his brother came back.

Mr Edwards came back into the room carrying a heavy tray. She forgot about Billy then, and his dead brother. On the tray was a teapot shaped like a house, a china house with a roof and a chimney, with windows and doors, with a spout growing out of one wall and a handle from another. There were three plates full of cakes, the most dainty, miniature cakes she'd ever seen. They were beautiful. Tiny, thumb-sized chocolate éclairs, marzipan fruits – oranges and lemons with tiny green leaves, bananas and bunches of grapes – butterfly cakes, tiny ring doughnuts that looked light enough to float around the parlour.

A feast. Food for queens and kings.

Not the sort of food Iffy and Bessie ever got to eat.

'Well, Bessie, you be mother.'

Bessie smiled proudly and carefully lifted up the beautiful teapot house and poured three cups of tea.

'Pour a cup for Johnny too. I expect he'll be wanting to wet his whistle.'

Bessie poured a fourth cup, but when she laid down the cup in front of the empty place her hand shook and the cup rattled noisily against the saucer. She blushed with embarrassment.

Iffy watched the curtained doorway with one eye in case Billy's brother should choose today to come back from the dead and join them at the table.

Mr Edwards beamed at them and offered around the plates of tiny cakes. They took a ring doughnut each, and ate carefully, licking the sugar from their fingers and lips.

Mr Edwards offered the plate again.

They ate steadily, slowly and politely, savouring every sweet mouthful.

The cakes and tiny fruits were delicious but when Mr Edwards laid out a selection of cakes on Johnny's plate, Iffy's appetite slipped away.

'Of course, I expect Billy's told you all about his brother,' he said nodding at the empty chair.

Iffy tried hard to swallow but couldn't. The marzipan grapes stuck in her throat. She thought Mr Edwards must be a mad man. How could Billy have told? Mr Edwards must know that his own son couldn't speak.

'It was Billy's birthday . . . his fifth. They went for a walk over the mountain to visit his auntie . . . his mam's sister, but of course they never arrived.'

The clock on the mantelpiece ticked sadly. The tulips in the silver vase dropped their heads.

Bessie began to wheeze, a slow rattle like a train going into a tunnel.

'There was a big wheel up the mountain, you've seen one like it I expect, it pulls the drams of coal along on wires.'

Iffy nodded.

Bessie rattled.

'It was just a game to the big boys – swinging on the wires.'

Across the table from Iffy, Bessie's chest clanked noisily.

Mr Edwards sipped his tea and stayed silent for a few minutes.

Iffy swallowed her tea loudly and felt herself go red.

'Eat up, girls.'

They helped themselves reluctantly to more cakes but the charm had gone out of them.

'Some dropped off straight away but the biggest and daftest hung on and just before they reached the wheel they let go.'

Mr Edwards's eyes brimmed with tears. The girls looked down into their laps.

'Eat up, girls.'

They ate unwillingly out of frightened politeness.

Iffy could hear Bessie's bony knees knocking together under the table.

'My boys stopped to watch.'

Tears dropped from Mr Edwards's eyes, big fat milky tears that ran over his round pink cheeks, down his neck and were soaked up by his shirt collar.

'One of the big boys dared our Johnny to have a go . . . but he wouldn't, he was sensible, see.'

Outside the window in another world a bird sang a cheery song.

Mr Edwards stood up so suddenly that the cups rattled on the saucers. He screamed out, 'Chicken!'

Bessie choked on her tea.

'Wark! Wark! Wark! Wark!' Mr Edwards flapped his arms against his sides like a demented bird. 'Chick chick chick chick chicken!'

Bessie's eyes grew huge and watery.

The room was a human chicken coop.

Iffy didn't know whether to laugh or to cry.

Then Mr Edwards stopped as suddenly as he'd begun. The clock began to tick again. He slumped back down into his chair. Underneath his white coat his chest heaved with exertion.

Still the tears rolled from his eyes.

'A boy called Walters lifted him up to reach the wires, he was too small, see . . . Billy should have stopped him!'

Bessie's chest was clattering dangerously. Mr Edwards didn't seem to notice. He was talking as though there was no one else in the room with him.

'He rode the wires like the big boys, higher and higher.'

Outside, in the sunlight, in that other world, someone whistled a tune.

His voice grew quieter, little more than a whisper, 'Higher and higher. Let go for Christ's sake. Drop, you daft bastard!'

Bessie gasped. Her face paled, as white as flour.

'But he didn't. Too afraid to let go he was.'

Silence. The clock held its tock.

'Somebody ran for his mam. She was shaving her legs. Luckily the men from the pit got to him first . . . They took him away in brown paper bags. Only his shoes were untouched . . . not a mark on them . . . brown sandals with crêpe soles that his mam hadn't finished paying for. The price was still on the bottom. Well, look at the time, I must get back to work. Any time you'd like some tea, come again. Come again.'

They stood up. Iffy's legs were shaking almost uncontrollably. They followed him silently back through the curtained doorway.

The gold rings jingled gaily. The air in the shop smelled sickly sweet. The bell tinkled above the door.

Iffy and Bessie stepped out together into the bright sunlight, and walked without talking all the way to the hump-backed bridge.

Bessie was sick first. Then Iffy.

Side by side the two small figures stood heaving and retching into the long grass.

The rain had stopped by the time he reached his destination; dark clouds scurried across the sky, blowing away over another valley. Will stepped down from the bus just as the town clock struck the hour. He stood for some moments looking up at the clock and soaking up the long-remembered smells of this town, similar to all the other towns in the Welsh valleys. There was still the heady scent of rich, oily black earth and of rain-drenched nettles that made his eyes water. The bitter-sweet essence of coal smoke that rose up from the chimneys was not as strong as it used to be.

The picture house had long-since closed and was now a discount furniture shop. He lingered for a while looking up at the building. Written on the stonework above the double doors he could just make out the faded letters O, Y and P. The rest of the letters had been worn away over the years. Olympia.

He took the faded photograph from his briefcase. A photographer from the *Argus* newspaper had taken it, he'd thought it would be a good 'heatwave' photo but it hadn't been used in the end. Someone else had snapped a bunch of well-dressed kids over in Ponty eating ice creams.

Will studied the photograph intently. A black and white photograph of four children sitting on the steps of the Olympia. Four kids sitting there on a boiling-hot day, sweating in the fierce heat, their eyes screwed up against the sun. Three scruffy-looking urchins and the fourth one done up to the nines. A few weeks later and one of them had disappeared forever.

Will booked into a pub. A spruced-up pub painted in rich dark green and gold with a sign that declared it to be the Firkin. It was a long way from the scruffy pub it had been when he had last visited the town. It had been called the Punch then.

He took a slow walk up through the town. Once it had been a thriving, bustling place, but was now a shadow of its busy industrial self. It had been a pit town then with the pavements ringing to the sound of colliers' boots and the pubs full of worn-out men on their way home from a shift, damping the thick dust in their throats with a few pints of ale. When he'd last been here there had been a Woolworth's, a busy Co-op and a host of butchers and bakers.

Now, almost every other shop was boarded up and To Let signs hung haphazardly above their windows. The few remaining shops looked to be on their last legs. It was a town decimated by the closure of the pits and the out-of-town shopping centres that had sprung up all over the valleys.

Only a few of the old shops remained. He stood outside one of them for a few moments. Curiously, Gladys's Gowns had escaped any signs of either modernisation or decay. It was from another age and just the same as the ladies' dress shops of his childhood. There were still the same white-faced dummies in the window wearing dated designs: tweed suits and olive-green twin sets, belted mackintoshes and day dresses. At the front of the window were a row of dismembered heads wearing wedding hats. There were still orange cellophane blinds to pull down in case of hot weather.

He walked on past a multitude of boarded-up takeaways, Indian, Chinese, kebab, Kentucky-style chicken.

It was a totally different place to the one he had known years before.

Halfway along the high street Will stopped. In the middle of the one-street town there was a sight that gladdened his eyes. The Italian café still stood there – Zeraldo's.

As a young man it had always fascinated him that so many Italians had ended up in the Welsh valleys running cafés and chip shops. He had often wondered why they should have left home and hearth in Italy and set off to a damp, industrial place like Wales to sell ice cream and chips.

Will peeped in through the misted-up window. A very old man stood behind the counter polishing glass tumblers. Looking up he saw Will and gave him a gold-toothed smile. Will smiled back.

A blue-eyed child in a window seat stared up at Will and smiled a gappy toothed grin. A child with a face smeared with ice cream and raspberry sauce. Ice cream melting slowly in a silver dish.

A little of the old place remained after all.

He wondered if there would be anything left of the past, any clues that would point him in the direction of finding out what really happened all those years ago. He doubted it. He thought that he had set out on a wild-goose chase, something to occupy a mind that didn't want to concentrate on dying.

Iffy and Bessie, bored to buggery, were sitting on the wall opposite the Old Bake House watching Lally Tudge who was skipping in the middle of the road.

Every time Lally jumped over the rope her thingies flopped up and down. Down. Up. Down. Up. Until Iffy felt giddy from watching.

Lally wasn't wearing a brassiere even though she had great big huge ones.

Brassieres were what grown-up women wore. Upper decker flopper stoppers. Over shoulder boulder holders.

She elbowed Bessie in the ribs.

'Stop it, Iffy!'

'She should wear a thingy.'

'What's a thingy?'

'A brassiere.'

Bessie went red and looked the other way.

'You shouldn't be looking, Iffy Meredith.'

Up and down went Lally's thingies.

Faster and faster. Titties. Bosoms. Tits.

There were two wet patches on the front of her blouse. The patches grew bigger as she continued to jump the rope.

Lally smiled at them. Iffy smiled back. Bessie didn't.

'Cowboy Joe from Mexico,
Hands up, stick 'em up,
Drop your guns and pick 'em up.'

'Bit big to be skipping, ent she?' Bessie whispered.

'She's twp,' Iffy said.

Lally skipped on, her big daft feet raising dust storms on the cracked road.

'Look!' said Iffy, nudging Bessie again, but Bessie wouldn't.

Lally sang the 'Cowboy Joe' song again and when she got to 'drop your guns and pick 'em up', she bent down to pick up her pretend guns. That was when Iffy saw that Lally didn't have any knickers on! She nearly fell off the wall and almost pulled Bessie with her.

'Careful, mun, you'll rip my clothes.'

Iffy hissed in Bessie's ear, 'She's got no knickers on.'

'Pack it in, Iffy!'

'Honest to God, Bessie, look!'

But Bessie still wouldn't look.

Iffy did.

'Drop your guns and pick 'em up!' sang Lally Tudge, and bent down again for the pretend guns.

Iffy saw her bum, her big fat arse. She saw it five times. It was huge and round and naked. It was white and greasy as lard. She even saw the black crack of it.

Then Lally changed her song.

'Nebuchadnezzar King of the Jews
Bought his wife a pair of shoes
When the shoes began to wear
Nebuchadnezzar began to swear.'

And Lally swore at the top of her voice, 'SHIT! SHIT! SHIT! FUCK! FUCK! FUCK!'

Bessie did fall off the wall then. Arse over tip she went in a flurry of lacy knickers and frothy petticoats, taking Iffy with her. They scrabbled together in the dust, Bessie trying desperately to pull her frock down over her knees.

'Discustin',' said Bessie, wiping dust from her frock.

It was too. It was real dirty. Filthy. It was great, but terrifying.

'Let's go!'

They went running off down the hill, Lally's filthy words whizzing past their burning ears like shrapnel, until they reached the bridge where they stood together, panting and blowing.

'Wotcha, girls!'

Fatty came up over the river bank.

'Where've you been? We been looking for you everywhere!'

He was dirtier than they'd ever seen him. He stood in

127

front of them grinning, his teeth white against the filthy black of his face, his eyes glistening under eyebrows that trailed cobwebs. His wet clothes were clinging to him, strands of weed wrapped round his bare brown legs.

'Bloody hell, Fatty! What've you been doing?'

Bessie sniffed and backed away from him.

'You'll never guess.'

'Down the pit by the smell of you,' said Bessie holding onto her nose.

'Licking a cow's arse?' Iffy guessed.

'Iffy!'

'I've been in the garden of the Big House.'

They stared at him. Didn't believe him.

'Liar! Liar! Your bum's on fire!'

'You wouldn't dare!'

'Honest to God.'

'Did anyone see you?'

'How did you get in?'

'Remember, Iffy, when Carty Annie said there was a way in? Well, I found it. I got in through the pipe.'

'Where is it?'

'Further up the river, just past the bridge. It's all over-grown. It took me ages to cut the brambles back and then it was easy.'

Iffy was bursting with admiration. He was one bloody brave bugger.

'Where does the pipe come out?'

'At the bottom of the garden in the bushes.'

'Was it dark in the pipe?' Bessie asked, she hated the dark.

'Ay, pitch black. And there were rats.'

'Ugh!' Bessie hated rats. They carried the plague. They had fleas and went for your throat if you cornered them.

'Did you have a torch?'

'No. Just a candle and matches, the rats kept jumping up to the light.'

Iffy pulled a face. She imagined rats' claws running up and down her backbone, the feel of their scratchy feet on her skin, the tickle of their busy whiskers.

'Weren't you scared, Fatty?'

'Nope.'

'What was it like in the garden?'

'I didn't see much. Just as I got out of the pipe I seen old Mrs Medlicott at the window. I scarpered then . . . but I'm going in again.'

The town clock bonged the hour. A horse clopped across the bridge above them. Bessie was late. Fatty was getting restless.

'Where the bloody hell is she?'

'I dunno, I told her seven o'clock.'

'I can't wait much longer.'

Billy, standing next to Iffy, held her hand. She let him when Bessie wasn't around. With his other hand he took some money out of his trouser pocket and showed it to Iffy. He mimed eating ice cream.

'Here she is!'

Bessie was coming down the hill ever so slowly. She was wearing shiny red wellies and couldn't walk fast because they were too big and her legs were too skinny to take the weight of them.

'Come on, Bessie, shift your arse!'

Bessie glared at Fatty.

Iffy giggled and gave Billy's hand a little squeeze, then let go.

'Right. Come on.'

Fatty led the way. They followed him in a crocodile, climbed down over the river bank and went under the dark bridge. It was gloomy there. A fish plopped, making rings in the dark water which spread wider and wider towards the banks. Somewhere a frog croaked. Iffy wondered if it was one of the magic ones that had fallen out of the sky.

They stepped out of the archway on the far side of the bridge into the fading sunlight.

'You lot wait here by the bridge. It'll take me about ten minutes to get through the pipe.'

They watched Fatty walk away towards the walls of the Big House. A lopsided sign on the wall said, 'PRIVATE. KEEP OUT.'

From the high wall was a steep slope leading down to the river bank, which was a thick jungle of weeds and brambles.

Fatty whistled to himself. The words to the tune went:

Hitler has only got one ball,
the other is in the Albert Hall.
His mother pinched the other,
now he ain't got none at all.

Bessie would have sniffed with disgust if she'd known the words to the tune.

He climbed the slope, whishing at the long grass with a stick. He turned round as he neared the top, and said, 'When I get through the pipe I'll whistle, right?'

They nodded silently. Bessie's mouth hung open catching gnats.

Billy made the sign of the cross.

'Be careful, Fatty,' Iffy called out quietly and she crossed her fingers behind her back for luck.

'Piece of cake, mun. See you in a bit.'

The three of them stood close together in the long waving grass and watched him go. A dragonfly hovered over the water, its wings beating rainbows. Jackie Long-Legs danced through the jungle grass and Bessie kept her skirts pulled tight around her bony knees.

'Want an aniseed ball?' Bessie said and took a screwed-up paper bag out of her pocket. She gave one to Billy. She gave Iffy two. Bessie smiled, showing her brown teeth. Iffy smiled back.

Fatty had reached the top of the bank and was scrabbling about near a clump of brambles. He bent down and pulled some branches to one side. They could just about make out the pipe, a black hole leading into the bank, hardly big enough for Fatty to get into. He turned around, grinned, and put his thumb up to them. Then he crouched down and moved towards the dark opening. Suddenly he ducked his curly head and crawled into the pipe. Iffy heard the strike of a match against a box. There was a flicker of light as he lit his candle. The last they saw of him was the crack of his bum peeping out of his baggy shorts. Smooth skin, soft and white against the dark brown of his back.

He was a hero all right.

It was so quiet as they stood there in the long grass waiting for him to whistle.

Whisshh! A bird flew up out of the grass nearby and Billy leapt into the air. Bessie squealed. Billy grinned at Iffy and pointed upwards. The bird climbed high into the evening sky, singing madly, dipping and soaring into the blue. Iffy watched it go until she felt giddy from the movement.

No one spoke.

They waited and waited. He must have been gone half an hour at least they thought. Bessie wanted to go home. So did Iffy.

A cool breeze came up the river rustling the long grass

131

that made Iffy's bare legs itch. Goose pimples pricked her arms and she shivered.

No whistle came from Fatty. He must have been in there by now. He'd been gone for ages.

The town clock bonged eight o'clock.

'Wee ooh wit!' Fatty's whistle! He was inside the grounds of the Big House.

The whistle came again louder, 'Wee ooh wi i i it!'

It was him! They knew his whistle anywhere. He was right there on his own in the grounds of the Big House.

'What if they catch him?' Bessie said.

'They might set the dogs on him.'

'Or the geese.'

'Or shoot him dead.'

'They wouldn't dare.'

'Would they?'

The sun dropped behind Carmel Chapel and the great arched windows burned with orange fire as if the whole building was alight inside. It looked eerie and frightening as if God had got in there and was playing with matches.

The water glugged and gurgled over the grey boulders of the river and swept on by. Invisible frogs croaked around them in the long grass and Bessie stamped her feet to scare them off. She did the same for snakes when they walked up the mountain. Thump thump thump she went, in case an adder had his eye on her for a quick bite.

The birds heard the noise before they did. They rose from the grass and the graveyard trees in a black explosion of squawking.

'BANG!'

Gunshot.

Bessie screamed and Billy had to put the flat of his hand over her mouth to shut her trap for her. Rooks and crows flapped and screeched above the burning chapel.

'They've kilt him,' Iffy said.

Billy's eyes were leaking pools of terror.

Bessie's face was as pale as the dummies in Gladys's Gowns' her mouth slack and hanging open behind Billy's tiny fingers.

Iffy thought of Fatty lying in a pool of crimson blood on the satin-smooth lawn, his guts scattered all over the grass, his lungs spread out to the size of tennis courts like they'd learned in science lessons at school.

'What'll we do?' Bessie said through Billy's fingers.

'They might come after us if they know we know it was them who shot him.'

Silence all around except for the glug of the river.

A silver fish plopped. Circles in the water grew ever wider. A crow cawed gruffly from a high tree in the graveyard.

They were too afraid to move. Running away meant turning their backs on a gunman.

Billy sobbed silently, his fingers searching out Iffy's hand.

Iffy's stomach rumbled noisily. Bessie farted, and coughed at the same time to cover up.

A second gunshot rang out.

They ran hell for leather for the cover of the bridge.

Still no sign of Fatty. He was a gonner. Bang bang you're dead fifty bullets in your head. Dead meat. They knew it.

Bessie's teeth chattered. Iffy's skin was a crawling map of goose pimples. Billy wiped tears from his eyes, fat, plopping tears that came without any noise. Iffy put her arm around his heaving shoulders and felt his bones shaking under his skin. Bessie rolled her eyes at the two of them.

'Haisht, Billy, it'll be all right.'

Muffled noises came from the pipe. It was someone come to get them.

'Bugger off, will you! . . . Ow! . . . Get off.'

Fatty's voice! He was alive! But someone was after him. He was being chased!

Bessie squealed and ran deeper into the cover of the bridge. Billy and Iffy followed her, peeping out from the archway. They could see the pipe, but if anyone came out behind Fatty they wouldn't be able to see the three of them. They'd have time to run.

Someone from the Big House was chasing after Fatty with a gun. Mrs Medlicott perhaps, who wasn't safe where kids were concerned, was following him across the lawns waving a shotgun. She must have missed him when she fired. What if she killed him in front of them? What if she killed them all?

Fatty came out of the pipe like the man they fired from a cannon at the circus, but without the bang. He shot out of the hole at a hundred miles an hour at least. He flew through the air and turned over and over, landing halfway down the bank with a hell of a crack that would have killed a normal boy.

He roly-polied over and over and over down the bank flattening daisies and dandelions as he went. Faster and faster. A blur of faded khaki and washed-out blue. He would have landed in the river if a thick clump of stingies hadn't broken his fall.

'Ow! Shit! Ow! Shit! Ow! F-f-f-uckinada!'

Bessie spluttered and went puce.

They heard a noise from the pipe. Someone *was* behind Fatty!

It was the maniac Mrs Medlicott for sure. A mad woman with a gun!

They looked up at the pipe in terror. Something peeped out of the blackness.

It wasn't a maniac. Or an English woman. It had an

orange beak, and two beady eyes, a long neck and a fat belly. It was a huge white goose. It glared down at them, looking from side to side. Then it opened its beak and let out one hell of a racket.

'Help me out, will you? I'm getting stung to death, mun,' yelled Fatty from the depths of the stingies.

Billy and Iffy rushed towards him, all the while keeping a careful eye on the goose.

Fatty swore and yelped.

The goose got fed up and waddled back into the pipe.

'Who fired the gun? Did they try to kill you? You was lucky.'

Fatty didn't answer. He was desperately trying to wriggle out of his T-shirt.

'Get me some dock leaves, quick. I'm fuckin' pickled.'

Iffy and Billy snatched up armfuls of dock leaves, spat on them, and Fatty stuck them all over his belly. Iffy and Billy did his back for him. Bessie kept her hands firmly in her pockets and looked the other way.

He was covered in lumps and bumps. All over his arms and neck, up his back and round his ankles. Iffy thought it must have hurt like mad, but he didn't even cry. He was lucky though. It was a wonder he hadn't broken his neck the way he'd come out of that pipe and catapulted down the bank. He was like a cat with nine lives.

Thank God.

The sound of the ice-cream man's bell clanged out, getting louder as he came up past Morrissey's shop. Mr Zeraldo always made his last stop near the bridge, even when it was nearly dark.

Mr Zeraldo was an Italian. He owned a café in town and he was the ice-cream man, too. He had a battered old van painted pink on the bottom half and cream on the top. Strawberry and vanilla. It had a bell, but nobody could tell what the tune was meant to be, it was just an awful racket.

Zeraldo's was the best ice cream in the world: strawberry, vanilla, chocolate, tutti frutti. Wafers. Oysters. Tubs with wooden spoons that set your teeth on edge. Zeraldo's ice cream had little slivers of ice in it that prickled the tongue.

Mr Zeraldo had been a prisoner in the war even though he hadn't done anything except sell ice cream. He had been sent away to pick hops on a farm up near Worcester. Mr Zeraldo's first name was Mario. He had gold teeth and wore a bracelet. The Italians had the best graves up in the cemetery – all photographs and flying angels.

Mr Zeraldo put raspberry sauce all over the top of a cornet, or chocolate sauce and nuts. A chocolate flake if you were rich. If you didn't have enough money Mr Zeraldo would give you a broken-off cornet and a little dollop of ice cream on it.

The sound of the bell came closer. Billy grabbed Iffy's arm, pulling at her excitedly. He beckoned to Fatty and Bessie to follow.

They hurried back under the bridge and scrabbled up the bank.

Zeraldo was parked up above them on the bridge. The bell faded into an echo, only the soft hum of the engine could be heard.

Mr Zeraldo leant forward through the window of the van. He stared open-mouthed at Fatty. His gold teeth glinted merrily.

'You bin inna de wars,' Mr Zeraldo said raising his black eyebrows.

Fatty looked a sight, as if he had walked out of a jungle after years of being lost. He was covered in spit-licked dock leaves. His filthy, scratched face was a mass of swelling bumps, black mud was smeared across every bare bit of his body.

'I had a fight with a gorilla, Mr Zeraldo!' Fatty said, grinning. 'I look bad but you should see the state of him!'

'It wasn't a gorilla, it was a goose,' said Bessie.

They ignored her.

Billy scrabbled in his pockets, stretched up on tippy toes and put some money on the counter of the van. He pointed at the board with the faded pictures of lollies, cornets and tubs.

He held up four small fingers.

'Foura ninety nines, eh?'

Billy smiled and nodded.

'You wunna da pools?' Mr Zeraldo asked Billy.

Billy smiled, his face full of dimples, and shook his head from side to side. He held his tiny hands up. Five fingers on one hand and five on the other.

'Data how mucha you won?'

Billy shook his head again.

Then Iffy twigged. 'It's his birthday, Mr Zeraldo. He's ten today.'

They stood together on the bridge in the growing shadows looking at Billy. A breeze rustled through the graveyard trees, sheep bleated up on the darkening mountain. Far away Barny the bulldog howled and rattled his rusty chains.

'Happy a birthday to you . . .' sang Mr Zeraldo.

They joined in,

'Squashed a tomatoes and a stew
Bread and a butter in ze gutter
Happy a birthday too oo oo oo yooooo!'

Mr Zeraldo drowned them all out. He had a huge,

beautiful voice even though he was only little. His voice hit the windows of Carmel Chapel and put the last of the orange fire out. His voice bounced back at them. It shook the trees and echoed under the bridge and chased after the river down the valley.

Billy bit his lip shyly. His huge brown eyes were wet and shiny.

Billy's birthday.

The same day as that awful thing had happened to his brother. The wheel turned . . . drop off . . . someone ran for his mam. They carried him away in brown paper bags.

Iffy didn't want to think about it.

Everyone clapped when they'd finished singing and Mr Zeraldo gave Billy his money back and gave them all free ice creams. He was dead kind.

'You buy yourself some-a-thing nice!'

'Thanks, Mr Zeraldo,' Fatty and Iffy said for Billy.

Mr Zeraldo drove slowly away over the bridge and the clapped-out old van creaked and rattled its way back towards town.

Fatty made them wait until he'd finished his ice cream and licked his lips.

'Bloody hell, I thought I'd had it!'

'We heard the gunshot.'

'Who was it who fired at you?'

'What? Nobody fired at me.'

'But we heard the bang.'

'Oh that! Probably somebody out shooting rabbits or foxes.'

'What happened then?'

'What's it like in there?'

'Did anybody see you?'

'Hang on, give us a chance.'

'Are there statues, Fatty?'

'Yep.'

'Were they . . . you know?'

'Naked? Yep.'

'Completely naked?'

'Yep. Starkers. You can see everything.'

'Everything?'

'Bums and titties!'

Bessie looked away, blushed from the knees up.

'And fannies.'

Bessie gasped. So did Iffy.

'And one of them's got no head.'

'No head?'

'No. Someone must have chopped it off.'

'Did anybody see you?'

'No. I seen her though.'

'You never!'

'She was having dinner. I could see her through the big window. Very posh. Lah di bleeding dah. There was candles in silver sticks.'

'What was she eating?' asked Bessie.

Fatty rolled his eyes.

'Fried liver and kidneys. Human ones.'

'Honest?'

'Don't be so dull. I couldn't see what she was eating.'

Fatty was as brave as a lion. Iffy couldn't imagine not being scared of the rats and the dark and the geese and dogs and the guns.

'Did you see the fishpond?'

'Yep.'

'Could you see to the bottom of it?'

'No, cause all of a sudden that fucking great goose come flying at me—'

'Fatty Bevan!'

'Sorry, Bessie. I'm going to go in again, though, when the

moon is full and I'm gonna see if what they say is true about old Medlicott coming out of the pond!'

Stark staring bonkers he was.

Will found his way to the bridge, a small hump-backed bridge spanning the river, a fast-flowing river now after the weeks of heavy rain. He felt strange standing there. He looked down into the water. He felt as if the past had conjured itself up again and wrapped itself about him. He thought that if he shut his eyes and wished, he could be drawn back into that long-gone summer with all its secrets.

He closed his eyes and leant back against the parapet. All around him was birdsong, the yammering of a disconsolate magpie, the querulous caw of a crow. A lone frog croaking down in the long waving grass, the sound of organ music drifted up from Carmel Chapel.

He opened his eyes. Rising up the hill, opposite where he stood were rows of identical red-brick council houses, houses with small uniform gardens and rotary washing lines. There were satellite dishes, television aerials and smokeless chimneys, vertical blinds and double glazing. In bedroom windows there were posters of football stars and rock singers.

The last time he was here there had been terraces of iron-workers' cottages with whitewashed walls and crumbling chimneys from which smoke curled into the blue skies, even though the weather was hot. There were sash windows that rattled in the wind, faded flowered curtains blowing in a draught, crucifixes and palm crosses in the windows of some of the cottages.

He turned his back on the houses and looked down into the water, absent-mindedly picking at the moss that grew thickly on the side of the bridge. It was soft and spongy, richly green, and came away easily in his hands.

He sighed deeply and was about to move away when

something caught his eye. He had uncovered the outline of a letter scratched in the concrete. He pulled away more moss, until he was looking at something he'd missed the last time he'd stood here. Not that it was of any importance but it gave him an eerie feeling just the same.

Lorence Bevan
William Jonh Edwerds
Elizabeth Gwendlin Meredith
Elibazeth Roof Tranter

After all these years the names were still there in the concrete.

The past was encroaching into the future, wrapping itself tightly around him, pulling him back to that distant summer, the hottest on record . . .

It had been unnaturally hot for weeks, although the weathermen on the wireless were warning of an end to the heat wave and thunderstorms were forecast. As he had sat in his office that afternoon he had hoped that the weathermen were right. The heat was overpowering, sapping the strength. He had been about to leave for home when the telephone had rung.

Sergeant Rodwell had sounded nervous, out of his depth. At first, Will had thought it was just a routine call: a child had gone missing up in one of the valley towns. He'd thought at the time that it was probably some kid who'd had a telling off for breaking a window or been given a pasting for stealing money from their mother's purse. It would be a frightened kid who had decided to hide away for a bit. Give their parents a scare and you could guarantee that a day's worry would assure them a warm, tearful homecoming. A storm in a teacup that would be cleared up in a few hours, all over by the following morning. But it hadn't, and thousands of mornings had passed and it still wasn't over.

Agnes Medlicott tilted her head backwards and sipped her wine and, as she put down her glass, a movement out in the garden caught her eye. A small boy, a very scruffy small boy, was emerging from the bushes at the far end of the garden. A curly haired boy, as brown-skinned as the Spanish boys from the village where she had lived for so long.

He stood still for some seconds, looking around furtively and then tiptoed across the lawn. She was about to ring the bell for Sandicock but thought better of it. The boy stopped in front of one of the statues. Maria Elena. He looked it up and down, taking in the whole of its nakedness with his greedy eyes. She reached again for the bell but once again her hand hovered, unwilling to take her eyes off the boy.

The statue was a good six inches taller than he was, but he reached up and, with one of the gentlest movements she had ever seen, touched the face, a delicate stroke of the cheek with his fingers. Then he stretched up on tiptoes and planted the softest of kisses upon the stone lips. The sleek brown muscles of his calves were taut with effort, the thin ankle bones almost delicate in contrast to the battered sandals. The nape of his neck was swathed with tight curls. She swallowed hard. He wasn't the child she was looking for, though she would have liked to sculpt this funny, grubby little boy with his sad, sweet gestures. He was a dirty cherubic figure and quite exquisitely beautiful.

The boy stepped back from the statue and crossed the lawn, looking about him, keeping low to the ground. When he got near to the fishpond he knelt down and bent his head to look into the dark, murky waters.

Agnes Medlicott rang the bell.

Iffy kept a check on the moon. A half moon. A three-quarter

moon. It grew slowly each night. She stood and watched it from from the upstairs bedroom window.

Down past the bridge, the graves in Carmel graveyard glowed in the moonlight. There were no signs of the graves cracking open yet. There were no skeletons clanking up the hill to find her. No more warnings sent from God. No locusts or famines or boils. No more frogs, leprosy or lightning bolts.

But one day soon when the moon grew to its full size the pond would start to stir and the bones of old Dr Medlicott would begin to rattle, the statues to move . . . and Fatty was going to crawl through the pipe to see if it was true.

He was mental.

Will stood on the river bank just beneath the bridge. It was damp, and a cold wind swept up the valley. It seemed like such a short time ago that he'd stood in almost same spot. Then, the sun had been beating down on his head, Rodwell had been standing beside him sweating profusely in his uniform. He remembered that he'd been astounded by the sound of croaking frogs, as if hundreds of them were thronging in the grass. He'd stood looking down at the clothes that had been abandoned. A small pile of clothes laid neatly in the parched grass. He'd picked them up, turned them over in his hands. They were warm from the sun and smelled very faintly of Fairy soap and lavender. A pile of kids' clothes but, strangely, there was no sign of any shoes.

Rodwell had told him that an old woman had raised the alarm. A Miss Bridget Thomas who'd been on her way home from Mass when she'd spotted the clothes. She'd been in quite a state apparently, ranting on to Sergeant Rodwell about God paying people back. Rodwell had to call a doctor for her, he'd told Will that she was a bit short-changed upstairs.

Now, forty-odd years later Will stood in the long wet grass

wondering what could have happened to the child. They'd thought immediately of drowning, of course. Most summers, particularly hot ones, claimed the lives of children tempted into the rivers and the mountain ponds. But the river levels had been very low after the weeks of hot weather, there hadn't been enough of a current to carry a body any distance downstream, although they'd checked the deeper pools further downriver but there was no sign of a child alive or dead.

There had been no sign of a struggle having taken place on the river bank and if some maniac had attacked or killed the child, God forbid, then surely the attacker wouldn't have left the tell-tale pile of clothes lying there to be discovered?

Days had passed and they'd been mystified that a child could apparently just disappear into thin air.

News had travelled through the town and three witnesses had come forward. If they were to be believed then they could establish that at between approximately three o'clock and four o'clock on the day in question, the child had most definitely been alive.

Will had interviewed the first witness. A Mr David Gittins, a middle-aged bus driver who lived locally. He stank heavily of sweat and stale beer and there was a peculiar smell of scorched cloth about him. He'd sat down gingerly in a chair and Will had wondered if piles troubled him. Will had thought him a shifty-looking bugger and an incredibly ugly bastard to boot. If Will was right, he probably had a bit of past form did Mr David Gittins.

They'd checked the records. He'd been had up on a couple of charges of burglary when he was a young man, urinating in a public place, handling stolen goods, but nothing other than that.

David Gittins claimed that he'd been driving the bus into town and, as he'd turned the corner by the rec, he'd nearly run over the child. It was about three o'clock, just before or just after, he'd heard the town clock chime the hour.

'Just come out of fuc— flippin' nowhere . . . must of jumped over the stile and run right out into the bloody road, not looking right or left, lucky not to have been killed I can tell you.'

It was a Sunday night. Billy, Iffy and Bessie met up on the bridge after Iffy had been to Mass with her grandparents and Bessie had been to evening chapel. Billy always went to early morning Mass. Fatty was dead lucky, he never had to go at all.

Voices drifted up from underneath the bridge. They all stopped still, kept quiet, just in case of ambush. Ambushes were always a worry, especially when Fatty wasn't around to help out. Sometimes kids from other parts of town hid under the bridge and waited. Then slimy mud bombs might be lobbed up in the air, coming down like fat rain. Any kids unlucky enough to be on top of the bridge would be splattered from head to foot with sticky black mud and weeds. And then there was all hell to be had at home when it wasn't even their fault.

They listened. Ears cocked. No sound of a lookout's whistle.

'It's only the Beynon twins, I think,' Iffy whispered.

They were afraid it was Mervyn Prosser, because everybody was scared of Mervyn Prosser. Even Fatty was a bit.

Mervyn Prosser lived up Donkey Lane. He was the roughest boy they knew. He was a bully and had his own gang: Dopey Thomas, Fido and Titch. Mervyn was the boss. They kidnapped kids and took them to their den and pulled the hairs out of their legs with rusty tweezers. Mervyn wasn't all there up top. Once he shot a woman up the arse with an air gun and the police were called and took the gun off him. It was Mrs Annie Caldwell whose arse it was and she was never right after.

Walter and Willy Beynon were just little kids from Balaclava. Harmless kids with snot running out of their snouts, down over their lips. Enough to make anyone sick. Snail trails all over their sleeves from wiping it.

They waited. Listened.

No bombs came over the top so they climbed up on the bridge and dangled their feet over the edge. Beneath them the water glugged and sucked and rolled away down the valley.

Music from a wireless escaped through an open window and floated on the soft evening air, *'Que sera sera . . . Whatever will be will be, the future's not ours to see . . .'*

'Oy! You lot!'

Mervyn Prosser came scrabbling up the bank. Behind him came Fido.

Shit!

Mervyn Prosser had a big red splash across his left cheek. A birthmark. His mam probably ate plums or damsons when she was having him.

Iffy thought fruit could be very dangerous: banana skins for broken bones, Auntie Mary Meredith had nearly choked to death on a monkey nut. And prunes. Prunes could make you shit through the eye of a needle.

'Look what we got!' Mervyn yelled running across the bridge towards them.

'A great big bugger,' said Fido, behind him.

They slid down off the bridge in panic. They were trapped. Not enough time to run. Bessie stood behind Iffy for safety.

Mervyn pulled his hands from behind his back.

'Look!'

'Urrgh!' Bessie stepped backwards with a yelp.

A huge fat frog peeped out from between Mervyn's filthy fingers.

Iffy thought the frog looked sad but not afraid.

'We found it in the grass. There's millions of 'em.'

'Wanna touch it?'

'Push off.' Bessie flew out the way. She knew that touching frogs gave you warts. Mervyn had them all over his fingers. Fido had one on his chin.

Fatty had told Iffy loads of cures for warts. Spit. Red match heads. Bacon. Slap a bit of bacon over the wart. Bury the bacon, and when it's rotted away the wart will fall off. Or else you could pee on them.

Iffy had read books where frogs turned into princes if you kissed them. Yet they never showed pictures of princesses with warty lips.

The smell of nettles and coal came up from the river, sweet and bitter and smoky. Dandelion parachutes blew in the breeze and floated over the bridge and away down the river to the sea.

Bessie didn't like dandelions. If you got the sap on your fingers it could make you pee the bed leaking.

Fatty once told Iffy that the French called dandelions pees on lee, which meant piss the beds. The French were very vulgar. Iffy would have liked to live in France.

Billy took the frog off Mervyn and held it. He stroked it on its head with his finger, ever so gently, putting his face really close to it. Iffy and Bessie looked on. Billy liked all sorts of creatures. He wasn't scared of any of them, even spiders and Black Pats.

Iffy hated Black Pats. They came out in the dark from cracks and holes. There were loads of them in the lav at night.

'Gis it back then,' Mervyn said.

Billy handed the frog back carefully.

Bessie shifted even further away, holding her skirt down over her knees in case the frog escaped.

147

'Right,' said Mervyn, 'Let's get the jar and take it home. See you!'

Mervyn and Fido went leaping and laughing back down to the river.

Iffy, Billy and Bessie climbed back up onto the side of the bridge and sat looking down into the water. Gnats gathered around them and a butterfly rested on the bridge, batting its wings. Iffy put out a finger to touch its wing. She liked butterflies. They did the day shift and their cousins, the moths, did the night one. She didn't like moths. They flew into candle flames and got burned.

The water burbled and glugged. No voices from under the bridge. Mervyn and Fido had gone. They must have gone further down the river and then cut up behind the back of the graveyard.

Suddenly they came running towards the bridge from the direction of Carmel Chapel.

'Oy, you three!' Mervyn shouted.

'What?'

'Cop hold of that!'

Mervyn threw something high into the air.

'Blast off!' Fido shrieked.

It wasn't mud. It wasn't a bomb. It was the frog.

It fell through the darkening skies.

Iffy put her hands to her mouth and prayed that it didn't twist its ankles when it landed on the concrete.

There was something peculiar about the frog as it came down through the air.

It came down right over Bessie, who screamed as it hurtled towards her.

There was a great red bang as the frog exploded. Green bits flying everywhere.

'Bullseye!' screeched Mervyn.

Frog bits dropped like rain: blood and guts and eyeballs.

Pieces of the frog stuck all over Bessie.

Mervyn and Fido hopped and squealed and danced up and down with delight. Their snot was like a river flowing down their pinchy little faces.

Skin and blood and intestines were stuck all over Bessie's Sunday-school frock. It was blue gingham with a white bow and puffy sleeves. Ruined now. Spattered with frog guts.

It was a cruel trick. Iffy knew what they'd done. They'd tied squibs to the frog's legs and poked gunpowder up its bum. Cruel buggers.

Bessie no longer screamed. She stood there like a big mama doll with her arms held out towards Iffy and Billy. Her mouth was wide open but no sound came out. Iffy could see her tonsils. Her face was a rainbow of colours: blue, green, shocking pink, purple.

Iffy ignored the outstretched arms. She didn't want to touch her because of the bits of frog. She stood at a safe distance behind Bessie and banged her on the back like grown-ups did with babies in case they were in danger of dying from not breathing. There weren't any bits of frog on Bessie's back. It took ages for any noise to come out of Bessie.

Billy began to cry. There was no sound. Just big tears splashing down his soft cheeks.

Mervyn and Fido stomped up and down, shrieking and pointing at Billy. 'Cry baby bunting! Cry baby bunting!'

Then Bessie sicked up her Sunday dinner. All down the bodice of her frock. Lamb and mint sauce. Iffy could smell the mint.

'Chick, chick, chick, chick, chicken!' yelled Mervyn.

Billy stopped crying. His body stiffened, he clenched his small fists by his sides. A pulse moved in his neck.

A long squeaky sound came out of Bessie. Her shoulders were going up and down. Quiet sobbing. Louder sobbing.

Fit to bust. Then she was shivering and shaking, trying to grab hold of Iffy but Iffy held her at arm's length so she couldn't get too close.

No one knew Billy could move so quickly. Mervyn and Fido weren't expecting Billy to go for them like a bloody mad thing.

Mervyn first. Biff! A fist in the chops. Mervyn's head rocked backwards, as it came forward droplets of sticky blood drizzled from his nostrils. Thwap! Billy's small fists battering the stupid face. There was blood on Mervyn's fat ugly lips: blood and snot mixed. Mervyn was hollering.

Whap! A left hander on Fido's snout. Bubbles of snot on Billy's tiny knuckles. More blood than snot now on Fido.

Billy went for Mervyn again, grabbing at his hair, twisting and pulling at it until clumps of it came away in his hands and blew over the bridge with the dandelion parachutes. Mervyn, face contorted in pain, squealed like a piglet.

Thwap! Thwap! Two biffs for Fido. One in the guts, one where his flies were.

Iffy gasped with shock and pleasure. Serve him right. Copped in the privates. Goolies. Clods. Balls. Nuts. Tentacles was the proper word.

Bessie was rolling on the ground.

The sound of voices came from the direction of the Mechanics. Carty Annie was trundling the cart behind her with Fatty close by her side, the two of them talking together, not looking up yet.

Fido was down in the dust, yelling, sobbing and blabbing.

Mervyn raced off up the hill, looking over his shoulder.

Fatty ran towards them.

'You wait! You bloody wait, Billy Edwards. You bloody fat arse you! I'll have you for this! I'll get my father down. He'll paste you!' yelled Mervyn.

That was a laugh. Mr Prosser only weighed about six stone wet through. He was as weedy as hell.

Iffy's nan once said the best part of Mr Prosser ran down his father's leg.

Fido got up and tried to run but his legs were wobbly, he was clutching at his dooh dah through his trousers.

Fatty was staring open-mouthed at Bessie.

'Bloody 'ell! Woss up with her?'

Bessie was wheezing and rattling nineteen to the dozen.

'What happened, Iffy?' Fatty said, looking from Billy to Bessie.

'They exploded a frog all over her.'

'What?'

'Put bangers up its arse and it landed on Bessie.'

'Bastards! You all right, Billy?'

Billy nodded, breathing fast, wiping the snot-streaked blood from his knuckles.

'Bloody hell, Billy! I didn't know you could fight.'

Carty Annie drew the cart to a halt on the bridge.

'You best have a lend of my old cart to get her home.' She nodded in Bessie's direction. 'She doesn't look very feckin' healthy.'

Bessie was crumpled up in a whistling heap. None of them had ever seen her in such a mess. Her frock was spattered with blood, there was snot on her face and dust on her sandals and socks.

Billy took hold of the reins on the cart. Iffy and Fatty cleared a space among the jam jars and the other junk in the cart.

Fatty nudged Iffy and pointed into the cart, 'Look.'

Iffy looked. Nothing special, only the usual old piss pot and stuff.

Fatty and Iffy took Bessie under the armpits and

151

managed to shove her into the cart between them. She was light, just skin and bone.

Billy pulled and Fatty pushed and they dragged the cart slowly up the rutted road.

Iffy ran on in front all the way to the steps that led down to Inkerman. Mrs Tranter was playing the harmonium when she knocked at the door. 'Rock of Ages'. Practising for a funeral. Bessie's by the look of her.

Mr Tranter limped across the bailey behind Iffy, grunting as he climbed the steps. His false teeth were clickety clacketing, pink and white castanets doing overtime.

Bessie was lying flat out in the cart like a landed trout. Bloody and squeaking, mouth opening and closing, her glassy eyes staring.

Mr Tranter puffed and blew, muttering between his dancing teeth.

Fatty's arm was around Bessie's shoulders and she wasn't even fighting him off. Her lips were purple, she was groaning and gasping for air.

Mr Tranter pushed Fatty roughly out of the way. 'Get your filthy dirty hands off her!'

'Hang on! I'm only trying to help.'

Mr Tranter lifted Bessie up out of the cart. He carried her all the way home in his arms. Iffy saw her knickers. Posh lacy ones with pink and white flowers. Iffy's were plain old aertex with baggy legs, and they went up the crack on hot days.

The three of them followed Mr Tranter, but when they got to Bessie's house he bared his clacking teeth at them, slamming the door without a word, and pushing the bolts home. They waited outside for ages for news of Bessie, but no one came out, so they trailed back down the hill to where Carty Annie was waiting by the Dentist's Stone.

Fatty thanked her for the lend of the cart and they

watched her as she trundled away, muttering to herself on her way back to the house in Dancing Duck Lane.

Bessie eventually recovered from the frog explosion and was allowed back out, scrubbed and disinfected. The blue gingham frock had been thrown out with the rubbish.

Iffy and Bessie were going for sweets. Bessie always had pounds of money for sweets. The baby teeth that she still had left were brown from eating too many.

Iffy's nan said Mrs Tranter would kill Bessie with kindness.

Iffy would've liked a mam who would kill her with kindness. Not a baggy-arsed, misery-guts of an old mam like Bessie had. Not a knitting, hymn-playing mam who smelled of Jeyes Fluid and hard toilet paper. She wanted a mam who smelled of Pond's cold cream and bent down without showing her stocking tops. A mam with her own teeth and a proper brassiere, not one big enough to carry the shopping home in.

Bessie always insisted on going to Morrissey's for sweets. Iffy wasn't supposed to go there, because Fatty had warned her not to. And her nan. Once her nan bought a quarter of Riley's Chocolate Toffee Rolls and when she opened them there were teeth marks in them and it turned her stomach to think of it.

Iffy knew that Bessie wanted to marry Morrissey when she grew up, but Bessie didn't know she knew.

All the way to the shop they argued about Morrissey's hair.

'It's a wig,' Iffy said. 'Any fool can tell that.'

'No it's not. If it was a wig you'd see the join,' said Bessie.

'I bet you ten bob it is a wig,' Iffy said even though she didn't have ten bob.

Iffy knew that Bessie didn't want to think the man she

was going to marry wore a wig, even if he did own a sweet shop.

'It is a wig.'

'Tisn't.'

'Tis.'

'Tisunt. Tisunt. Tisunt.'

'Tis. Tis. Tis.'

'Right, I'm going home!'

Iffy gave in then because she didn't have any money and Bessie had two bob.

'Okay, so it's not a wig,' she said but she looked the other way and said, 'Tis. Tis. Tis,' under her breath.

'When I grow up,' Bessie said, 'I'm gonna live in a sweet shop and eat sweets all day long.'

'Your teeth will fall out.'

'I don't care. I'll get false ones.'

Bessie's mam and dad had false teeth. Their gums were as pink as Blackpool rock.

'You'll be gummy like Dai Full Pelt.'

Bessie didn't care. She was going to marry Morrissey the Sweet Shop when she was older because he always called her darling and said he'd wait for her to grow up.

Iffy didn't like Morrissey. Once she'd bought some dolly mixtures and the pointer on the scales went just past two ounces. Morrissey had taken a dolly mixture out and cut it in half.

Morrissey's shop was in the middle of Armoury Terrace, squashed in between all the other little houses. It had thick, green, dimpled-glass windows. When the shop door opened a rusty bell tinkled high above your head. Then there was silence for a few seconds. Then *up* would pop Morrissey like a bloody jack in the box. It made Iffy jump every single time, even though she knew it was going to happen.

154

Morrissey was a very queer man to look at. He had pointy pixie ears, and eyes the colour of Parma violets. His nose was long, thin and peaky. He had thick black curly hair that was a wig, whatever Bessie said.

Syrup of figs – wigs
Apples and pears – stairs
Hampton Wick – Dick

That was proper English. Fatty had told her.

The English lived through the Severn tunnel that was seven miles long. It was a long train ride to get there. On the other side of the tunnel lived the English. The English had a very swanky way of talking. They had fluffy lids on their toilets and said mummee and daddee, and her nan said they'd never learn to make gravy as long as they had a hole in their arse.

Morrissey's mouth was very tiny and his voice was a strangled squeak.

He always wore the same clothes, day in and day out. Very dapper in his dressing but not too clean about himself. He wore a red dicky bow, a fawn shirt, brown trousers and a yellow waistcoat the colour of lemonade powder.

He thought he was the goods, did Morrissey. Iffy didn't like the smell that came off him, wet biscuits, brown sauce and cough drops all mixed together.

Inside Morrissey's shop it was as dark and mysterious as a wizard's den. When your eyes got used to the dim light they could feast on the rows and rows of sweet jars that stretched right up to the ceiling. All types of bon bons: Lemon. Strawberry. Chocolate. Aniseed balls as red as blood. Rainbow drops. Sherbet pips. Chocolate eclairs. Rum and butter. Coconut macaroons. Pineapple chunks. Toasted teacakes. Pear drops. Humbugs. Everton mints.

Barley sugar. Sherbet lemons that gave you ulcers on your tongue from sucking too hard.

On top of the shiny wooden counter there were boxes of Spanish, which the English called liquorice, Flying Saucers, Black Jacks, Milk Gums, gobstoppers, bubblegum, tiger nuts, sweet tobacco, shrimps, Fry's Five Boys, banana splits, everlasting strips, Jamboree Bags galore.

In front of the counter there was a bran tub as deep as a well. It was thruppence a go.

It was heaven apart from Morrissey.

On the right-hand side of the shop, close to the door, there was a huge cream-coloured fridge that hummed like an angry bumble bee. Iffy'd seen inside and it was deep and dark and full of snow. It contained ice-cream blocks and Mivvies, choc ices, tubs and Jubbly's. If you bought ice-cream blocks, Morrissey wrapped them in newspaper.

Morrissey was so short he had to stand on a box and on tippy toes to reach down into the fridge. Iffy liked watching him disappearing down into it. When he came back up for air his black wig was sprinkled with frost and his thin nose was blue with the cold. Iffy wondered if he fell into the fridge whether it would be like falling down a frozen well and if he'd come out where the Eskimos lived, where there were polar bears and igloos and seals balancing balls.

Bessie went into the shop first. The rusty bell tinkled high above their heads.

Iffy held her breath and clamped her feet to the floor. She was determined that she wasn't going to jump.

Up popped Morrissey behind the counter. Iffy's feet left the floor.

Bugger. Bugger. Bugger. Shit. Shit. Damn.

'Good morning, lovely girl,' Morrissey said to Bessie. He ignored Iffy.

Bessie smiled her best smile, all dimples and gappy

teeth. She stank of double helpings of baby powder and cod liver oil. She always spoke to Morrissey dead proper and never dropped her aitches. Iffy knew that was because Morrissey thought he was a cut above and Bessie wanted him to think her posh.

'And what can I do for you, little princess?'

Ugh! thought Iffy.

'A quarter of pineapple chunks, please, Mr Morrissey.'

A quarter! Iffy could only ever afford two ounces. Gutsy pig.

Morrissey climbed up the rickety ladder to reach the jar. Pineapple chunks were on the second shelf from the top in between Pontefract cakes and chocolate bon bons.

He climbed back down the ladder, smiled again at Bessie, tipped up the jar and the pineapple chunks clattered into the metal weighing dish. The arrow on the scales pointed to four ounces. He lifted the dish, tilted it and the chunks slid into the triangular paper bag he held in his left hand. Morrissey twisted the top of the bag shut.

'There you are,' he said handing them to Bessie, and stroking her hand as he did so. 'For the most beautiful little girl in the valley.'

Iffy thought he must be blind.

Bessie giggled and grinned like a bloody Cheshire cat.

Iffy looked away. Sometimes Bessie could be dead soppy, as daft as arseholes. Bessie thought she was IT. If she was made of chocolate she'd eat herself.

Anyway, Morrisssey called lots of people beautiful girl. Iffy'd heard him. He'd never said it to her though, and she was glad.

'Two ounces of sherbet lemons, please, for my friend Iffy.'

She had to let Morrissey know she was buying Iffy sweets to show how nice and generous she was. Morrissey weighed the sherbet lemons out. The arrow on the scales went just over the two ounces mark. Fat chance he wouldn't notice. He took one sherbet lemon out and popped it back into the jar.

Tight as a camel arse in a snowstorm.

The red arrow on the scales wavered just before the two.

Bessie gave him her money. Morrissey put it in a box under the counter and when he gave Bessie the change he squeezed her fingers tight and blew her a kiss through his cat's arse lips.

Bessie giggled and turned pink.

Behind the kiss, Iffy caught the smell of his breath which stank of cough drops.

'Goodbye, Mr Morrissey,' Bessie said with a plum in her mouth.

'Goodbye, princess.'

'Yuk!' said Iffy under her breath.

'I'll wait for you to grow up!' he called after Bessie.

Double yuk.

Iffy went out of the shop first. Behind her the bell tinkled. Bessie waved to Morrissey with her fingers, like a baby.

If Bessie did marry Morrissey when she grew up she'd live above the sweet shop and be able to eat sweets all day long. Bessie Tranter, Queen of the Sweet Shop. Lucky gutsy pig!

She'd have to kiss him though on his cat's arse lips and rub their belly buttons together if they wanted babies.

Treble yuk!

And a baby would come out of Bessie's bum.

Urrrgh!

Serve her right.

Will climbed wearily up from the river bank, walked up the hill and turned left towards the rec, if there was still a rec after all this time. He was astounded by the sight that confronted him.

The walls of the Big House were overgrown with ivy and brambles and behind the walls the house was a charred shell, the roof had fallen in, inhabited by crows and magpies. The wrought-iron gates were intertwined with brambles, and a sign warned, KEEP OUT! It had once been a glorious house with a particularly fine garden. He had been invited to sit in the garden and take tea by Agnes Medlicott, the woman he had called the second witness.

He could still conjure up a picture of Agnes Medlicott in his mind. She had been an elderly woman, with thick coiled plaits flattened over her ears, a fashion rarely seen these days. He remembered thinking at the time that she must have been a strikingly handsome woman in her younger years. She was strong boned, with intelligent deep-brown eyes. Her nose was large and hooked but this did not detract from her looks. She had been out of the top drawer. She had explained to him that her late husband had been the local doctor years before. She'd moved abroad after his death but had come back about nine months earlier.

It had been one of the most stunning gardens he had ever seen. The lawns were mown to absolute perfection, the flowerbeds were carefully tended and the flowers were a riot of harmonious colours. He could remember the soothing sound of falling water from concealed fountains, the humming of contented bees.

At one side of the garden close to the wall bordering the river there had been a steep rockery, resplendent with morning glory, lobelia and periwinkle. There was a large pond with giant-sized goldfish, and in alcoves and shady corners were an assortment of exquisitely beautiful statues. He'd commented on them and she'd said, 'Ah yes, all my dear children . . . they remind me of the good times.'

He'd been shocked by her words and had counted up the

statues, there were well over twelve of them. Surely they weren't all her daughters?

She must have noticed the puzzlement on his face because she'd smiled sadly and said, 'Not my own children, Inspector. I'm afraid I wasn't blessed with a family. I lost my only child.'

Will had looked at her closely and seen a slow ripple of grief pass across her features. Then she'd swiftly changed the subject.

'When my husband was alive, I ran a small school here, a sort of finishing school for young girls.'

'And the statues?'

'They were just a hobby of mine.'

'A hobby of yours?' he'd said astonished.

She could easily have made a very good living as a sculptor and he'd told her so.

She'd sighed softly, her hands clasped tightly in her lap. Outwardly, she gave the impression of supreme serenity, but he guessed that this belied a very great inner turmoil, a life unfulfilled. He noticed too that in contrast to the rest of her body, her hands were hard, strong and sinewy, used to heavy toil.

'My husband was an old-fashioned sort of man in many ways,' she'd said. 'I don't think he would have approved of me making a living by sculpting.'

Will had thought that it was a great pity that her husband's approval had had any bearing on her life as an artist.

'But you ran a school, that was profitable no doubt?'

'Well, not really. I did that as a sort of hobby too . . . I'd lived abroad, you see, for many years before we were married. In Spain. I was fluent in the language and still had contacts over there. My girls came on recommendation. I taught them English and other things considered useful. I was never lonely, Inspector.'

From the tone of her voice he knew that he was talking to a

very lonely old woman, a woman living more in the past than the present.

'Is there any news on the missing child?' she'd asked and she'd lowered her eyes and turned slightly away as though she wanted to hide her face from him.

'No, I'm afraid not. Can you be definite about the time you say you saw the child?'

'Oh yes, most definite. You see I'd asked Sandicock, he's a sort of general dogsbody who's worked for us, me, for years, to serve tea at three o'clock on the dot and by a quarter past three I was rather annoyed. I'm a stickler for punctuality, Inspector. I always take afternoon tea in the first-floor drawing room. While I waited for Sandicock I stood by the window. I saw the child down on the bridge, leaning over as if looking for someone.'

And Will had wondered for many years just who that someone was.

When Iffy came up the road from the Cop where she'd been sent to buy milk, Fatty was sitting on the bridge, eating cockles out of an old newspaper.

'Where d'you get them from?' asked Iffy.

'Mrs Baker. Always trying to fatten me up she is. Want some?' he asked Iffy as she jumped up next to him.

'No thanks.'

She'd been sent out to buy extra milk for visitors who'd come from down the valley so she couldn't stay long to yap. Auntie Blod and Cousin Eirwen. She'd never met either of them.

'Guess what, Iffy!'

'I dunno. Give in.'

'My wish is going to come true.'

'What wish?'

'You remember – when we drank the holy water.'

Iffy turned her head away, she didn't like thinking of that.

'What did you wish for?'

'A puppy. And now I'm gonna get one.'

'Where from?'

He pointed towards the Big House.

'Old Gravelwilly's black Labrador's having pups.'

The black Labrador that belonged to Mr Sandicock was a pedigree. Pedigrees knew more about their ancestors than people did.

'How do you know she's having pups?'

'Cos I heard them talking ages ago.'

'Who?'

'Dai Full Pelt and Gravelwilly.'

'What did they say?'

'Dai was going to take the Labrador to get it covered.'

'You make it sound like a settee.'

'Don't be dull! Covered by another black Labrador.'

'Why?'

'So she'll have pups!'

Iffy didn't ask him any more in case he explained. She got embarrassed. Nothing ever embarrassed Fatty at all.

'When is she having pups?'

'Any day now, but they won't be black Labradors.'

'How come?'

'Cos a couple of days before Dai took the dog to be covered, the Labrador got out and done it with Barny the bulldog. I seen 'em, so they'll be half bulldog and half Labrador.'

Barny the bulldog lived on Old Man Morgan's farm. He was tied up to a post most of the time, but sometimes when the moon was full he escaped and took himself off on adventures. They called him Barny the bulldog, but he was much bigger than the pictures of bulldogs they'd seen in books, nearly big enough to ride on.

Whenever he escaped he came along Inkerman dragging the chains and the post behind him.

Bessie was terrified of him. She always ran inside and pulled the bolts across the door.

'I'm gonna ask if I can have one when they're born,' Fatty said.

'How much will they cost? Pedigrees are expensive.'

'That's the point, Iffy, they won't be pedigrees, they'll be mongrels and they give mongrels away.'

'Great!'

Iffy wondered if the wish she'd made that night would come true too, but she knew it wasn't possible. Dead people didn't come alive. Then she had to go in case the milk turned sour.

Iffy was told to call her Auntie but Auntie Blod wasn't a real auntie. She was just someone that Iffy's nan had known for years. She kept a home for bad girls down the valley.

Iffy thought it a scary-sounding place. Fatty'd told her that it was where unwanted babies came out of girls' bums in the middle of the night.

Auntie Blod was an old maid even though she had a daughter. Cousin Eirwen wasn't Auntie Blod's own baby, but Auntie Blod had felt sorry for her because all the other babies had been adopted, but no one had wanted Eirwen and she would have had to go to the orphanage, so Blod had adopted her instead.

Auntie Blod was cross-eyed so it was hard to tell who she was looking at or who she was talking to. She looked Iffy up and down when she arrived in the kitchen. At least Iffy thought she looked her up and down. Iffy didn't like the look of Auntie Blod. She was hard-faced and thin about the lips.

'Give Auntie Blod a kiss, Iffy.'

Iffy flinched. She hated being told to kiss people. Grown-ups told you never to talk to strangers one minute and then asked you to kiss them the next.

She gave Auntie Blod a swift peck on the cheek. She didn't like the smell of her: fresh perm lotion and stale wee. She was dressed all in brown like someone out of an old photograph: brown skirt, cardie, stockings, shoes. Even her teeth were brown.

'She's the spit of her mam,' said Auntie Blod looking at Eirwen.

Iffy stared at Eirwen. Her mam must have been dead ugly.

Nan coughed and clattered cups and saucers.

Best china. Posh teapot. Apostle spoons.

'Got her father's eyes mind . . . got a nose like that cat.'

Iffy peered at Eirwen. She had a nose more like a pig than a cat, with big black nostrils. She also had a slack-lipped mouth that hung open showing sharp pointy teeth.

'She's got her own bloody nose, Blod . . . Take Eirwen into the pantry and give her some biscuits, Iffy,' said Nan.

Iffy pretended she hadn't heard. She didn't want to take Eirwen into the pantry. She didn't like the look of Cousin Eirwen any more than she did her mam.

'Nan, Fatty Bevan's going to get a puppy.'

'Use his proper name, Iffy! It's not nice to call him Fatty all the time. A puppy? It'll never survive in that house.'

'He is though. Can I have one?'

'Not on your nelly! I've got enough to be doing without clearing up after a puppy!'

'Who's Fatty?' said Auntie Blod.

'Lawrence Bevan. You won't know him, but you'll remember his mam, she was the midwife round here.'

'Which midwife?'

Nan didn't reply, but coughed a sharp little cough.

'Oh. Ellen Bevan. Is she still living round here?'

'Ay, but she hasn't worked for some years. She had trouble with her nerves. Too much of the old pop and being married to that hopeless article. She should have left him years ago. Don't stand there gawping with your mouth open, Iffy. Go and get some biscuits.'

'There was talk she had a fancy man years ago. She fell for him hook, line and sinker.'

'Iffy! Move!'

Iffy moved reluctantly. She beckoned Eirwen to follow her, but across the kitchen Eirwen stood rooted to the floor, staring at Iffy with her small, queer eyes. Iffy smiled, a weak smile of half-hearted encouragement. Eirwen made no sign of moving. Iffy stared back. Iffy guessed Eirwen was about thirteen. She was a big beefy girl with skin the colour of old chip fat. She grunted through her open mouth, like Bessie did when she was constipated.

Iffy sighed, turned on her heel and lifted the latch to the pantry. All of a sudden Iffy felt Eirwen's hot breath on the back of her neck, large as she was, Eirwen had made no noise crossing the kitchen floor. Iffy shuddered. Feeling Eirwen that close without being able to see her made Iffy feel unsafe.

It was dark and cool in the pantry, only a little light came in through the high small gauze-covered window. Iffy loved the smell of the pantry. Sometimes she hung around in there for ages soaking up the smells: Fairy soap and Reckitts blue; block salt and pickled onions; cooking apples and mud-crusted potatoes; runner beans and peas in the pod waiting to be shelled. When Nan was well out of the way Iffy took sly nibbles from cold cuts of lamb or beef, snaffled pork crackling, or slipped her hand quietly into the biscuit jar and picked the currants from rock buns and the icing from cakes.

She turned round to face Eirwen. Eirwen stared back at

her. Iffy thought her eyes were the oddest she'd ever seen: pink-rimmed with white lashes that blinked too fast, stared too hard and too long.

On the other side of the door Mrs Meredith and Auntie Blod were whispering together.

'When did she come back?'

'November. Out of the blue . . . Never thought she'd set foot in that house not after . . .'

'Have you seen her?'

'No. She keeps to the house. She's not even been to Mass, though God knows she needs to go to confession if anybody does. She must have known what he was up to.'

'Who'd have thought she'd ever come back?'

'I've told our Iffy to keep away.'

'She must have known what he was doing with those young girls. And what sort of girl was *she* anyway, giving her own flesh and blood away. Dear God, if the child hadn't been the spit—'

'What if she realised?'

'The old doctor said she didn't want to know. Took one look at the baby and said, take it away.'

Snippets of conversation like all adult conversation – completely unintelligible. Sounds of cups and spoons clattering.

Suddenly Eirwen smiled. The pantry grew cooler with that smile. It was a twisted, sly smile that didn't join up with her eyes.

Iffy stretched up and took down the biscuit tin from the top shelf. She pulled off the lid and took out three biscuits and gingerly held them out to Eirwen. One broken custard cream, two fig rolls.

Eirwen held her hands behind her back and shook her big lollopy head slowly from side to side.

Neither of them spoke.

Iffy ate the custard cream and put the fig rolls back in the tin.

Then, quick as a wink, Eirwen pushed past her and grabbed hold of a bar of Fairy soap that was kept on the scrubbing board next to the tin bath. She held the soap in her fat, dimpled hand and began to tear at the wrapper. She peeled back the paper until half the bar of green soap was uncovered. Then she lifted it to her mouth and began to bite greedily into it. Lumps of green soap disappeared into her mouth as she chomped away with her pointy teeth. Iffy gawped in disbelief. Eirwen ate soap as if it was chocolate! She munched and crunched until foam billowed out of the sides of her mouth.

She was nuts.

Then Eirwen poked out her tongue at Iffy, threw down the half-eaten bar of soap and snatched a bottle of dandelion and burdock pop from under the table and drank half the bottle without coming up for air.

She burped loudly and glared at Iffy. Then she yanked the biscuit tin from the shelf, drew out a fistful of biscuits and stuffed them all into her mouth at once.

Iffy sidled past her, breathing in so as not to touch her, but Eirwen followed, her feet padding on the stone floor. Too close for comfort. Iffy felt the hairs on her neck shoot out warnings.

She sat back up at the kitchen table as close to Nan as she could get, as far away from Eirwen as possible.

'Nan, that girl's just ate the soap,' she whispered from behind her hand.

Nan ignored her.

'Go and play in the parlour,' said Auntie Blod. 'Eirwen's got a nice new doctor's set and your nan and I have got a lot of catching up to do.'

Auntie Blod pulled a paper bag out of her basket and thrust it at Eirwen.

Eirwen took the doctor's set out. It was a little white case with a red cross painted on the side.

'Go on,' said Nan. 'You don't want to sit here listening to women's talk.'

Iffy did, though. She didn't want to go in the spooky room with the soap-eating Eirwen.

They stood in silence facing each other in the back parlour. Outside, sunflowers nodded by the grey garden wall. A bee fizzed against the window trying to get in. Iffy was dying to get out.

Granny Gallivan looked down from her picture frame and gave Iffy a knowing look, as if to say, 'Look out behind you!' On the stiff-backed settle the invisible bones of the ghosts creaked and their movement sent up the smell of moth balls. Iffy kept one eye on the wooden biscuit barrel half hoping the hand would come out and grab Eirwen by the rude bits and drag her screaming and wriggling into its magic depths.

Eirwen spoke first, 'That's my mammy,' she said to Iffy pointing at a painting of the Virgin Mary that hung on the wall. She spoke as though she were pushing the words out through her nose, more a snuffle than speech.

'That's Our Lady,' Iffy said.

'My mammy,' said Eirwen glaring.

Iffy went back into the kitchen.

'Nan, that girl said the Virgin Mary is her mam.'

'That girl's got a name, Iffy.'

'Eirwen says that the Virgin Mary is her mam, but she's not, is she, Nan?'

'Sometimes she says daft things. Take no notice. She's not all there, poor dab. Go and play, there's a good girl,' said Auntie Blod.

Back in the parlour, Eirwen was looking at the picture of Napoleon.

'That's my daddy,' she said.

Iffy smiled and bit her lips so as not to laugh. She didn't feel brave enough to argue.

'I know a good game,' said Eirwen.

So they played Eirwen's game. Iffy was too afraid not to. Eirwen gave the orders. Iffy had to be the doctor first. Eirwen was the patient. She sat on the high-backed settle between the moth-ball ghosts. Iffy took invisible splinters out of her chubby white arm with the pretend tweezers and listened to her chest with the stethoscope that didn't work. But she could only hear the sound of the bleeding heart pumping away behind her as it dripped blood over the chair backs.

When it was Eirwen's turn to be the doctor she ordered Iffy to lie down on the couch. The black, cracked leather was cool against her legs. Horsehair, escaping from a rip, tickled her neck. She giggled.

'Shut your eyes,' said Eirwen very solemnly.

Iffy shut her eyes.

'Tighter,' said Dr Eirwen.

Behind Iffy's tightly squeezed eyelids the world went black and red. She could hear Eirwen's heavy breathing somewhere in the blackness.

'It won't hurt a bit,' said Eirwen.

She took ages. She must have taken a run up from the back door at least.

'Aaaargh!'

Suffering doughnuts!

The plastic syringe quivered in Iffy's arm like a Red Indian's arrow.

'Now I'm going to take that baby out of your bum.'

But Iffy was up and off the settee like a shot. She flew into the kitchen roaring.

169

Her nan had to pick out the plastic with a pair of tweezers, and dab her arm with iodine in case it went septic. Iffy was going to have a bruise for weeks after.

When Auntie Blod and Eirwen had gone Iffy showed Nan the bar of soap with the teethmarks in it. Nan said Eirwen couldn't help it, she wasn't normal.

Iffy showed Fatty the bruise and the hole where the needle had gone in.

'Bloody hell,' he said. 'Good job she didn't give you the injection in your bum!'

She told him about Eirwen eating the soap.

He laughed and said, 'Next time she farts bubbles will come out of her bum hole. Ha ha ha!'

They rolled about laughing and called her Eirwen Fairy Hole after that but not to her face because she only came the once.

Will walked on past the walls of the Big House, following the curve of the river away past the recreation ground. The recreation ground was a euphemism for a barren wasteland where a solitary rusted roundabout turned slowly in the wind. He climbed over the rotten stile. It was over this stile that the child had leapt and almost been run over by the bus driven by David Gittins. He had always wondered why the child had been running so fast, like a ghost had been on its heels, David Gittins had said. What had the kid been so afraid of? Had someone been chasing the child? Had that someone caught up with the child down by the hump-backed bridge? And then what had happened?

Will walked past a withered tree that overhung the path, casting its stark shadow over the ground. The wind grew cooler and rain began to fall. It was eerie standing there in the darkening day, knowing that the child had raced past this very spot only minutes before disappearing off the face of the earth.

He turned round, climbed back over the stile and headed towards town thinking as he went about the third witness. She'd been a really comical old girl. A true eccentric. In his notebooks he'd written her down as the Woman with No Name. Even Sergeant Rodwell, a fellow who'd been born and bred in the town, had been unable to enlighten him. He said no one in the town knew her name. She'd told Will that names were just a feckin' irrelevance. Just call me Old Missus she'd told him, like the rest of the world did. She'd spoken with a southern Irish accent but she had been unwilling to give anything away about herself or her past.

Rodwell had told Will that all kinds of myths had grown up around her: she was from an aristocratic family but had got herself pregnant; that she was a nun who'd escaped over the convent wall; a child murderess on the run.

She'd had a foul tongue on her and Rodwell had blushed deeply at her colourful use of the language, but beneath the rough exterior Will had realised he was talking to a well-educated woman. Everywhere she went she dragged an old cart full of rubbish behind her. She swore, hand on her heart and may the Lord strike her feckin' dead if she told a lie, that she'd caught a peep of the child hiding in the long grass down by the river. At about four o'clock she'd said. And she'd said that the child had been talking to someone, someone hidden in the grass. That someone had been the last person to see the child and they had never discovered who that someone was.

Fatty kept the head in a box. It rested on a piece of cotton wool that he'd found in the ash tip. He carried the box everywhere with him for fear of his old man going through his room and finding it. It wasn't valuable, he didn't think, but that wouldn't matter to the old man. He'd seen the head in Carty Annie's cart the night Bessie'd had the frog explode on her. He'd seen it there many times before, but hadn't realised what it was or where it had come from. It just looked like an old stone covered in moss but when he'd looked more closely at it as they'd lifted Bessie into the cart, he'd seen the shape of a nose, the indent of an eye socket.

That night he'd lain in bed thinking about how he could get his hands on the head and have a proper look at it. He wouldn't steal it because that would have been wrong. He wondered why Carty Annie had bothered to carry it around for so long, it must have been dead heavy.

The next morning he'd had just the stroke of luck he'd hoped for.

He'd seen Bessie and Iffy coming down the rutted road alongside the Three Rows and was going to run and join them, but he'd spotted a water rat swimming below the bridge and stopped to watch it for a moment. By the time he reached the Dentist's Stone, Iffy and Bessie were further down the road and going into Morrissey's shop. He would not set foot in there. He'd told Iffy not to go in, only she wouldn't listen. He hated Morrissey. He was a filthy old pig. He'd done some dreadful things, and if mad Bridgie Thomas was right then he'd be due for a lightning bolt, boils or a plague of locusts in his shop. Fatty had hung about waiting for the girls and while he'd waited he'd seen Carty Annie come up the lane towards the bridge. He walked towards her and called out, 'Mornin', Old Missus.'

'Morning to yourself, handsome fella!'

Fatty grinned, and Carty Annie looking up at him thought that he truly was the most beautiful child she had ever clapped eyes on. Gorgeous enough to eat, he was.

'Where you going?' he asked, his hands in his pockets.

'Away off home to me bed. I been out half the night looking for them little bastards.'

Fatty looked down. He didn't want his eyes to give him

away. He knew what she was talking about; he knew what she had in her house.

'Want some company?'

'Sure, to the stile though and no further.'

They walked along together, an odd-looking couple, towards the Big House. As they came alongside the gates Carty Annie took a detour, a wide arc out into the road.

'Why d'you always do that?' he asked.

'Just because,' she said tapping her nose with her finger.

'Because what?'

'That nose of yours will get you into trouble.'

'Just wondered, that's all.'

'Master Bevan, it seems to me you wants to know the ins and outs of a duck's arse.'

Fatty laughed out loud.

'I keeps me distance, that's all, and you should too.'

'What's that?' he said innocently, and pointed into the cart.

Carty Annie stopped and looked down to where he was pointing.

'What's what?'

He pointed to the head.

'Ah, that now is a missing piece of a jigsaw.'

He scratched his head.

'Doesn't look like a piece of a jigsaw.'

'Well now, that all depends on the types of jigsaws you're used to. Are you good at jigsaws?'

'Yep,' he lied. He'd never had a jigsaw, but he knew what they were.

'Well, if you can put together the rest of it, if you find all the other pieces, this head will complete it.'

'Have you ever tried to finish the jigsaw?'

Carty Annie looked him in the eyes. He had quite unfathomable eyes. Deep, deep blue eyes that reminded her of a restless sea. He was a very special boy this one.

'No,' she said with a sigh. 'I think I was waiting for someone else to come along. I'm tired of jigsaws. Here.' She bent over and prised the head out from the tangle of piss pot and tinselled Pope. 'It's yours.'

She handed him the head as though she were a headmistress handing out cups at speech day.

Fatty swelled with pleasure. He cradled the head with both arms as he looked up at her in admiration. He didn't care what people thought about Carty Annie, he liked her. She was a bit like him really, people took the mick because she wasn't like everyone else, because her clothes were ragged. They didn't know what went on inside other people's heads, just looked at the outside and made their minds up. Carty Annie had a lovely face, it was darkened with age and weather, but her eyes were young and alive, deep greeny-blue eyes, eyes that looked right into him as though they might winkle out his deepest secrets.

The moss covering on the head was soft to the touch, but he could feel the hardness of stone beneath.

'Thanks, Old Missus.'

He held the head to one side, leant towards Carty Annie and, swift as a wink, he kissed her on her wrinkled cheek.

Carty Annie smiled. A wide arc of a smile that lifted her face, a radiant smile Fatty would remember for a long time.

'Now feck off out the way, I've things to mind to.'

And she was away, trundling the cart on up the road.

Fatty stood quite still for a few minutes and then turned away, unaware of the eyes that watched him from an upstairs window of the Big House.

Iffy sat beside Fatty on the river bank, idly running slivers of shale through her fingers.

Fatty knelt down, leant over the edge of the bank and

held the stone head under the water with both hands. He'd carefully peeled away all the moss from the face but it was still stained green with mould. Air bubbles rose up from the nostrils and ears.

He lifted the head carefully out of the water, dried it on his T-shirt and laid it gently on the river bank. It was still hard to tell what it looked like beneath all the green.

The slender neck was jagged as if it had been knocked off with violence when it had been parted from the rest of its body.

'She's pretty, ent she?' said Fatty.

Iffy threw a handful of shale into the river, looked down at the head and sniffed. 'She's all right, I s'pose.'

Iffy was bored with the head. As far as she could see it was just a dirty old broken statue's head and there was nothing that interesting about it. It had staring eyes, a chipped nose, a ghoulish green-lipped smile and a small bird's feather stuck fast to the chin.

'She is though, ent she, Iffy?'

Iffy turned away from him and began to break off daisies' heads.

'S'pose,' she said without much interest.

'I got to get something to clean it up properly. What d'you reckon?'

'Soap?'

'Where can I get some from?'

'Your house?'

He shook his head.

'I could get some off the washing board at home.'

'Shh. Somebody's coming.'

Fatty put the head back into the box and disappeared into the bushes. Iffy raised her eyebrows. She couldn't see what was such a secret about a silly old head and yet he'd made her swear not to tell anyone that he had it.

Lally Tudge came waddling along the river bank. She was carrying a baby in a shawl, rocking it gently from side to side, her puckered lips crooning down at the covered head.

'Hey you!' she called out.

Iffy looked behind her but there was no one there. She didn't want to speak to Lally on her own.

'Want to see my baby?' Lally asked

Iffy hoped Fatty wouldn't be long.

She stood up and peeped nervously into the shawl. It wasn't a baby, it was a doll. An old battered doll that had pen marks on its face from where it had been jabbed, and holes in its head where its hair had been pulled out by the roots.

'He's ever so good,' said Lally, smiling down at the doll.

Iffy wondered if Lally'd remembered to put her knickers on today.

'You can watch me feed him if you like.'

She began to unbutton the front of her blouse. Iffy looked away quickly.

'Oh, he's still sleeping, I'll wait a bit.'

Iffy sneaked a look. The buttons were done up again. No titties hanging out.

Close up Lally smelled of over-boiled cabbage and burned fat.

'He's called Zachariah and he's a month old.'

She rocked the doll from side to side in her dimpled arms.

Iffy had never been so close to Lally before and she took a good long look at her. Lally's hair hung down to her shoulders, straggly hair the colour of parched grass. The fringe was greasy and fell into her eyes so that she blinked a lot. Beneath the fringe her eyes were large and round, green speckled with brown and grey. Iffy thought that they were quite nice eyes.

'Rock a bye baby on the treetop,
When the wind blows the cradle will rock,
When the bough breaks the cradle will fall,
Down will come cradle, baby and all.'

Iffy hated that song. It was scary. How could a baby sleep at night thinking it might crash out of the trees at any minute?

Lally finished her song and smiled at Iffy with her honeycomb teeth.

'Go on, hold him,' she said pushing the doll towards Iffy.

Iffy didn't want to hold it or pretend that it was a baby. It was only a doll. Besides, Lally was too old to play make-believe with. Lally Tudge was twp but not nasty twp.

Nan said pity for her and God help. Poor cow.

Iffy took the doll from her reluctantly. It was wrapped up in a grubby knitted dishcloth.

'You'll have to rock him else he'll wake up.'

Iffy rocked the doll.

'Take him for a walk if you want to. I've got to get the dinner on for my old man.'

Lally didn't have an old man.

'I got to go,' Iffy said. 'Here's your baby.'

She held the doll out for her to take.

Lally stared at her with wide speckled eyes, eyes narrowing from circles to slits.

'What you say?'

'Here's your baby,' Iffy said.

She held the pretend baby towards Lally again and smiled.

Lally bared her rotten teeth.

'I never had no baby! Don't you go saying I had no baby!'

Her eyes were bulging and her cheeks grew crimson with anger. Just as Iffy was afraid that Lally was about to fly at

177

her, Lally began to cry, great shiny teardrops plopped onto her fat cheeks and slid down her big quivering face.

'Don't you go telling I had a fuckin' baby. I'm a good girl. I am!'

Iffy held on to the doll wondering what she'd done to upset Lally.

'Don't you go telling I been with men. Lally's kept her hand on her ha'penny, Lally has.'

Iffy was bewildered, she'd never said anything to her about being with men or about ha'pennies.

'You want pasting, you do! Saying things like that!'

Lally stopped crying. She put her fists up in front of her wet face. Iffy stepped back out of the way. Lally was fat enough to hit hard, but fat enough not to be able to run fast.

'I'll give you what for for saying I done those dirty things!' she yelled.

She dropped one fist and snatched at the doll. Its head came away in Lally's hands. A bald holey head, the bright-blue eyes rolling back into their sockets.

'Mama. Mama. Mama,' cried the doll.

Iffy jumped in alarm, dropping the rest of doll, and watched in dismay as it rolled out of the dishcloth and fell onto the grass.

Fatty stepped out from the bushes.

'It's all right, Lally,' his voice was quiet, soft. 'Iffy didn't mean nothin'. I 'spect you're just feeling sad because they took your baby.'

Lally dropped the head of the doll. It bounced once and came to rest in the grass.

'Look what you done. You killed it!'

Her hands hung limply by her sides as she stared at the broken doll and her huge body shook, from her feet to her head. Great tears welled up again in her eyes and splashed onto her cheeks.

Iffy looked at Fatty.

He bent down and picked up the doll's head and twisted it back onto the body.

'There,' he said. 'It's all better now.' He winked at Iffy.

'No. It's dead now,' said Lally. 'I don't want it any more.'

'We better bury it proper then,' said Fatty.

Lally smiled at him, blinking away her tears. And then she was off, waddling away up the river bank without looking back once.

'God, she frightened me then. I thought she was going to hit me,' said Iffy, breathing hard.

'Pity for her, Iffy.'

'Pity for me if she'd hit me! She's mad, Fatty. She said I said she'd been with men and she swore!'

'You don't know, do you?'

'Know what?'

'She had a baby.'

'No, she never.'

'She did, Iffy, a couple of weeks ago, that's why she's been away.'

'But she's not married.'

'She was down the home for bad girls.'

'Where's the baby?'

'They took it off her and that's why she's pretending the doll is her baby.'

'Oh.'

'You mustn't tell anyone, Iffy. It's a secret.'

'How do you know, then?'

He tapped the side of his nose twice. Iffy hated it when he did that.

The grass in the graveyard was carefully mown, the early evening sunset bathed the crooked headstones in a pink wash.

The lights burned brightly behind the windows of Carmel

Chapel. From inside came the mournful strains of a hymn, 'The day Thou gavest, Lord, is ended, the darkness falls at Thy behest . . .' And darkness fell around the graveyard, creeping up from the river like bonfire smoke.

Will wondered to himself if there was any point in carrying on trying to solve the mystery. It had probably been a straightforward drowning accident and it was just a quirk that the body had never been found. If it had been murder, sooner or later the body would have been discovered.

He lingered for a while, reading the headstones of the graves.

DOLORES TRANTER. AGED 28.

The grave was one of the few untended in the graveyard. Whoever she had been, she had no one to mourn her.

Will shivered. It didn't seem right to read the names of the young on headstones.

Suddenly, he became aware that there was someone close by. He stood quite still and listened. Nothing. He wandered over towards the walls of the chapel. Again, he heard a sound, the fall of a heavy footstep in the damp grass. The graveyard was full of shadows and somewhere in the grounds of the Big House an owl called. He turned around quickly and thought he saw someone move behind a grave. The hairs on his neck lifted in trepidation.

A figure appeared and shuffled towards him. A large middle-aged woman holding a baby wrapped in a shawl, softly crooning to herself. As she got closer, she smiled at him revealing a mouthful of rotten brown teeth. Her lank grey hair hung about her white face, tears trailed from her eyes smudging her dirty cheeks. Then, without warning she thrust the baby towards Will, but he didn't react quickly enough and he watched in horror as the shawl spilled open and the baby dropped towards the ground.

'Jesus!'

Will bent down towards the baby.

'Mama! Mama!'

A grimy doll lay in the grass. Its lifeless eyes were an unnatural blue in the gloom of the graveyard. He picked it up, and looked up, but already the woman was a moving shadow among the graves.

An owl flew low, just above his head, its eyes bright in the growing dark, and the soft whispering of its wings like a shiver in the darkness. He laid the doll down gently in the grass.

He pulled his jacket closer and left the graveyard. The moon was high above the hill, and a cold wind blew through the tall trees in the gardens of the Big House.

Bessie refused to go: she wasn't going anywhere near Lally Tudge.

'Up your arse then!' Fatty called out.

'I'm telling my mam on you,' she said, head up in the air, ringlets bouncing. But she wouldn't have. She'd never have said arse to her mam.

Iffy and Billy sat together in the long grass with Lally and made daisy chains, miles of them, while Fatty bent twigs this way and that and whittled away with his penknife. He built a small cradle and filled it with corks to make it float. Then he picked up the doll and handed it to Iffy, who bound it round and round with daisy chains. Lally watched intently as Iffy worked. Iffy handed the doll to her.

'Iss lovely,' Lally said, and smiled at Iffy. She lifted the doll up to her face and kissed it very gently.

'Maaama! Maaama!'

She handed the doll back to Iffy. Iffy kissed the doll on the cheek. Billy took the doll next, made the sign of the cross on its forehead and handed it to Fatty.

Fatty laid the doll gently on the cradle and secured it with some cord and white wool that Iffy'd pinched from her nan's sewing box. He left a long enough piece of cord to hold on to and then slowly lowered the cradle into the river.

The doll looked quite beautiful in its daisy shroud as it bobbed on the moving waters.

'Hold the cord for me, Billy.'

Billy stood up very straight and took hold of the cord.

'Now, we all sing,' said Fatty.

'What shall we sing?' Iffy whispered.

'My old man's a dustman,' said Lally.

'Iffy?'

Something from church, she thought, something sad. She stood up, clasped her hands in front of her and cleared her throat.

'O salutaris hostia
Quae caeli pandis ostium'

Her voice rose high and clear above the sound of the rushing waters.

Fatty took out his penknife.

'Qui vitam sine termino'

The cradle bobbed dangerously.

'Nobis donet in patria.'

The doll's eyes opened, blinked up at the blue skies above, then closed softly.

Fatty cut the cord.

The doll sailed away down the river gently at first, then gathering speed and shedding daisies as it went.

They watched until it turned the bend in the river and

headed off down the valley to the faraway sea. When they looked around, there was no sign of Lally. Just the imprints of her big daft feet in the damp grass.

Earwigging was a difficult game to play, but one of Iffy's favourites. First she had to check that the kitchen was clear, then crawl underneath the kitchen table, resting her back against the wall with the oilcloth tablecloth as cover. She had to remember to shut the cat in her bedroom so it couldn't give her away. Then she had to steady her breathing and wait, and wait . . .

At last, Nan came shuffling into the kitchen from the back parlour. She lifted the kettle from the hob, swilled out the teapot with boiling water and tipped it into the bosh.

Although Iffy couldn't see her, she knew that she would be scooping out tea from the tea caddy which had a picture of an old king on the front. She heard the hot water splashing onto the leaves and smelled sweet fresh tea.

She kept very still, her knees tucked up tight to her chin, not daring to move an inch because Nan's feet were almost touching her own. One move, sneeze or giggle and she'd be a dead girl.

Quietly she sniffed up all the secret under-table smells: cracked old linoleum, ancient cat hairs, disinfectant, wood-worm dust, Fairy soap and lavender coming from Nan's skin.

Iffy kept her eyes on Nan's slippers in case she stretched out her legs and discovered Iffy. They were prickly tartan slippers, with pom poms and beady-eye buttons, which she had bought in Briggs' shoe shop in town. Even in the summer Nan wore thick brown stockings, wrinkled round the knees and coiled like sleeping snakes round her ankles.

Iffy'd seen Nan undressing lots of times, down to her vest and drawers, but never naked. She'd never seen a naked grown-up. Bessie had only ever seen her mam in her dressing gown and once, by accident, in her petticoat.

Nan didn't wear suspender belts like other women and her stockings only reached her knees and were held up by thick elastic garters. From the knees up there was a small gap of lily-white leg that stuck out of her salmon-pink knickers. Knickers as big as bedsprerads. Knickers knackers, Christmas crackers! The crotch of the knickers sagged down almost to Nan's knees. Iffy thought that if she ever fell or got pushed off a high bridge, the knickers would work like parachutes.

Sometimes Nan hid money up her knickers. Once Iffy had seen a ten-bob note tucked in them, but next time she'd looked it was gone.

The queen of England's face was on bank notes. Fatty had shown her how to fold the paper to make a bum out of the creases in the queen's face. Bessie wouldn't look.

Fatty had sung, 'In nineteen fifty-four the queen dropped her drawers, she licked her bum and said, "Yum yum", in nineteen fifty-four!'

Bessie had called him a dirty filthy pig and had run home crying.

Bessie's mam had a picture of the queen above the mantelpiece in their back parlour. The Merediths had one of Napoleon. He was French and a dwarf, but a very clever dwarf.

Mrs Bunting came huffing and puffing through the doorway, dragging her wooden leg up over the step. The chair groaned as she sat down. Iffy stared hard at Mrs Bunting's legs, trying to remember which was the wooden one. The right one facing her, she thought.

Up above the table, Nan poured tea. Cow's milk and no sugar for Mrs Bunting, she had die-or-beat-us, so she couldn't eat sweets or sugar. It made her leg go bad and she'd had to have it cut off. Fatty said they tied her to the kitchen table and did it with a rusty saw and stuffed up her mouth with old rags so she couldn't scream. She said she still felt the false leg itching and in damp weather it squeaked.

Mrs Bunting was nice. She lived a few doors down from Iffy and she kept coconut biscuits in a wooden biscuit barrel, and she gave Iffy five at a time. She wore a hat even when she was indoors and in bed in the winter. She smelled funny. Nan said it was because she kept moth balls in her drawers but you couldn't hear them rattling when she walked. Iffy'd followed her once, all the way across the bailey and listened.

'She's got another one on the way, by the look of her,' Mrs Bunting said.

'Good God,' said Nan. 'Twelve now, is it?'

They were talking about the woman who made babies. She was called Mrs Watkins and lived in Mafeking Terrace and didn't have the sense she was born with.

'Don't know how he knocks them out! There's nothing of him.'

'All skin and bone. You'd think if he had a hard-on he'd fall over!'

That must have been a joke, because they laughed and spat tea.

'Make a baby a year they do.'

'Wants to tie a bloody knot in it.'

'Mind you, she've stood by her kids, I'll give her that. Not like some people we know,' said Nan with a tut.

'Duw,' said Mrs Bunting. 'Never got over that. Never seemed the type to leave a child like that. Them foreigners are supposed to be mad about kids.'

Iffy grinned under the table. When she was little and didn't know anything she'd thought Mrs Watkins made the babies with her hands, out of clay. She'd imagined her rolling out arms and legs, making bottoms, belly buttons and dimples. Putting an extra bit of floppy clay for the boys' bits or making a neat little mark with a palette knife for the girls'. She'd pictured Mrs Watkins holding up the babies she had made, turning them over and admiring them, then putting them to dry on a huge Welsh dresser with millions of babies on it the way other people had Toby jugs. Iffy had wondered if she made them for other people and sold them like Mrs Williams who was famous for pickled onions and gherkins.

Iffy knew all about babies now.

Nan poured more tea. Iffy smelt the butter melting into freshly baked Welsh cakes. Her belly rumbled and her mouth filled up with spit.

The talk changed tack.

'There's a state on that Mrs Bevan. God, she's looking bad. I seen her coming out of the Punch – eight sheets to the wind she was – went white when she seen me, must of thought I was someone else. Said it wasn't right what she done – ranting on nineteen to the bloody dozen.'

'The drink have addled her brain. Pity for Fatty, mind. He's got no life, poor little dab. That father of his isn't up to much either, he's a right nasty piece of goods.'

'Fancy,' said Mrs Bunting slurping her tea, 'they come and took Mrs Prosser's cooker last night.'

'Her new one?' Nan sniffed. She had no truck with cookers. They were new-fangled nonsense.

'Had a win on the horses, so she says. She only paid the deposit. Never made no more payments. The man from the Cop come to take it back.'

'Dopey 'aporth. Don't know what she wants a cooker for, she can't cook to save her life. All packets and tins with her.'

'Well, there was all hell up. The man come at teatime. She was cooking Albie's tea.'

'Hotting up a shop pie, if I know her.'

'Crying she was, begging the man to wait until the tea had finished warming.'

'Up to her eyes in debt.'

'Where's your Iffy?' Mrs Bunting said.

Iffy sat tight under the table, closed her eyes and held her breath.

'Oh, out with Bessie Tranter somewhere.'

'I seen Bessie and Mrs Tranter in town, in the Penny Bazaar. Iffy wasn't with them,' said Mrs Bunting.

Iffy hoped that they wouldn't lift the tablecloth and find her out. Fingers crossed. Eyes shut. Count to ten.

'I s'pect she's out with Billy then.'

They didn't look under the table.

'She's like her father, that Bessie, mind. The spit of him.'

'No mistaking where she come from.'

Bessie didn't look like her father at all. He was bald and limped. He had false teeth that clattered and chattered when he walked.

'I was behind Dulcie Davies coming up from town on the bus. There's a whiff off her.'

'Filthy rotten, she is.'

'Like a bucket of last week's whelks.'

Dulcie Davies was a lunatic. She lived in Iron Row. There were lots of lunatics in the town. Grancha once told Iffy that if ever Mr Hitler had invaded England and got as far as their town he would have taken one look at some of the daft buggers in the valley and run like hell.

'Something I meant to ask you, I've had a bit of trouble with mouth ulcers again. Don't suppose I could have a little drop of that holy water, just to dab on them.'

'Ay, course you can. I'll just get you some.'

Iffy put her hand across her mouth. She wanted to shout out, 'Don't drink it, Mrs Bunting!' but she couldn't.

'Damn, it's strong stuff that water.' Mrs Bunting made smacking noises with her lips.

The two old women talked for hours. Iffy was stiff as a poker by the time she got out from under the table and she hadn't heard anything interesting at all.

The Catholic cemetery was at the top of a long steep hill over-looking two valleys. It was the burial place for Catholics from miles around. The climb was arduous, the road winding away up out of the town. Will passed the last of the houses, a few straggling pigeoncots and a row of dilapidated sheds. The road narrowed, the bends grew sharper, the climb steeper. At the top of the hill there was a wonderful view down into the next valley, but he didn't stop to look. He pushed open the high wrought-iron gates and stepped into the cemetery.

It was a long time since he'd been there, but his feet knew the way, he'd walked this path many times in his darkest dreams.

The wind was keen and rain clouds were banking above the distant hills as he went on through the cemetery. An old man was kneeling in front of a grave, his head bowed. As Will got closer the man stood up and made the sign of the cross. When he saw Will, he smiled. It was the old man from the Italian café in town. His eyes were damp with tears, his lips quivering with emotion. He hurried away towards the gates. Will looked down at the grave. Fresh flowers had been placed there, deep-red tulips and white rosebuds. He read the inscriptions.

Lucia Maria Zeraldo. Aged seven. Tragically taken from us.

The second inscription read:

Rosa Maria Zeraldo. Mother of Lucia, wife of Luca.

She had died less than three months after her child.

Will shivered as he took the last few steps.

The grave was overgrown and he had to break the stranglehold of weeds and ivy from the headstone. He pulled at them until his hands were chafed and sore from the effort.

The lettering was faded now, eroded by many winters. He slumped forward and had to rest his hands against the headstone for support.

For the first time in years he spoke her name out loud. 'Rhiannon.'

He had never been able to hear the name without a cold band gripping his heart in a vice. He had never been able to say it before.

'Rhiannon!' His voice echoed loudly among the graves.

He had been a husband for only a few years. And it had all been wiped away one cold, merciless November night when all his joy had turned to grief. He had held her hand, had brushed his lips across her bruised head. Her eyes had closed, dark lashes falling across her cheeks like shadows. Her fingers had gripped his own nicotine-stained fingers as though she would never let go.

He thought of the old Italian, who made his regular pilgrimage to the graves of his own wife and daughter all these long years. He would know what it was like, living the half life of those who had lost their greatest love.

The name on the gravestone wobbled through his brimming tears.

Rhiannon Louisa Sloane. Aged 25 years.

Oh, Christ. That night when she'd been taken ill, collapsed with a brain tumour, he'd been . . . he'd been . . . He couldn't bear to think of it. He had betrayed her utterly.

He bent his head and wept properly for the first time, while the rain fell like a benediction of nails on his neck.

Fatty took the lid off the box. The head of the statue sparkled in the sunshine. He lifted it out and laid it gently in his lap.

All the green moss had been scrubbed away with a bar of Fairy soap that Iffy had stolen from home. Fatty had dug the mud and dirt out from the nostrils and ears with his penknife. Now the head was as white and smooth as a new candle.

He turned it over in his lap. The stone hair was carved into a tight cap of curls around the head. He turned it back over. The nose tilted upwards towards the sky. The eyebrows were raised, the white lips smiled a secretive sort of smile. They were pretty lips.

'You're lovely,' said Fatty.

He bent over and kissed the statue full on the lips.

Iffy blew out through her nose and looked the other way. Disgusting.

'It's just a stone head, Fatty.'

'I'm gonna give it back to her,' he said, laying the head tenderly back in the box.

'To Carty Annie?'

'No!'

'What do you mean then?'

'I'm gonna sneak in there,' he said pointing towards the Big House, 'and I'm gonna stick it back on . . . they say she comes looking for her head. P'raps she'll be at peace then.'

'You're mad! What if you get caught?'

'You can't get done for mending something, can you? I'm doing her a favour.'

'You don't even know who she was.'

'Carty Annie knew her. That's why she kept the head.'

'Where did she get it from?'

'She found it down in the grass by the river. She reckoned old Medlicott went berserk, smashed the head off and threw it over the wall.'

'Why?'

'Carty Annie said he was in love with the girl – that she was having a baby by him – only she wasn't.'

'She wasn't having a baby?'

'No, she *was* having a baby.'

'You just said she wasn't!'

'No. Listen. She was having a baby, but it *wasn't* old Medlicott's, it was somebody else's who she was in love with. Old Medlicott found out and went nuts.'

'He didn't chop her head off in real life though, did he?'

'No. Carty Annie said she thinks they took the baby down to the home for bad girls.'

'What happened to her?'

'The baby?'

'No, the girl.'

'They sent her back to where she came from.'

'Where was that?'

'Spain. It's dead sad, isn't it?'

Iffy didn't answer him. She was sick of the stupid head and his daft ideas.

Fatty stood on the step of Iffy's house in Inkerman Terrace, hopping up and down, bursting with excitement.

'Guess what, Iffy! The puppies have been born!'

'Honest?'

'Yep! And one of them looks just like Barny! You wanna see them?'

'Will Mr Sandicock let us?'

'No, course he won't, but they're out in one of the old sheds, there's a way to get round the back and see them through the window. Come on, I'll show you!'

'I'm not going in the grounds, Fatty!'

'You don't need to, come on.'

Fatty led the way, skirting the walls of the Big House until they came into the cover of trees alongside some out-buildings.

'Up there!' Fatty said, pointing to a window that had bars on it but no glass. 'I'll climb up first and take a decker, she's used to me, she don't bark any more when she sees me.'

'How do you mean, she's used to you?'

'Cos I been coming for ages to get to know her, so's when she had the pups she wouldn't be afraid of me.'

Iffy thought that animals always loved Fatty, so did kids unless grown-ups interfered and told them not to bother with him.

'How you gonna get up there?'

He tapped the side of his nose and winked. Then he disappeared back into the bushes and came out pulling two wooden pop crates behind him. He put one below the window and stacked the other one on top of it. Then he climbed up on top of them. He was just tall enough to look in through the window.

'Hello, old gel . . . we've come to have a look at your pups . . . beautiful they are too, I brought Iffy to see 'em . . . Iffy won't hurt them. She's nice.'

Fatty jumped down from the crate.

'Have a look, Iffy. See if you can guess which one I want.'

Fatty gave her a leg up onto the crate. He had to steady the crates for her.

At first she couldn't see much at all. She screwed up her eyes and peered into the darkness. Then she saw! In one corner of the shed a big black dog lay curled on a pile of old blankets. She stared at Iffy with soft brown eyes.

Iffy was afraid she'd bark and that Mr Sandicock would come running, but the dog just whined at her. When Iffy's eyes grew used to the dimness she saw the pups. Five little humps of fur lying close to the mother dog's belly. Their little tails were wagging, their wet noses snuffling.

They were really beautiful. Four of them were dark like the mother but one of them was the exact colour of Barny, and it was the most lively one of them all. It would suit Fatty.

'Can you guess?' Fatty asked.

'Yep! The brown wriggly naughty one! When you gonna ask if you can have him?'

'They got to be about six weeks old before they can leave their mam.'

Then, with a crash, Iffy fell off the crate.

Fatty grabbed her and she put her finger to her lips, 'Someone's come in the shed,' she hissed.

'Stay still,' Fatty whispered. 'Get up against the wall in case they look out of the window.'

They flattened their bodies against the wall. Iffy could hear her heart beating and hoped that whoever was inside couldn't hear it knocking against the wood.

They kept quiet and listened. The sound of angry voices came through the window.

'Take a look at them, you half-baked clot! Get her covered by a bloody black Labrador! It wasn't a bloody black Labrador that covered her or I'm a bloody monkey's uncle!' said Mr Sandicock.

'Honest to God! It was, mun, I watched them at it!' said Dai Full Pelt.

'I'll tell you what, Dai, I want my bloody money back! I paid you good money to get that bitch covered by a pedigree and what have I got? A litter of bastard mongrels!'

Fatty nudged Iffy and whispered in her ear.

'Told you so. You watch. They'll give them away when they've been weaned.'

'Honest to God, Mr Sandicock, it *was* a black Labrador. On my mother's life!'

'On your mother's life! Your mother's been dead for years. You must be a bloody dull bugger! You couldn't tell a black Labrador from a bloody polar bear. I want my money back!'

'P'raps you can sell them a bit cheaper, Mr Sandicock.'

'Sell them! You can sell pedigrees, Dai! Mongrels are two a sodding penny. These you'll have to bloody give away. I'll leave that up to you, you stupid bloody article, you.'

'Told you,' Fatty said, grinning. 'And when they're old enough I'm gonna ask for one. I'm saving up for a lead and a collar.'

He would ask too. Fatty wasn't afraid of anyone or anything. He'd be dead lucky to have a pup all of his own.

They waited until the voices died away, checked that no one was about and scuttled off back up the lane.

Bessie had five shillings to spend, and Iffy was going with her to buy sweets, but when they got to Morrissey's shop the blinds were pulled down on the windows, so they went for a walk to pass the time until he opened up.

Iron Row was narrow and dark, it wasn't a proper street just four little cottages joined together. They would have been pretty if they'd been whitewashed, but they were caked with black dirt and moss grew from the cracks in the walls. There were slates missing off the roofs and the chimneys were crooked.

The flagstones in Iron Row were loose and a smattering of black mud sloshed up over Bessie's new socks. They were nice socks, shiny white cotton with two pale-pink bands around the tops.

Bessie made it worse by rubbing it. She said her mam

would kill her, but she always said that. Her mam hardly ever even told her off.

A skinny brown dog with three legs followed them and tried to sniff up Bessie's frock. It belonged to Mrs Maloney who lived down in town. She had a husband called Custard Lungs although no one could remember why.

Bessie squealed as the dog's nose disappeared up her frock.

'Sniff, sniff, sniff,' went the dog.

'Eek, eek, eek!' went Bessie.

She ran round and round in circles trying to get away from him but he thought it was a good game and carried on until he got giddy and fell over. He hopped away down the Row, peeing as he ran.

Two girls came out of the second house along and stood on the step looking them up and down, especially Bessie. They raised their eyebrows at her posh clothes. Done up like a dog's dinner she was, even for playing out.

Iffy thought they looked a right rough pair of bruisers. They were twins. Red-haired and white-skinned with thin pale-pink lips like kittens.

Bessie stared back at them.

'Don't stare, Bessie! Look the other way.'

Bessie always gawped and it made people mad.

'Oy, you! You dropped something!' one of the girls shouted as they drew level.

Ifyy didn't look round, she wasn't going to fall for that old trick.

Bessie did.

'Too late, the flies are on it!' yelled one of the girls. They laughed and pointed and stuck out their tongues.

Bessie glared at them.

'Keep it shut, Bessie! Just keep on walking.'

'What do they mean, the flies are on it?'

Iffy spoke between clenched teeth, staring straight ahead, 'They mean you've just shit.'

'Ugh! You dirty filthy pigs!'

The girls were already halfway down the Row.

Iffy pulled Bessie roughly by the arm, 'Run, Bessie!'

Bessie was hopeless at running and the twins were hot on their heels. Iffy looked behind her. Their pink eyes were deepening to red, sharp teeth, fists like bananas. The Price twins!

'Shit!'

She'd heard of them. Rosalind and Rosemary Price – they were nutcases – they'd even beaten up Mervyn Prosser. They were gaining on her and Bessie by the second.

Then, suddenly, they stopped dead in their tracks.

'Go on, piss off back up your own end! You carrotty pair of bastards.'

Iffy recognised the old woman as soon as she saw her because she'd met her once with her nan outside the wet fish shop in town. Disappointed, the twins hotfooted it away, back up the Row.

Iffy nudged Bessie, and whispered, 'That's Dulcie Davies.'

'Who?'

Iffy knew loads more people than Bessie did because Bessie's mam hardly spoke to anyone.

'Dulcie Davies! She's a lunatic. She used to do *it* with sailors for money and she pees in milk bottles.'

'Ugh.'

Iffy thought it would be hard to pee in a milk bottle.

'Once she took all her clothes off in the Black Prince and danced a hornpipe.'

'She never did! She's about ninety. Come on, let's go.'

Dulcie Davies stood on the step of the last house squinting down the Row towards them. Fatty had told Iffy that she ate live eels and fish eggs and sucked raw fish heads like they were sweets. Fatty said he'd seen her and that if you cut open her belly it would be full of millions of tiny fish that had hatched out from all the eggs she'd eaten.

Iffy knew they were trapped: the twins were behind them; Dulcie was in front. She walked on quickly, telling Bessie to look the other way, but they weren't quick enough. Dulcie Davies came off her step and came towards them. She walked sideways like a crab. She stopped in front of Iffy.

'Come in, pretty girls, and give an old lady a hand to light the fire,' she said, and before they had a chance to run she snapped her bony hand over Iffy's wrist.

'Don't go in!' Bessie said.

Dulcie Davies held on to Iffy tightly and though she was nothing but a bag of skinny bones, she was very strong. Iffy grabbed hold of Bessie's sleeve and tried to drag her along too, but Bessie wriggled her arm out of her fluffy bolero and was off and running, her skinny pins going nineteen to the dozen.

'Just a little hand to light the fire. My poor old hands are too weak to strike the match these days,' Dulcie said.

Too weak! She had a grip like a navvy.

Iffy's knees shook with fright. Dulcie was a lunatic. Iffy wasn't sure if she was a dangerous one or not.

The smell inside the house smacked Iffy full in the chops as Dulcie lugged her struggling through the door. It stank in there like nothing she'd ever smelled before. The smells went in through her nose and came out through her ears. Then they went in again. Round and round they went until her whole body was full of them. She felt sick to her stomach. The house was scruffy enough on the outside but inside it was even worse. It was filthy, stinking dirty. There was straw on the floor and lumps of dried cat shit. All the walls were cracked and peeling, wooden bits stuck through the broken plaster like the ribs of a ruined ship.

The light inside the house was strange. Green, moving light, as if it was underwater.

The floorboards rolled under Iffy's feet. The house rocked, pitched and tossed until waves of sick bashed against the inside of her ribs.

Under a table in one corner of the room a red-eyed, scabby cat coughed up fish skeletons in a pile. There was a tin bath standing on an old milking stool, it was full of brown water and scum and bubbled as if it were a magic cauldron.

Dulcie Davies loosened her grip on Iffy's arm, but not enough for her to escape. She pushed a box of matches towards her. Iffy took them. The box felt damp and greasy. She wasn't much cop at lighting matches at the best of times. She tried to stop her hands from shaking, but soon a pile of burned matchsticks lay in the hearth.

'We need something to help it along a bit, I fancy,' said Dulcie with a cackle.

She stared into Iffy's face. Too close for comfort. She smelled of boiling haddock and sardine oil. She had a face like a codfish, round glazed eyes, wet lips and a mouth that opened and closed even when she wasn't speaking.

'Who are you belonging to?' she said, her mouth close up to Iffy's.

'M-M-M-Meredith.'

'Old man Meredith from up Inkerman?'

Iffy nodded.

'Brave old bugger, he is . . . I remember him years ago giving that dirty old doctor a pasting.'

Iffy stared at her.

'Aha! Wop, he went, smack! Took the smile off the evil old bastard's chops. Whose kiddie are you then?'

'Ch-Charlie's.'

'Ay, damn I can see that now, round the eyes. Wicked boy, he was. He give me a kiss one New Year's Eve in the Mechanics. Good-hearted he was, mind. He give me a pound note once, bless him . . . down under the bridge. Sad about him. Not the sort you'd have thought would do himself . . . Now, this'll get it going!'

She waved a bottle at Iffy. A bottle full of pink-coloured water. She popped the cork. An evil smell rose from the bottle. Iffy swallowed hard. It was probably deadly poison and she was going to force her to drink it.

Iffy shut her mouth tight. Dulcie chucked a great slosh of the pink stuff over the coals in the range.

Iffy managed to light a match. She pushed it gingerly towards the papers and the few lumps of coal in the grate.

Whoosh!

A roaring and rushing noise filled the room. Wax flew out of her ears. Wee escaped from her bladder. Her screams hit the rafters, so did her eyebrows. She was out of there in a flash.

She heard Dulcie the lunatic laughing somewhere behind her in a cloud of smoke.

Iffy ran and, as she ran, she thought angrily that her dad would never have kissed an ugly old thing like Dulcie Davies.

She reached the end of Iron Row panting and sweating, her face as hot as hell. She ran and ran as if the devil himself was behind her.

Bessie was waiting halfway down the next road.

'Why didn't you help me?' Iffy sobbed. 'It was all your fault. If you hadn't stared at those two girls . . .'

Bessie didn't answer, but screamed and then gawped with her mouth wide open.

'Why didn't you help me? She could have killed me.'

Bessie started crying. 'Your face is all black and there's bits of you missing!' she said.

Iffy left her there catching flies in her mouth. She ran all the way home without stopping. She wouldn't wait for Bessie, who couldn't keep up on her lucky-not-to-snap legs.

Nan looked up as she hurtled into the kitchen.

'Jeevrey fathers! What in God's name have you been up to, girl!'

Iffy told her.

Nan gave her murder. 'What the hell were you thinking of, going in there in the first place! Dulcie Davies is a bloody lunatic, mun. I've told you often enough! You're lucky you didn't get killed.'

She wiped the grime from Iffy's face with a warm flannel and trimmed her singed fringe with nail scissors.

'It'll take weeks to grow back. You look a bloody sight! Dopey 'aporth! I told you to keep out of there! Don't listen, that's your trouble!'

She put cream where Iffy's eyebrows used to be. And she kissed her after she'd stopped being angry.

But she kept her in all the next day.

Will stood outside the Big House looking through the rusting gates. There was a padlocked chain to keep the gates shut, but the chain was long and with a little bit of jiggling Will was able to squeeze through into the garden.

The house was derelict, the roof cracked open, blackened beams exposed to the sky. The high arched windows were nailed across with wooden slats.

The once well-tended lawns had long since disappeared. The grass was coarse and waist high. Dandelions and nettles grew in abundance.

Organ music drifted up from Carmel Chapel.

'Shit!'

Brambles.

He bent down gingerly, feeling the scratches on his flesh. He winced, the pain between his shoulders was more acute than usual.

Something caught his eye in the grass. He pulled back the layers of overgrown weeds and saw the nose first, then the sightless eyes, then an open mouth. A head severed from the body.

'And what the fuck do you think you're up to!'

Will jumped with fright, his heart raced and as he struggled to his feet his spectacles slipped from his nose.

A man stood in the long grass staring at him. A man with his arms around the neck of a girl . . . a naked girl.

'Can't you read?' the man said. 'Keep out. Can't make it much plainer than that, can I?'

Will kept silent.

He had a terrible urge to laugh at the absurdity of the situation. Just for a moment, without his spectacles he had thought the girl was real.

The man looked brazenly at him, a glint of challenge in his eyes. He took his arms from around the statue and let her fall with a heavy thud into the long grass.

Will, his glasses back in place, stared back at a thick-set handsome man, with a large red splash across one cheek, a strawberry birthmark.

'Little beauty, isn't she? Now what do you want?'

'I'm sorry for trespassing. I was just hoping to take a look for old times' sake.'

'Not from round here, are you?'

'No, not any more, but I spent a fair bit of time here in the past. I didn't mean to cause any offence, old policemen never die.'

The man's eyes narrowed.

'In the force, are you?'

'Not any more. Retired.'

'So what's so fascinating about this old place?'

'I came here once, years ago. Sat just over there.' He pointed across the jungle of garden towards the dilapidated house. 'I remembered the statues and wanted to take a look.'

'Some proper beauties. The old doctor had a fondness for statues, naked ones mainly . . . bit of a dirty old sod, by all accounts.'

'The gardens were beautiful when I was here last.'

'Well, they will be again in a few years time . . . a bit different though. I've bought the place, I start work in a few weeks. Mervyn Prosser, builder.'

The man held out his hand to Will. Will shook the hand and felt the enormous strength of the fellow.

'Going to build a pool here for the kids. They're grown up a bit now, grandchildren in a few years, no doubt. I'm gonna dig up that ugly old fishpond, get rid of these bloody old statues. First thing my wife said to me, "Get shot of them spooky old things, Mervyn." '

Will cringed silently.

'Got big plans for the house, double glazing, weights room, jacuzzi, pine kitchen . . .'

It occurred to Will that this man would be about the same age as the lost child.

'My wife . . . she didn't really want me to buy it, but she came round when I showed her the plans. I told her, I said, you won't know the place when I've finished with it.' He cocked his head in the direction of Carmel Chapel. 'That's my wife you can hear playing the organ over in the chapel. Practises every day. Very talented lady.'

'I can hear that,' Will said.

'Tell you what, call in and see her one morning. I'll tell her to expect you. Come round for some tea.'

'Really, I don't want to put you to any trouble.'

'Tell you the truth, I'd be glad if you did. You could tell her how beautiful the Big House used to be, might make her a bit more keen about things.'

'Thanks,' Will said, but he felt less than enthusiastic.

Iffy was up at the kitchen table rubbing lard into where her eyebrows had been because Fatty had told her it would make them grow back quicker. Grancha was drinking tea behind the *Argus*. He always got behind the newspaper when Winnie Jones came in. He couldn't bear her. She lived further down Inkerman, near Bessie. She had a husband who kept pigeons and a son who had gone to Australia and never ever wrote. She was always on the cadge. Cups of sugar, a couple of slices of bread, fags, holy water.

Nan poured tea for Winnie Jones. Fussell's milk. Four sugars.

'Someone broke into Mrs Clancy's parlour and pinched her budgerigar,' said Winnie taking out her top teeth and slipping them into the pocket in her apron. Iffy looked away in disgust.

'There's a funny thing to pinch,' said Nan, banging down the teapot on the oilcloth.

'Ay, wouldn't make much of a meal for a family would it?' Grancha said, his breath rustling the newspaper.

Iffy peeped at him over the paper to see if he was joking. His face was like a poker.

'Mr Meredith, you are a one!' lisped Winnie, her mouth puckered up with sweet tea.

'Take no notice of him, Iffy!'

'There's been a spate of it,' said Winnie helping herself to a fifth spoon of sugar.

'Pinching budgies?' Iffy asked.

'No. Breaking into people's houses and stealing. They

203

took Mrs Edwards's rib of beef from the pantry and the clock off the mantelpiece!' Winnie said.

'Never to God,' Nan said into her cup.

'And Mrs Tudge had her knickers pinched off the washing line last week.'

Grancha laughed. 'Must have been desperate!'

'Oy!' Nan threw him a dirty look.

'Mind, you could clothe a family from Mrs Tudge's knickers if you was handy with a needle.'

'Oy!' said Nan again.

'When Mrs Tudge hangs her knickers on the line you'd think they'd put the clocks back.'

'Pack it in,' Nan said and tried to sound cross, but Iffy knew she wanted to laugh.

Iffy thought her grancha was very funny.

Sometimes Iffy made jokes without knowing it. Once when Nan was talking about Mrs Tranter, she said, 'Whatever anyone says about Mrs Tranter being a funny old cow, she's spotless. You could eat your dinner off her floor,' and Iffy had said, 'Why? Haven't they got any plates?' Grancha had fallen off his chair laughing and kept saying over and over, 'Haven't they got any plates?' like the needle had got stuck on the gramophone. Iffy still didn't get what was so funny.

'Poor Mrs Tudge,' said Winnie. 'She've had her fair share of hardship this last few months what with Lally and that lazy arsed son of hers.'

'What's up with Lally?' Grancha said.

'Your eyesight wants testing I fancy,' said Nan pouring more tea.

'I haven't seen much of Lally lately.'

'No, she's been away for a bit.'

Nan looked hard at Grancha, nodding towards Iffy who pretended she wasn't interested.

'Where's she been?'

Nan coughed. 'A bun in the oven.'

'Never to God! Poor little dab. Who the hell done that to the little gel?'

'Your guess is as good as mine, but the talk is it was the same one as put a bun in Hilary Tranter's oven all them years ago.'

'The dirty old bas—'

'Not in front of Iffy!'

Grown-ups talked arse backwards sometimes. So what if someone had put a bun in Lally Tudge's oven. It was quite nice of them, Iffy thought, especially after having to give her baby away and all that.

'Guess what?' said Winnie, helping herself to more tea without being asked. 'Mrs Tudor Yabsley has gone.'

'Gone where?'

'Well, that's just it. Upped and gone. Packed her bags in the night and when Mr Tudor Yabsley woke up – no sign of her. Talk is she've run off with that Mikey Muscles from Merthyr. Bit of a wrestler he's supposed to be.'

'Well, well,' said Nan. 'She always was one for the men. Talk of the town she was in the war, dirty, fausty old cow.'

Grancha snorted over the top of his paper. 'Mikey Muscles is all of four foot six.'

'Well, like they say, little dogs have big tails.'

Iffy didn't get that. Jack Look Up's little dog hadn't got a tail at all.

'She was supposed to be a pillar of the chapel,' said Grancha. 'I thought she was quiet.'

'Quiet my arse! You know what they say, quiet sows sup the most swill!'

'Been funny ever since she went off meat.' Winnie sighed.

'All them vegetables can't do you any good, it's not natural, mun, that's why we got teeth to chew a bit of steak.'

Nan didn't have any teeth.

'Poor Mr Tudor Yabsley.'

Iffy went out in the end. Grown-ups talked dead daft most of the time.

Days had passed after the child's clothes had been found and still there was no sign of a body, alive or dead. The local men had turned out in force and joined the police officers in the search. Gangs of them had scoured the river banks, searched sheds and outhouses, checked the deep pools, but there was nothing to be found.

Up on the mountain the top ponds were dragged and six ancient skeletons were dredged from the mud: two dogs, three sheep and a headless donkey. It was all to no avail.

The photograph taken outside the Limp was reprinted in the form of a thousand posters.

MISSING
Have you seen this child?

Later, the posters had been pasted up all over the valleys. Then later still, as far away as Bristol and even London. Until they finally peeled away after many months when hope had died.

Iffy's eyebrows grew back slowly. Nan had pencilled some in for her but her hand shook while she was doing it and that made Iffy look worse, as if she was surprised all the time. Nan plastered Iffy's curls down over where the eyebrows should have been, wetting them with spit and rubbing them flat with a flannel.

Iffy saw hardly anything of Fatty for days. He was so bothered about the stupid head and the puppies down at the Big House that he didn't have time for anyone else.

Nan was upstairs, Grancha at work, the kitchen was empty so Iffy slipped under the kitchen table, and then everyone in the world came visiting, so she couldn't get out. Winnie Jones came in first on the cadge for gravy browning. Then Mrs Bunting for her daily chat with Nan.

They didn't talk about anything interesting, just went on about pickling onions and Mrs Bunting's waterworks playing up and a woman down the valley who died when the toilet cistern fell on her head. It was all boring stuff but it livened up a bit after Mrs Bunting left.

Iffy was listening to Mrs Bunting's wooden leg squeaking as she crossed the bailey, when she heard a familiar voice. She could tell that voice a mile off: Auntie Mary Meredith. She had a voice that sounded as if she was dragging wet words over big boulders. It took her ages to get things out and sometimes people got bored and finished her sentences for her, which got her hopping mad. Auntie Mary Meredith was funny. She was a bit like a kid and said things she shouldn't.

'Auntie Mary had a canary up the leg of her drawers.

When she farted how it started! Shot out the leg of her drawers!'

Auntie Mary Meredith lived down the valley and was a bit twp.

Once, she trod on a frog in the outside lav. She was so fat the frog made a farting noise when the air came out of it and she fainted. She had a son called Norman who had shellshock from the war. He was nice but a bit scary. If he heard a bang he began to shake, threw himself on the ground and covered his head with his hands. People laughed at him, but he couldn't help it.

He wasn't twp though like his mam. He had a clever head on him and was good with figures. He did the books for shops.

'Yoooooo hooooooo,' called Auntie Mary as she came in over the step.

'Mary! Come in, love,' Nan said. 'There's a nice surprise! Smelled the tea, did you? Come on in and sit yourself down.'

Auntie Mary sat down at the table and the chair creaked noisily under her weight. Her legs came under the table towards Iffy, who had to squeeze up tight against the wall. Auntie Mary had huge flabby legs and the skin hung down in pink flaps over her shoes.

'Oh, damn, I'm weary,' she said. 'My arse is making buttons from sitting on that bus so long.'

Iffy bit her lips so as not to laugh. She wished Fatty was under the table with her. Fatty always went into fits when he heard Auntie Mary talking.

He was really good at taking people off. He could do all the teachers in school, and Father Flaherty. When he mimicked Auntie Mary he sounded just like her.

Nan poured tea. Cow's milk and three sugars for Auntie Mary Meredith.

'I've just seen that Hilary Tranter's daughter, coming up the hill behind that big fat piece from the Old Bake House,' Auntie Mary said.

'Oh, that's Lally.'

'Good God!' said Auntie Mary Meredith. 'There's a pair of tits on her.'

Iffy rammed her fist in her mouth so as not to laugh and bit her knuckles hard.

'Mary,' Nan chuckled, 'you mustn't say things like that.'

'Well, she have! Huge they are. Like bloody big pumpkins,' said Auntie Mary.

'I know she have,' Nan said, 'but you mustn't say so.'

It was no good telling Auntie Mary though because she said things like that all the time, the first thing that came into her head.

Iffy wondered what Hilary Tranter's daughter was doing with Lally. Hilary Tranter never came near Bessie's house because her mam had disowned her after she ran away from home, dyed her hair and changed her name to Dolores. And Auntie Mary must have got it wrong anyway because Hilary Tranter didn't have a daughter she had two boys. Iffy and Bessie had seen them. It was a secret because Bessie wasn't supposed to have anything to do with her sister.

One day they'd seen Dolores coming out of Morrissey's shop and they'd followed her. She wore high heels that clicked as she walked and her skirt was so tight she had to take very small steps. She was pushing two sleeping babies in a battered old pushchair with buckled wheels. Bessie said the babies were twins and were called Cliff and Adam.

They followed her down over the bridge, past Carmel Chapel, along a lane that led to a farm where the farmer had a gun and a bad temper. She'd turned a bend in the road and as they rounded the corner she was standing facing them, hands on her hips.

They'd stopped dead in their tracks.

'You'd never make a pair of bloody spies!'

They shuffled their feet and looked down at the ground.

'You want to come in or what?'

Bessie shook her head.

'Don't worry, Bessie, I won't tell mam you've been. I don't speak to her, remember?'

Hilary Tranter's house was wedged in between two wrecked ones. There were still fireplaces in the upstairs walls and scraps of flowery wallpaper flapped in the breeze.

Hilary went into the house and the girls followed. There were clothes thrown all over the floor and a brassiere hung over the banisters. Hilary stepped through all the mess as if it wasn't there.

The kitchen was worse than the hall. There were boxes on the floor full of empty tins and beer bottles. White flour spilled out of a paper bag onto a pile of dirty socks. There were knickers with brown marks on and, on a newspaper in one corner, there was a piece of half-eaten fish that buzzed with flies. There were fag ends and burn marks on every surface. Greasy plates were piled high on the kitchen table.

'We can't stay long, Lurry,' Bessie squeaked.

'I'm Dolores now not bloody Lurry.'

Bessie began to wheeze.

Iffy wondered if she was putting it on to get out of there but there was a mangy-looking cat asleep on top of the draining board. Cats always made Bessie wheeze. So did maths.

Dolores said, 'Please your sodding selves. Don't wake the bloody babies up on the way out.'

But she smiled kindly at Bessie and she stood on the step and watched them as they walked back down the lane.

On the way home Bessie said Hilary must have been burgled, but she hadn't been else she'd have called for the police. Bessie only said that because she was embarrassed.

She'd made Iffy swear not to tell her mam.

Auntie Mary Meredith said, 'Wasn't it that queer-faced little man in the sweet shop, that Morrissey fellow who put Hilary Tranter in the family way in the first place?'

'Well, that was all the talk at the time,' Nan said.

'Only fourteen, wasn't she, when she had the baby?'

'Ay, fourteen or fifteen. Hot in the knickers she was, that Hilary. Calls herself Dolores now. Soft cow. She got a couple of dark babies off a sailor from Newport.'

'Mrs Tranter took on the one she had by Morrissey, didn't she?'

'Oh ay, been rearing her as if she was her own. Mind you, I don't think Mrs Tranter has a clue about who the father is, so don't go opening your trap, Mary. Bessie, the girl is called, she plays with our Iffy. Nice enough little girl but mollycoddled.'

Bessie! Nan meant Bessie Tranter!

Iffy sat very still under the table trying to make sense of what she'd heard. She rolled the words round in her head. She still didn't understand. Then she did. It couldn't be true!

She wished she hadn't heard. Perhaps they'd made a mistake, but she'd heard them.

That meant Bessie's sister was really her mam. And her mam wasn't her mam at all, she was her nan.

Iffy's head was spinning just thinking about it.

And Morrissey was the man who had done it with Hilary Tranter. Morrissey and Hilary Tranter had rubbed belly buttons and Bessie hadn't come out of Mrs Tranter's bum, but out of her sister's, well, her sister who was really her mam.

It was awful. And Bessie didn't know.

Poor Bessie! She couldn't marry Morrissey now. He was her dad. And who she thought was her real dad was her grancha. And the chocolate babies in the pushchair were her brothers, sort of.

Iffy felt sick. It was the worst secret ever. She knew she must never tell Bessie, even if they argued. Even if she wanted to for spite. Bridgie Thomas had been right about there being secrets in the town.

Iffy was glad there were no secrets about herself, she was sick of secrets.

Auntie Mary Meredith stayed for ages and when Nan went out to the lav, and Iffy could finally crawl out from under the table, her legs would barely move they were so stiff.

Iffy didn't call for Bessie all the next day and when Bessie

211

came knocking she hid under the bed. She didn't want to see her now she knew. Things didn't feel the same any more.

Iffy kept the secret, but knowing it made her feel bad. It was always ready on the tip of her tongue to spill out. Whenever she and Bessie argued, Iffy thought about telling Bessie the truth, but she daren't.

It was horrible having a secret and she'd always thought it would be nice.

It was too big a secret. It made her afraid and it made her chest hurt. It grew inside her until she was afraid she'd have to let it out. Telling the secret would be like a snowball: small at first but getting bigger as everyone knew. Bigger and bigger, as people whispered it behind their hands, until it was so huge it would roll away and flatten Bessie. Even kill her.

It was a hunch. Coppers' instinct.

Will opened the door to Gladys's Gowns and went inside. It was like stepping back into another age. The shop even smelled the way life had forty years ago.

A smartly dressed woman in her fifties came forward and smiled at Will. Behind her in a wicker chair a very old woman sat wrapped in a plaid shawl.

The older woman looked Will up and down with bright-eyed interest despite her great age.

'How may I help you?' the younger of the two women asked, clearly quite surprised to see a gentleman in the shop.

'I wondered . . .' said Will. 'I was looking for a hat.'

'For any particular occasion?' said the younger woman politely.

'Well, it's rather difficult. I have an old aunt, she's in a home now, but she was always so particular about her hats.'

'Not so easy these days to get a good hat,' said the old

woman. 'In my day we wouldn't go out without one. These youngsters go flying about the place with their heads un-covered, no wonder they're all suffering from these funny diseases we never had years ago.'

'That's just what my aunt says. She's very fit really, apart from her legs, she's eighty-nine.'

Just then the telephone rang in the back of the shop and the younger woman excused herself and went out the back.

'I'm ninety-two. Your aunt has the same problem no doubt with her legs as I have. I can't stand for long periods. Still do a lot of my own cooking, mind. My Marlene has a heavy hand with pastry.'

'Ah, now that's one of my weaknesses – pastry,' said Will.

'I can't bear all this low-fat, no-fat nonsense,' said the old woman.

'Wimberry tart, nothing tastes like that. Wimberries seem to have gone out of fashion,' said Will.

'Not if you know where to look. There's an old boy who brings me wimberries. Marlene laughs when I call him an old boy, he's only seventy-five – years younger than me. If it *is* wimberry tart you want, Inspector?'

Will smiled. 'It's that obvious, is it?'

'I can tell a policeman at fifty paces. My husband was in the force, over in the next valley, a bit before your time. Now, if it's just wimberry tart that you're after, maybe I can help.'

Will had taken a liking to this old lady, there wouldn't be much that she didn't know about the happenings of years ago.

'It's half-day closing on Thursday. Marlene goes to visit a gentleman friend – she thinks I don't know! I'm not as green as I'm cabbage-looking! You come round the back about three o'clock – I'll get her to leave the door on the latch.'

Jack Look Up flew his kite when the moon was full. They called him Jack Look Up because he looked up every

213

couple of seconds. It was a twitch. They used to watch him and count: One, two, three, and Jack's chin twitched twice. His head jerked up towards the sky and one eye winked. One, two, three, then it happened all over again. Over and over.

The children were watching him from the bridge. The big red kite was like a badge against the darkening sky above Blagdon's Tump. Jack Look Up held on to the reel of string and danced backwards and forwards across the Tump. Mad as a hatter, Jack was. Nan said he was a gentleman and a scholar. He lost his only son in the pit. He was only sixteen. They were working on the same shift. There was a bad fall and the son got trapped. Jack had to cradle him in his arms and watch him die. He was never right after. There were lots of people in the town who were never right after.

Jack Look Up wouldn't set foot down the pit again. He said thank Christ the days of coal were nearly over. They'd sucked the valleys dry and spat out the bones. And one day when they'd had all they wanted, they'd shut up shop and leave them to scratch about for a living.

No one believed him, though. It was just daft talk. Grancha said there was tons of coal left in Wales. There'd always be a pit in the town and all the other towns. Like it or not, coal was the lifeblood.

Jack Look Up might have been mad, but he was very clever. He built giant matchstick castles and cathedrals and sold them in the markets in Merthyr and Swansea. Iffy wondered how he managed not to drop all those matchsticks when his chin twitched and his head shot up.

They watched him flying his kite until it was too dark to see him any more. Just a glimpse every now and then of his kite passing across the big milky moon.

Fatty and Billy walked Iffy and Bessie back to the steps of

Inkerman. On the way Fatty showed them the little lead and collar he'd bought ready for when he got the puppy. It was tiny and made of red leather, attached to it was a little silver barrel. Carefully Fatty unscrewed it and took out a small piece of folded-up paper. They could just make out the writing in the light of the lamp post: This dog belongs to Lawrence Bevan, Coronation Row.

'What you gonna call the puppy?'

'Yapper!' Fatty said.

Bessie sniffed.

'Why Yapper?' Iffy asked.

'Cos he's always yapping every time I go down and look through the window.'

As they came level with Inkerman, Fatty pointed up towards the Black Band. 'Look, there's Dai Full Pelt!'

Dai was creeping across the Black Band. He had a sack slung over his shoulders, he was looking all around him as if he was worried about being followed.

Fatty pulled them back into the shadows of the houses, and they watched him. He went past Iffy's grancha's chicken coop and on up towards the ponds.

'Probably been out burglaring,' said Fatty.

'No,' said Bessie. 'Burglars wear striped jumpers and masks when they're working.'

'Only in comics, you daft sod,' said Fatty. 'Otherwise everybody'd know who they were!'

Bessie sniffed and turned her back on him.

Bessie-O!

Second time of calling.

'G'night.'

The girls ran hell for leather.

Down in the graveyard the Old Bugger hooted and Barny the bulldog howled and rattled his chains like a ghost.

*

Fatty called for Iffy in the morning, standing on the step red-faced and puffing.

'Iffy, I got something important to tell you!'

'What's up! Not about that bloody head again?'

'Shhh! No.'

'Ask him if he wants some toast,' shouted Nan from the kitchen.

'Yes please, Mrs Meredith.'

Fatty always said please and thank you even though he was rough. Bessie didn't always and Billy couldn't.

They sat side by side on the step and Nan gave them huge culfs of toast and butter.

'Thank you, Mrs Meredith.'

Fatty ate the toast hungrily and in between bites he said, 'You know we seen Dai last night going up the mountain with a sack?'

Iffy nodded and licked butter from her lips.

'Well, after you'd all gone in I hung about for a while, and after a bit Dai come back down, but guess what?'

'Give in.'

'He didn't have the sack with him.'

'So?'

'So, he's hidden it somewhere. And coming up through town just now I heard that someone broke into the presbytery the other night and pinched the silver. I reckon it was Dai and he's hidden the swag up the mountain somewhere.'

'What shall we do?'

'Find it and get the reward.'

'Is there a reward?'

'Bound to be, mun, for silver.'

Fatty hid round the corner while Iffy called for Bessie but Bessie's mam, who wasn't really her mam, opened the door and said she was otherwise engaged.

That meant she was in the lav having a pwp.

Iffy banged on the door of the Tranters' lav but Bessie wouldn't answer.

Iffy called out, 'Bessie!'

Bessie grunted. 'Go away, Iffy Meredith!'

'Bessie, it's important.'

'I'm on the lav. Now get lost.'

'Get lost yourself,' Iffy hissed. She wanted to say more, but instead clamped her mouth shut and ran after Fatty, leaving Bessie there grunting and blowing.

Billy came up the hill and Fatty told him the plan.

'We'll look round the shale tips,' Fatty said.

They climbed up onto the Black Band and walked up the hill towards the shale tips. They searched all round the huge grey tips, but there was no sign of the sack.

'Tell you what, let's spread out and walk towards the pond, see if we can find any clues,' Fatty said.

They spread out and walked, heads low, towards the blue lake searching the ground for clues.

Billy started jumping up and down and beckoned to the others. He pointed to a fag end on the ground.

Fatty picked it up and sniffed it. 'Fresh, my dear Watson. No more than a day old!'

He gave it to Iffy and Billy to smell. It stank. Capstan Full Strength.

'Well done, Billy!'

Billy grinned from ear to ear.

'Which way do you reckon he went?' Iffy asked.

Billy pointed towards the blue lake.

They went at a run and found another clue. There were footsteps in the sand leading to the edge of the lake and footsteps leading away again.

'He's hidden the loot in the lake!' yelled Fatty. 'Let's get in and look for it.'

Iffy shook her head and so did Billy. The lake was full of drowned wild boys and drunk men.

Iffy and Billy kept a lookout, while Fatty paddled out into the murky waters. He told them to keep their eyes peeled for Dai or anyone else who might come along.

'Chuck us a stick, Iffy.'

Iffy scrabbled about, found a stick and threw it out to Fatty who was up to the top of his legs in the water. He poked about for ages.

'Geronimo! Got it!'

Whatever it was, it must have been heavy because he was tugging at something under the surface of the water that didn't seem to want to budge.

'Gonna have to drag it out, it weighs a ton!'

Iffy thought that it must be the stolen treasure from the presbytery. A bag full of precious silver! And maybe even gold!

Fatty dragged the sack to the edge of the pond. It was an old coal sack tied at the top with string.

Iffy grinned as she thought of the reward. They'd be rich. Have their pictures in the paper. Bessie would be dead mad that she'd missed being a hero!

'Open it, Fatty! Quick! Untie the string before someone comes.'

Iffy and Billy hopped about in excitement but still kept a wary eye out for Dai.

'Hang on, Iffy. Give me a hand to drag it into the dip out of the way in case anyone sees us.'

Iffy grabbed a corner of the sodden sack and helped him drag it down into a hollow. Fatty was soaked to the skin, his legs were streaked with weed and scum, black mud squelched out from the holes in his sandals but he didn't seem to care a bit.

The three of them stood close together staring down at the sack hardly believing their luck.

'Go on, Fatty, open it!'

Billy was so excited he was clapping his hands and jumping up and down on the spot.

Fatty cut the string with his penknife.

Iffy wanted to pee.

'Ready?' said Fatty.

'Yep.'

Iffy sang a hymn from school, 'Daisies are our silver, buttercups our gold. This is all the treasure we can ha a a ave or hold!'

Fatty bounced the sack onto his knees to take the weight and shook the bottom corners to tip out the treasure. Any minute now and the silver would fall onto the green grass. Billy grabbed hold of Iffy's arm and shivered. Fatty heaved up the bag to his chest and the treasure tumbled out.

Billy gasped.

A bird piped out a tinny song and a fish jumped and plopped back into the blue lake.

Fatty squealed.

Billy stared down at the grass open-mouthed, eyes wide.

Iffy looked from the grass to Fatty's face. He stood as still as stone looking down at the treasure. His face was mud-streaked, his blue eyes were staring. A wide-eyed statue.

There was no silver, or gold. No reward to be had.

On the green mountain grass, among the daisies and the buttercups, lay a pile of broken bricks and five drowned puppies.

Billy tucked his small hand into Iffy's, which was shaking.

Fatty dropped down onto his knees beside the puppies. He cupped his dirty hands around one of them and lifted it up. It was soggy and limp. Its velvety little face was crumpled up and its eyes were closed tight. The tiny, tiny mouth was twisted into a sad little smile showing two white pointed teeth.

It was Fatty's puppy. The miniature Barny lay dead in his trembling hands. Yapper.

A terrible noise came out of Fatty. It made Iffy's whole body quiver. It was a sob, a shudder and a moan all at once. It was the worst sound she'd ever heard. He lifted the puppy up to his lips, like Father Flaherty lifting the sacred host at Mass, and he kissed it so softly.

His mouth crumpled as he said, 'I was gonna put a collar on him and teach him to walk on the lead I bought . . . and teach him to sit . . .'

Fatty's eyes were a blur of blue tears that squeezed between his thick black eyelashes. The tears slid down the sides of his nose, magnifying his freckles and making muddy rivers of his cheeks. His tears fell onto the wet puppy.

'And teach him not to chase sheep . . . and let him sleep with me so's he wouldn't be lonely and neither would I any more.'

Fatty's nose was running, a waterfall of snot, all over his top lip.

Iffy looked across at Billy. Billy's eyes were two dark ponds bursting their banks. Her throat felt as though it was stuffed full of sharp stones.

Fatty rubbed away the snot and tears with the back of his hand. His face was a smudge of sorrow.

Iffy let go of Billy's hand and knelt down beside Fatty. She put her arm around his shoulders. She felt the pain run off him and pass through her fingers like electricity. She held him close against her for a long time until his body stopped shaking and the fierce pain that came out of him turned into a dull throbbing ache.

Billy ran all the way home for a shovel and a candle and

came back bringing a red-faced and puffing Bessie Tranter with him.

They buried the puppies one by one down in the little hollow. Yapper was the last one to be buried. They made daisy chains and hung them over wooden crosses made from lollipop sticks. Fatty lit the candle but it kept on going out.

All day they stayed on the mountain keeping watch over the graves. As the sun dipped behind the Sirhowy Mountain they stood up. Fatty said, 'May the souls of the faithful departed puppies rest in peace.'

'Aremen.'

They made the sign of the cross:

Ace
Jack
King
Queen

Walking slowly down over the Black Band towards home it was as though the whole world was on fire. An orange-red glow filled the sky and the clouds were lined with gold and silver. The windows of Carmel Chapel blazed with fire and sparks from the dying sun singed the trees with light.

No one spoke. Even Bessie seemed to know when to keep her trap shut sometimes.

Down in the valley Zeraldo's bell rang, but none of them was in the mood for ice cream.

As they reached the steps that led down to Inkerman, Fatty was first to break the silence, 'I know one thing,' he said.

'What's that?' said Bessie.

'Dai Full Pelt is a bloody dead man.'

Billy nodded. So did Iffy.

'We'll swear an oath,' said Fatty, his eyes bright in the growing darkness.

'I'm not swearing,' said Bessie.

They ignored her and swore with their hands on their hearts, 'Dai Full Pelt is a bloody dead man!'

Even Bessie.

PART THREE

PART THREE

Fatty called a meeting, he said they had to do it properly. It was no laughing matter. It was tamping down with rain so they'd sneaked round the back of Mr Edwards's bakery and crept into Billy's coal shed.

'We could boil up bags of mushy peas and pelt him on the way home from the pub,' Iffy said.

'Where we gonna get all those peas from, stupid?' Bessie said.

Iffy glared at her.

'You think of something better then!'

'We'll make bombs out of horse shit!' said Fatty.

Bessie sniffed.

'Dynamite,' she suggested.

Iffy roared with laughter. Fatty stared at Bessie.

'Got some have you?' he asked.

Bessie sulked.

'Fireworks,' Iffy said.

'I'm not going in Shanto's shop after what the dirty pig done to me with that discustin' false eye of his,' said Bessie.

Then Fatty yelled. He whispered something to Billy, who grinned and his eyes lit up.

Fatty whispered to Bessie. She went white and shook her ringlets.

'No,' she said.

Fatty whispered in Iffy's ear. They couldn't! They'd get killed if they got caught, or go to jail. It was terrifying! It was brilliant! Fatty was a genius! Or a nut case.

The door to the chapel was well-oiled and opened with barely a squeak. Will stepped into the gloomy interior. Diluted sunlight filtered in through the high arched windows and he shivered in the chill air. The pungent smell of disinfectant and polish made his eyes water.

At the front of the chapel a plump middle-aged woman sat at the organ, swaying gently from side to side as she played.

Will's footsteps rang out loudly on the stone floor. The organ music petered out and the woman turned to face him.

'Oh, hello. You must be Mr Sloane. How do you do?'

Will stared at her, his head began to spin and the painful thump of his heart reverberated in his ears.

The ringlets were gone. They had been replaced by a fierce tight perm, the dark-blonde hair was greying at the temples. She was much fatter than she had been all those years ago but the wheezing noises still came from her chest.

'Bessie Tranter?' said Will, and his voice wavered with surprise.

'Ugh! It's years since anyone called me that! I prefer to be called Elizabeth.'

She still had that squeaky tremulous voice. She held out a hand to Will.

"My husband Mervyn said you were going to call and tell me how beautiful that garden used to be. Mervyn asked me to invite you to tea. I thought Friday perhaps?'

'That would be fine, thank you. Where do you live?'

'We're rather tucked out of the way. I'm going home now, and if you fancied a walk I could show you, it's not too far.'

Will walked with Elizabeth Prosser through the graveyard. Suddenly she stopped at a well-tended grave, knelt down and straightened a vase that was filled with freshly cut flowers.

'My mother's and father's grave,' she said. It was of black marble, polished to shining, the gold inscriptions on the headstone gleaming in the weak sunlight.

'There's another grave over there,' Will said indicating the far end of the graveyard. 'Dolores Tranter. Any relation of yours?'

Bessie stood up stiffly and straightened her skirt.

'No,' she said and brushed an imaginary fleck of dust from her jumper.

They walked a long way in silence. The only sound was the wheezy noise that came from Bessie's chest.

As they turned a corner she said, 'Here we are, Mr Sloane, our humble dwelling. Of course once the Big House is ready we'll put this on the market.'

Will stared at the house in fascinated horror.

'All Mervyn's own work,' Elizabeth Tranter said proudly.

Dear God! Will had a fleeting vision of the architectural horrors that Mervyn would soon inflict on the Big House.

It was an old house, really a row of three small terraced houses that had been joined together into one at some stage. It had been covered in cladding and painted a ghastly, luminous strawberry pink. All the old sash windows had been ripped out and replaced with mock-leaded double glazing. A monstrously huge satellite dish was attached to the roof.

'Well, now you know where we are, do come for tea on Friday. About four?' said Elizabeth Tranter.

'Thank you,' said Will, with more enthusiasm than he felt.

*

Fatty was in charge of the plan: the boss, the general.

'We have to get to know our enemy,' he said.

'We do,' said Bessie. 'It's Dai Full Pelt.'

'I know it's Dai. But we need to know everything about him, what he does, every move he makes. We can't afford to make a mistake. Now, listen.'

And they did. All ears.

For days they followed Dai to find out all his habits. Everything he did was written down in Bessie's notebook until they knew his movements by heart.

At six o'clock he parked the bone-shaker of a bus down near the town clock. It took him fifteen minutes to walk home. They followed him through town, ducking and diving into doorways if he stopped to light a fag or looked behind him. They stalked him past Morrissey's shop, left down the hill, over the bridge, and watched him go in through the doors of the Mechanics.

They hung around for ages outside the pub, hidden behind wooden beer barrels waiting for him to come out, checking the time on Bessie's Cinderella Timex.

Bessie wrote, one hour and thirty minutes and five pints, in the notebook.

Three minutes, while he stopped to piss in the river.

Ugh. Poor river. Poor fish.

Five minutes to waddle back up the hill to his house in Sebastopol. Close on his heels they crept across the bailey behind him, weaving between washing lines hung with dancing clothes that acted as camouflage.

Outside Dai's house Fatty stood on a battered bucket and then one by one, except for Bessie, they took a turn on the bucket and peeped through Dai's filthy window.

They watched as Dai kicked the cat off the grandfather chair and sat down by the fire. His wife Ruby served tea at eight. She stumbled across the kitchen and launched a chipped plate bearing a mountain of bubble and squeak and scorched sausages, all drowned in brown sauce towards the table.

It took five minutes for Dai to shovel it down his neck, then there was forty-five minutes of sleeping.

At ten to nine Dai came out the back to the outside lav.

Each day they watched and made more notes.

They made the final plans in Billy's coal shed. Fatty sat them down in a half circle as if they were kids in school. He drew plans on an old piece of wallpaper he'd found up at the ash tip. He put on a really posh voice, swanky English with plums, the way they talked on the wireless.

There was a lady on the wireless who Fatty copied. She sang dead daft songs. 'I love little pussy. She's so soft and warm. And if I don't hurt her she'll do me no harm!' It made them roar with laughter the way she sang it. They had to bend up double and hold their bellies. She sounded like a mental case.

'Are you sitting comfortably?' said Fatty.

They grinned up at him from the coal-littered floor where they sat, except for Bessie, who was wearing wellies and was perched on her hanky on top of a box.

'Right! Shut your traps, and then I'll begin!'

And they listened. Goggle-eyed and open-mouthed, hardly believing they were going to do such a fearsome thing.

'Fatty, I'm afraid!'

'Just stand by the gate and keep your eyes peeled. Whistle if anyone comes. You can see the house from there,' Fatty hissed.

'What if the dog barks?'

'She won't. She knows me by now.'

'Fatty, don't leave me.'

Iffy stood by the gates of the Big House, too close for comfort. Fatty had been into the grounds of the Big House several times and pulled away some of the overgrown bushes that shielded the house from outside view. There was a small gap now and if Iffy got up close enough she could see the French windows.

Iffy was shaking uncontrollably with fright.

'I'll be in there in a couple of minutes, just the time it takes to get through the tunnel.'

He disappeared over the river bank with the statue's head under his T-shirt and, in his pocket, a small bag of concrete mix he'd scrounged from some builders in town.

Curiosity made Iffy look into the grounds. She only had a small view through where Fatty had managed to tear away a few branches. The lights behind the French windows were burning brightly. They were fancy lights, loads of them hanging from the ceiling like dripping tears.

Seconds slowly built into minutes.

The lights were like a magnet, drawing Iffy in like a moth to the candle flame.

Barny the bulldog howled from Old Man Morgan's farm. The Labrador in the Big House howled back hopefully. Iffy turned her back on the window.

The red kite sliced across the moon above Blagdon's Tump. Red as blood.

'Whee ooh wit!'

He was in.

'Hurry up, Fatty!'

The Old Bugger hooted.

Iffy leapt with fright. A light had gone on in an upstairs window of the Big House.

She saw a black shadow cross the lighted window, a hooked nose, coiled plaits, a Bible.

'Hail Mary full of grace. Shit! Shit! Fatty, come on!'

The light went out in the upstairs room and she heard the sound of a window opening. Torchlight shone into the blackness of the garden.

There was a shout from the house.

Someone screamed, a wild mad scream.

232

Iffy was paralyzed with fear. She heard the waters of the fishpond begin to stir and the soft pad of a statue's feet in the damp grass. Bubbling noises filled her ears.

All the lights in the Big House went on.

A hand came out of the blackness and grabbed her.

On his way back through town it began to rain heavily and Will decided to take shelter. There were only a few people in the café when Will entered. He sat down at a table and the old man he had seen in the cemetery came out from behind the counter to take his order.

He smiled at Will, a gold-toothed smile of welcome. He took his order and then disappeared back behind the counter singing softly to himself.

He delivered the ice cream and coffee to Will's table with a flourish.

'I hope a you enjoy. Iss a long time I think since you have a knicker a bocker a glory, eh?'

'A very long time,' Will said. 'Too long.'

The old man laughed, and retired behind the counter. He busied himself washing and polishing cups and glasses. Then he settled himself on a high stool behind the counter, took up a battered book and began to read.

Will glanced at the book cover. Laurie Lee's *As I Walked Out One Midsummer's Morning*. He'd read it himself many years ago. He'd always thought he might try and follow in the writer's footsteps and walk the route from the north-west of Spain down to the south, but like so many other things in life he'd put it off.

Will got up, paid his bill and held open the door for a young woman who was carrying a small child into the café. The child was soundly asleep in her arms. His head lolling backwards, a sweet smile of contented relaxation on his flushed face.

'Hiya, Mario! Give us a coffee please,' the woman said. 'I'm knackered. I been all over the place with him to buy new trainers. You need a mortgage with the price on them!'

Will glanced back at the child. He was wearing pristine white trainers and Will blanched when he caught sight of the price tag stuck fast to one of the soles.

As he left the café the sun slid out from behind grey clouds and a glorious rainbow hung above the houses of the town.

The hand that grasped Iffy's wrist was strong and the fingernails were sharp against her skin. The scream that grew inside her chest never made it to her lips. As she opened her mouth the sound died away inside her. She stiffened with fear.

The face that stared back at her from behind the gates of the Big House was old Mrs Medlicott's. The face was close enough for Iffy to reach out and touch and was contorted with terror, with wide staring eyes and lips stretched back over yellow teeth.

The hand loosened its grasp. The eyes closed, the bushes folded together like curtains, and she was gone.

Fatty was suddenly behind Iffy, pulling her arm, dragging her down over the river bank and shoving her under the black archway of the bridge.

The Labrador began to bark again in the grounds. Old Sandicock was shouting out to someone. The geese began to honk.

They stood together catching their breath. Fatty could feel Iffy's heart pounding through her T-shirt.

There were muffled voices close by, in the darkness. Fatty put his finger to Iffy's lips. Someone else was there under the bridge, hiding in the shadows.

Fatty squeezed Iffy's hand tightly.

Somebody groaned.

'Now, I think you'll do what I want. You wouldn't want

me to spill the beans to that little bastard son of yours.'

There was a rustle of clothes and a whimpering noise like that of a wounded animal.

'So let's have it nice and easy.'

'Let me alone. He's a good boy.'

'Your old man knows, does he? It's a wise child who knows its own father.'

More grunting noises and the sound of a woman sobbing somewhere near them. The groaning noises came faster. It was a man: Dai Full Pelt; and a woman crying quietly.

Fatty pulled Iffy up over the bank, the sound of his wild sobs hung on the night air.

Far in the distance could be heard the ringing of an ambulance bell.

Will sat in his room at the Firkin looking through his old notebooks and thinking about the moment when Elizabeth Tranter had closed the front door and left him standing in a daze looking up at the house.

The last time he had been there he had been on police business. He'd visited the middle cottage in Coronation Row with Sergeant Rodwell. Coronation Row where Lawrence Bevan had lived out his short life.

He and Rodwell had called round at the house looking for Mr Bevan. There had been no sign of anyone at home and yet the front door was unlocked.

Will had pushed open the door and he and Rodwell had stepped inside the darkened house. There had been an unpleasant, fausty odour about the place, an uncared-for, dirty smell.

Each room on the ground floor was strewn with discarded clothing, piles of old racing papers, empty milk bottles and fish and chip papers screwed into balls. A mountain of beer flagons filled the floor in the pantry.

They had climbed apprehensively up the uncarpeted stairs. There were two bedrooms. The largest was a mirror of the downstairs rooms. The smell was rank, of sweat and greasy bedclothes. A brimming piss pot festered beneath the bed. On the bedside table cigarette butts overflowed from a saucer and a cup of long-cold tea was surfaced with mould.

When they'd entered the smaller bedroom across the landing it was as if they were in a different house. There was an iron bed against the wall nearest to the window. The sheets on the bed had been made from old flour sacks, slit down the sides and tacked loosely together with pink thread. The makeshift pillow was made from a roll of newspapers wrapped round with an old ripped towel and tied with string. The bare wooden floor was scrubbed clean and was dust free. There was a bookshelf cobbled together from old wooden cider crates.

Will had picked up one of the books. The *Waverley Medical Encyclopedia*. It was a battered old copy, and where the spine had broken it had been carefully mended with adhesive tape. Lollipop sticks had been inserted between some of the pages.

'A queer sort of book for a kid to read,' he'd said to Sergeant Rodwell.

'Well, if you don't mind me saying so, sir, he was a queer sort of kid.'

'In what way?'

'Well, scruffy as hell for a start. Always up to something.'

'Takes a bit of gumption, though, to keep your room clean and tidy like this when the rest of the house is a bloody tip,' Will'd said.

Will had turned to one of the pages of the encyclopedia which had been marked with a lollipop stick. Page 614, SPEECH. He'd read the text that had been underlined faintly in pencil.

When the voice is lost suddenly and there is no obvious abnormality to be seen in the cords, the cause is hysteria.

The second lollipop stick marked page 369, and carefully underlined were the words:

Thus . . . successive generations of human beings may have an excessive number . . . or a deficiency of fingers and toes.

Will sat very still, thinking.

He looked back at the notes he'd made all those years before. He'd recorded that in the margin of the book someone had written 'MEASURE BOTH CATS FEET'.

Will remembered raising his eyebrows at the time, he had closed the book and placed it carefully back on the bookcase. Then he'd looked quickly through the rest of the books. There was a school atlas, a boys' annual, a well-thumbed copy of Robert Louis Stevenson's *Treasure Island*. Not the usual reading matter for a ten-year-old, he'd thought at the time.

On the top of the boy's bookcase had lain a small red collar with a silver barrel attached to it.

'Did he own a dog?' Will had asked Rodwell.

'Not as far as I know, sir. No, I don't think so. He was mad about animals though. One of those kids who'd pick up birds with broken wings, kept snakes and toads in his pockets, that sort of thing.'

'He wasn't known to you for any criminal activity?'

'No. He wasn't into thieving or anything like that. Couple of things we suspected him of but never caught him for.'

'What were they?'

Sergeant Rodwell had coughed. 'I think it was him who . . . er . . . tipped a bag of manure over a woman in town.'

Will had laughed, an echoing laugh in the sparsely furnished room.

'What?'

'Somebody got into one of the empty flats above one of the shops. Along came this particular woman and Bob's your uncle, someone emptied a sack of the stuff all over her. Still steaming it was too. Miss Riley, she's a local schoolteacher. Gave her a right turn I can tell you!'

'Nice woman?'

It was Sergeant Rodwell's turn to laugh.

'Ah, no, sir. She taught me. A right old dragon.'

'The case is closed then?'

'Yes, sir.'

'Any other crimes?'

'Well, Mrs Carmichael, the Sunday school teacher swears she saw him mooching about the church the day somebody sabotaged the nativity scene.'

'Sabotaged! That's a strong word, Sergeant.'

'Well, there were sixteen bangers strapped to the shepherd's leg, sir. Did quite a bit of damage, as you can imagine. Straw blown everywhere and knocked the stuffing out of the Virgin Mary.'

'Sounds quite a boy.'

'Ay, he was, sir.'

Rodwell's use of the word 'was' had filled Will with acute despair, as though the boy had already been consigned to the past.

He had knelt down and looked under the bed. There were two boxes pushed up against the wall. He had slid them out, and lifted the lid on the first box. It was empty except for a layer of dirty cotton wool, indented, as though something very heavy had lain on it. He sniffed, the smell of strong soap rose from the cotton wool. He replaced the lid and opened the second box. It contained two jam jars with holes punched in the metal lids, and a copy of a Shakespeare play, *Hamlet*. Will's favourite. He had opened the book. It was on loan from the local library and the ticket showed it to be ten years overdue. There had also been two new candles in the box, a third half burned, and six bangers tied around with string.

Will had slipped the copy of *Hamlet* into his jacket pocket, replaced the lid on the box and slid it back under the bed. There was no wardrobe or chest of drawers in the room, no clothes of any description lying around.

'No clothes anywhere. Looks as though he's taken everything with him,' he'd said.

Rodwell had cleared his throat.

'Only ever seen the boy in one set of clothes and they were the ones he left behind on the river bank. He's been wearing them for the last few years. Funny thing I noticed . . .'

'What?' Will had asked.

'There was no cricket belt. He always wore a red and white cricket belt to keep up his shorts. They were about five sizes too big.'

Will had sighed and wondered. Had the boy been strangled with his own belt? But without a body they weren't going to find any answers. It was probably only a question of time before the body was discovered. Children didn't just disappear off the face of the earth.

'Well, there's not much to see, nothing to give us a clue as to what's happened to him.'

Will had gone down the stairs of the house in Coronation Row with a heavy heart.

Fatty had done what he'd meant to do: he'd given the statue her head back. Iffy had thought that might have made him happy but it hadn't and it wasn't like him to be miserable. He never spoke about the puppies again, but Iffy knew he would never ever forget, and he didn't once mention that night under the bridge when they'd heard Dai and his mam messing about.

239

He seemed different somehow. Paler. Like all the hot air had been let out of him.

He mooched about for days. He barely spoke. Head down, hands in the pockets of his huge shorts, kicking out viciously at stones on the road. He only cheered up a bit when one afternoon Billy came running, pulling them by the sleeves, pointing excitedly, dragging them down to show them the queue down by the Dentist's Stone.

Carty Annie was holding court, telling fortunes. A tanner a go if she didn't like you. Free if she did.

Bessie ran off home. She didn't want her fortune told.

Iffy made Fatty go first. He spat on the palms of his hands and tried to rub some of the dirt off.

Carty Annie saw him and grinned. She took his hand in hers and drew her finger across it this way and that. Fatty giggled. He was very ticklish.

'I see women . . .'

Fatty looked at Iffy and winked. Iffy nudged Billy in the ribs.

'Women all around you . . . A half-naked woman in the water.'

Iffy giggled and put her hand over her mouth. Fatty gave her a look over his shoulder, a shut-your-bloody-trap look.

'I see a cap.'

That meant he'd work down the pit.

'And a gown.'

Operations. Poor bugger.

'And a place of learning.'

School.

Iffy didn't think Fatty would stay in school long. The teachers picked on him because he was scruffy and they didn't seem to like him even though he was really clever.

Carty Annie let go of his hand for a moment then quickly

took it back. 'I see a large expanse of water, a restless ocean. Someone coming across the ocean looking for you, looking for a long time without knowing why. Water rippling . . . a figure slipping away.' She looked hard at Fatty then and a troubled look stole across her face, a long dark shadow of sadness. 'You will need to forgive.'

Iffy was next.

Her hand shook when Carty Annie took hold of it. She felt the heat in the old woman's touch. Carty Annie squeezed up Iffy's hand into a fist and held it tightly for a long while without looking at the palm. Then she raised the hand to her lips and kissed it very tenderly, a soft whisper of a kiss that made Iffy shiver. Slowly she uncurled Iffy's tiny fingers and her bright-blue eyes looked carefully at the lines on Iffy's palm.

After a while, she said, 'Iffy, you have a long and winding path to take. I see mountains and eagles on the wing.'

A mountaineer! Carty Annie meant she'd climb Everest and be as brave as Fatty!

'You will have a good guide. A brave and handsome guide paving the way for you.'

Ugh!

Carty Annie closed her eyes but carried on speaking as though no one was there, 'There will be much sadness, but then great joy. This will be the greatest journey of your life.'

A tear slipped from the old woman's eyes and ran down a deep wrinkle on her weather-beaten cheek. It reminded Iffy of a river after a drought. An ancient woman with a face full of rivers, travelling down towards the sea.

'I see a woman. I see tears trailing.'

And more tears rolled down Carty Annie's face, breaking the banks of the rivers.

'I see the laying down of a head on a damp breast.'

Carty Annie stopped speaking and sat very still for a while and then looked around her as if she couldn't remember where she was or why they were there.

Iffy looked over her shoulder at Fatty and rolled her eyes at him, but he ignored her. He was staring down towards the Big House as if he had seen something that had shocked him. His face was very pale. He looked back at Iffy, but his eyes were faraway and clouded as though he was looking at her and through her, at the same time. There was a strange, troubled look about him that she had never seen before. He shook his head, blinked, saw her looking at him and smiled. Iffy grinned back.

She was disappointed that Carty Annie hadn't said that she'd live to be a hundred or be stinking rich or famous. At least she hadn't said she'd have babies coming out of her bum by the bucketful and a smelly husband.

Billy took his turn after Iffy.

Carty Annie put her hand on his head and ruffled up his curls.

Iffy knew why she did it, because it was what everyone wanted to do to Billy. He was so lovely you could eat him.

Billy looked up at Carty Annie, his lips were sucked up inside his mouth, which he always did when he was shy or excited. His eyes were wide, his eyelashes glistened in the sunlight.

Carty Annie took his hand and Iffy thought it looked little and pale against the old woman's dark skin.

'You will live a long life, Billy. I see two children. I see twins.'

Iffy thought of Rosemary and Rosalind. Billy's twins would be nice though. She imagined two little dimpled Billies in a pram, smiling.

'I see a foreign place, a wife . . .'

Iffy wondered who Billy would marry. She hoped it

would be someone nice and kind who didn't mind about him not talking.

'I see a crossroads in your life, Billy.'

There was a crossroads at the end of the Dram Road. There were four different ways you could go: Abergavenny, Merthyr, Trefil or back the way you'd come.

'You must take one of the roads. You must stop looking backwards, Billy. You must put your foot on the road. And walk until you find peace.'

Iffy thought he was a bit young to be thinking about going off on his own, his mam and dad would never let him. Anyway, they weren't allowed to walk that far. It was miles to the crossroads.

'There's something you need to get rid of. Something you must give away before you can move on, Billy. But remember, you may have to take the road on your own if no one else will follow.'

That was daft. His mam would never let him walk all that way on his own, somebody could grab hold of him and do him in.

It was growing colder. A restless wind blew through the trees and a few dying leaves began to fall. The sun was going down fast; deep-red fire burned behind the windows of Carmel Chapel and shadows crept stealthily up the valley. The town clock bonged the hour and Carty Annie shooed them away. They went running and skipping down to the river, shrieking and laughing through the long waving grass.

They had picked up the boy's father in a pub over in the next town and brought him down to the police station. He'd been on a five-day bender. Will had disliked him on sight.

He was of medium height, a fat, sweaty, hard-nosed man with a dying cigarette stuck to his lips.

'So, Mr Bevan, you didn't know your son had been reported missing?'

'No.'

He stared defiantly at Will across the table.

'You haven't picked up a paper in the last few days?'

'Now, do I look like a man who reads the newspapers?'

'And you don't know the last time you saw your son?'

'No, I don't. Is that a crime?'

'And you've no idea where he could be?'

'No.' Mr Bevan spat out a strand of tobacco, re-lit his dead cigarette with a match and blew smoke across the table into Will's face. He showed not the slightest interest in the where-abouts of his son.

'He'll be back. You'll see. He's always pissing off and turning up again.'

Will's patience had worn thin.

'And you think it's perfectly normal for a ten-year-old boy to go off around the countryside on his own?'

'He's not what you'd call a normal sort of boy, is he?'

'I don't know, Mr Bevan. You tell me.'

'He's odd. A bit missing. Picking up half-dead animals and trying to cure them, reading bloody doctors' books.'

'It doesn't occur to you that reading that sort of book might be the sign of a very intelligent lad?'

'Ay, well, if he's that intelligent he'll find his own way home, won't he? And then he'll feel my belt round his arse! Now if that's it, I'd like to go.'

Will had walked out of the room then, because he'd had an enormous desire to reach across the table and split the man's fat nose across his arrogant face.

They'd checked out his whereabouts though and he'd been where he'd said he'd been. Numerous landlords and fellow drinkers had vouched for his drunken presence in a multitude of pubs from Neath to Merthyr.

244

*

Iffy woke with a start to the sound of someone hammering at the back door. Upstairs the big bed creaked as her grandparents stirred. The noise grew louder. Someone was coming down the stairs two at a time. The hammering carried on, as though someone was battering at the door with a big stick.

Then came a great bashing on the tin bucket.

'Suffering piss pots!' said Grancha as he stepped down into the parlour.

Iffy opened the bedroom door a crack and peeped cautiously round it. Grancha was wearing only baggy underpants, one blue-veined leg stepping into his trousers, braces trailing, hopping and stumbling through the darkened room.

Still the awful racket went on.

Iffy slipped on her shorts and top, pulled on her black daps and followed him into the kitchen.

He bent down and unbolted the back door; daylight came flooding into the kitchen. Quarter past seven on the lop-sided clock that once was pawned.

Billy came falling into the kitchen along with the daylight. His small face was twisted with fear, his dark eyes were wild and wide. He pulled at Grancha's arm and didn't even seem to notice Iffy.

'What's up, little fellow? Dear God, it's not half past seven yet. Is somebody after you?'

Billy'd been to early Mass. Iffy knew because she could smell the candle smoke and polish on him.

He began to pull at Iffy's sleeve, yanking her out over the step and into the deserted bailey, dragging and pulling her roughly up over the steps and on down the hill. Grancha followed behind, puffing and wheezing. Slipping and sliding down over the river bank, past the spot where they'd launched Lally's baby into the river. Away on down towards the Leaky Pool. Billy pointing and sobbing.

'Jesus Christ!'

Grancha made the sign of the cross.

'Turn away both of you! Iffy, take Billy with you. Run. Run to Morrissey's and ask him to telephone for an ambulance.'

She was floating face down in the deep water of the Leaky Pool. Her pale arms stretched out wide, like Christ on the crucifix. Her clothes spreading out around her. Close by a silver fish jumped and plopped.

Grancha went into the water, losing his footing, turning her over onto her back, pulling the weeds from her face. A soft white breast slipped from her unbuttoned dress.

Iffy and Billy ran. Ran and ran and banged on Morrissey's shop door. Hammered, screeching for him to open up.

On Thursday afternoon Will walked to Gladys's Gowns. True to her word Gladys Baker had asked Marlene to leave the door on the latch and he called out as he entered the back entrance of the shop.

'Straight up the stairs and the room in front of you,' she called out cheerfully.

Gladys Baker sat in a high-backed chair near the window. Will looked around him and he felt as though he had stepped back into a bygone age. The room was like a set from an old-fashioned stage play. *Arsenic and Old Lace* sprang to Will's mind.

Will was in seventh heaven as he went against doctor's orders and indulged himself in three slices of wimberry tart and cream, served up on beautiful old china. He didn't see the point in worrying any more about his cholesterol levels, his allotted time was running out fast.

'Does your wife make pastry?' Gladys asked.

'My wife has been dead for years. She's buried up in the Catholic cemetery.'

Gladys Baker nodded, smiled sadly and said no more on the subject and Will was glad.

The old woman was fascinating company. She'd opened her gown shop before the Second World War. Her daughter Marlene had worked there from the day she left school. Never married, see, the old woman said, got let down badly.

'Now, what is it that you really wanted to know? Not the price of hats, I'm sure.'

Will smiled and blushed, there were no flies on Gladys Baker.

'Yes, well,' he said. 'Actually, the old aunt story was rather a ruse,' and he told her about his quest.

She listened, her eyes closing from time to time as though she was dropping off to sleep, but Will knew she was listening intently.

'And it's been bothering me subconsciously all these years,' he finished.

'And you have to know before you . . . a heart problem, I suppose?'

Will was taken aback, he nodded.

'I have a problem like that. Had it for years. I take herbal stuff for it, kept me going well past the time limit the doctors gave me. I got the herbal cure from an old Irish woman, long dead now. Marlene makes it up for me. I'll give you a bottle of it sometime.'

'Thank you. What I can't understand,' said Will, 'is that from that day to this there's never been any sign of him. No sightings. No news. No body. It's as if he vanished into thin air.'

'There was another case like that back in the thirties. A toddler disappeared from a farm up Worcester way. Terrible thing. It was said that the gypsies had taken him. Never found him until years later when they were doing some improvements on an old farm worker's cottage. Found his skeleton

247

down an old disused well . . . Most things have a rational answer.'

'Yes, I'm sure you're right. I read about a similar case in Spain. I suppose sometime, tomorrow, next year, maybe in a hundred years the skeleton will be found. Long after anyone will remember the case of Lawrence Bevan.'

'There was a skeleton found a few years ago further down the valley,' said Gladys.

Will stiffened with interest.

She smiled sadly.

'Not your boy, I'm afraid. It caused quite a stir, though. They reckoned it was about forty years old. They couldn't match it with anyone reported missing from around that time. Besides, it had no head.'

Will sighed. 'Do you remember Lawrence Bevan, Mrs Baker?'

'Call me Gladys. Oh yes! A hard boy to forget. He was well-known around here. A bugger of a boy he was. Bright lad, he would have done well for himself if he'd had a chance. Course a lot of people had a downer on him.'

'Why was that?'

'Well, the family was rough and ready. The boy got blamed for things he never did. Then again he never got caught for a lot of things he did do!' Gladys Baker laughed.

'You liked him?'

'Couldn't help but like him. I used to feed him up a bit. He used to come round here and I always gave him chocolate or sweets if I saw him about the place. He never asked for anything, mind. Very well-mannered he was.'

'What did he look like?'

'Oh a handsome-looking boy he was, the most beautiful eyes you've ever seen. Dark, dark blue. I felt for him. A lot of people pick on kids like that, make a scapegoat of them, makes them feel better about their own devious offspring. I would have been proud to have had him for a son.'

'What was his family like? I met the father briefly when we eventually found him. Drunk over in the next valley. He'd been on a bender, didn't even know the kid had gone missing.'

'He was a good for nothing waster. He was in the army for years, a big bully of a man.'

'The mother killed herself, didn't she?'

'Yes. Threw herself in the Leaky Pool just down from the bridge. Got fished out, but it was too late. Very sad affair that.'

'What was she like?'

'Fine, until she married that old thing. A beautiful girl she was. She used to do a bit of acting in the thespians. She was good too. I remember her playing Ophelia. I think I've still got some old programmes somewhere, with her photograph. She was trained as a midwife, but something went wrong. The drink got to her. Picked up with the wrong sort of man. She went to pieces after her old man came out of the army. There was talk that she'd had the boy by someone else. He certainly didn't look like he was out of the same bloodline as his no-good father.'

'We had the father down as a suspect but he was well out of the way at the time, out of his head on drink. We checked, and he was where he said he was.'

'My guess is, Will, that if the boy didn't drown, then he ran away. He was a resourceful little bugger, streetwise as they say nowadays. He was used to fending for himself. He had to be.'

'He didn't have any other relatives who would have taken him in?'

'No. They would have put him in Bethlehem House with the Sisters Without Mercy and that would have finished him off!'

'I took a walk round where he disappeared the other day. It's changed beyond all recognition.'

'Yes, well, they pulled down all the old ironworkers' houses in the sixties. Built them horrible council-box things. Not the same at all. All the old neighbourliness went when they did away with the baileys. They were great them old baileys, everybody out having a chat, sitting out on a summer's night keeping their eye on the kids. It's all gone now.'

'It was a better place in the old days?' said Will.

'In some ways, in other ways it was worse.'

'In what way?'

'Well, I don't agree with all these young women having babies outside of marriage like they do today. It's not the marriage bit that bothers me. That's not always all it's cracked up to be. I just think it's better if a kiddie has two parents, but I wouldn't want to go back to the way it was.'

'In what way?' Will asked again.

'There used to be a home for unmarried girls further down the valley. For the poor little buggers who got pregnant. They were carted off there, whisked away out of sight, then they took their babies away. It caused a lot of unnecessary misery. Misery that still goes on today for those it happened to.'

Will didn't want to talk about the home for bad girls. He changed the subject, but he was sure that Gladys Baker knew he'd done it deliberately. 'I met a chap called Prosser and his wife the other day.'

'Oh! Mervyn Prosser. Bloody horrible child he was. Nasty, sneaky thing. He married that peculiar little girl, all ringlets and dull as a Toc H lamp. Done well for himself moneywise. A bit of a wheeler-dealer by all accounts. He's bought the Big House, hasn't he? You watch, he'll ruin that place.'

'It's pretty ruined now.'

'Ay, I know, but damn, in its day it was beautiful. I knew Mrs Medlicott, you know. Nice woman she was. We did a lot of trade with her and the girls from the school she ran.'

'Did you know Dr Medlicott?'

'Knew him as much as I wanted to. He was a queer old thing. We used to call him the Horse Doctor. Never let him near me or mine. I never liked him. Wandering hands he had. A friend of mine, Esther Jones, worked as a maid there in the war. She had to spend a night in the air-raid shelter on her own with him and she had to fight him off all night!'

Will stayed talking to Gladys until Marlene came back, then he took his leave.

'Come back another time,' said Gladys. 'It's done me a power of good talking about the old days.'

Bessie was kept at home with her dad, but Iffy and Billy watched the funeral from the bridge.

Someone had lent Fatty a suit, an old-fashioned suit, the sort posh boys wore to make their first Holy Communion, and shiny lace-up shoes. He looked strange and awkward and too grown up. They'd never seen him in any clothes other than the khaki shorts and blue T-shirt. They wanted to wave at him but he never once looked up, he kept his eyes on the ground.

Billy turned away as the coffin was lowered into the grave.

Iffy watched in horrified fascination. She flinched as the first handful of black soil was thrown onto the coffin. Through her tears Fatty was a wobbling figure at the graveside. A hand came out of the suit and dropped a bunch of yellow poppies into the gaping grave.

Fatty took a step backwards and as he did he seemed to fold into his clothes until he was just a crumpled suit on the grass. A woman stepped forward from the crowd, then another. Iffy's nan and a woman from Sebastopol, another woman she didn't know. They scooped Fatty up and he was lost from sight.

Fatty's father stood very still and made no move to go to Fatty. The mourners split ranks and began to drift away. Fatty's father walked away from the grave and out of the

gates. He stopped, cupped his hand to light a cigarette and then walked off in the direction of the Mechanics.

On Friday afternoon Will took a leisurely walk up from town, pausing on the hump-backed bridge. The sun was dipping behind Carmel Chapel and the windows were lit with an eerie orange-red glow. An early moon rose over Blagdon's Tump and somewhere on a hill farm a dog began to bark.

He was always drawn back to the bridge. He looked down again at the spot where the boy's clothes had been found. In the old photograph taken outside the Limp they had been black and white, but Will still remembered the colours vividly. The stained khaki shorts, the faded blue of the ripped T-shirt. The lingering smell of Fairy soap and lavender.

A pile of clothes left neatly on the river bank.

Will's mind was full of jumbled half-memories. Disjointed thoughts flashed through his tired brain. And he could make no sense of any of them.

Random thoughts that surely had no significance: the old Italian reading his book at the counter; a child stepping into a pair of shoes. But there had been no shoes left on the river bank. And yet . . .

He thought of the sleeping child in his mother's arms. Brand-new trainers that cost a fortune.

Damn! Something didn't add up. He couldn't make any sense of it at all.

Looking down at Carmel Chapel he remembered the morning when he and Rodwell had taken a walk in the graveyard and come across the grave of the boy's mother.

The newly dug grave was close against the walls of the chapel. There had been a mound of damp, black earth. The funeral flowers had been cleared away, but a few stray curling petals were embedded in the soil.

A simple, cheap wooden cross bore the words: Ellen Jennifer

Bevan. He remembered that as he'd stood there he'd felt as though someone had been watching him and he'd swivelled round, but the graveyard was empty. A piece of card, the type attached to wreaths had been trodden into the damp earth. He had prised it from the ground and turned it over. The ink had smudged and the black soil had stained its whiteness.

'To Mam. Love. . .' but the rest of the childlike script had been obliterated into an inky stain. Will had slipped the card into the pocket of his trousers and had walked away through grass that was still wet with the early dew.

It was all such a long time ago. He wondered what temporary madness had made him think that after all this time he could solve the mystery. The case had been closed for years and yet for some inexplicable reason he'd never really been able to let it go.

Now, forty odd years later he pressed the doorbell of Coronation House and jumped in alarm at the racket that ensued. A loud rendering of 'Que Sera, Sera' emanated from somewhere close by. Elizabeth Tranter opened the door and Will stepped across the threshold of the house feeling the strange sensation of the past mingling with the present.

'Well, Mr Sloane, come in do. Tea? With sugar or without?'

'Please. No sugar, thanks.'

Elizabeth Tranter showed him into the sitting room and left him alone while she busied herself in the kitchen. Will looked round the immaculately tidy room. Large ornately framed photographs of two children adorned the walls. One was of a boy with a swede-shaped head, dressed in a boy scout uniform, a boy with a small mean mouth, sly eyes and, by the look of him, a bit of a bully, Will guessed.

There was a picture of a girl about the same age as Bessie had been when he'd first met her, she was wearing a pale-pink ballet tutu and clutching a silver cup. This child had no ringlets but a fussy hairstyle, adorned with scrunchies, slides and other such paraphernalia. The expression 'done up like a dog's dinner' came to mind. Another picture of the same girl was of her wearing a fussy Bo-Peep style wedding dress with a crowd of Bo-Peep bridesmaids, and one of the boy dressed in a morning suit.

Elizabeth Tranter came back into the room with a tray of tea.

'Course they're grown up a bit now. Derek we called him, after my brother, he's doing very well for himself, lecturing in woodwork in the Tech, and our Leanne is a nursery nurse. Last year she got married to a boy from a nice chapel family down the valley. Mervyn was telling me that I've met you before, but I've got a terrible memory!'

'It was a long time ago when we met, Elizabeth. You were only a little girl.'

'I really don't remember.'

'I interviewed you and your friend, another Elizabeth as I recall.'

Elizabeth's eyes clouded over and she screwed up her nose in an effort to remember.

'Elizabeth? Elizabeth. Oh, you must mean Iffy!'

'That's right. Iffy Meredith.'

'Sounds daft now, doesn't it? Iffy! They called me Bessie, as you know. Quite revolting! That was years ago. Why were you interviewing us?'

'About a boy who disappeared.'

'Disappeared?'

'Lawrence Bevan.'

Elizabeth Prosser bit her lip in another effort to conjure up memory.

'Oh yes! I'd forgotten all about that. Well, I didn't know him that well. We called him Fatty. You haven't found him, have you?'

'No. The police stopped looking for him years ago. I was just in town on some business and it reminded me of the case.

Policemen are notorious for remembering cases they failed to solve. As I say, I was just passing through and I met your husband in the garden of the Big House, I always liked that house.'

'Oh, I wasn't keen on Mervyn buying it at first. I found it a bit scary and gloomy you know, but it's the biggest house around here. Mervyn's done very well for himself and he's fancied that house since he was a boy. It'll be nice when it's modernised, I suppose. More cake?'

Will accepted.

'It was sad about the boy, Fatty. But he was probably better off. His father was a dreadful man and as for his mother, well, she was no sort of mother at all.'

'What do you think happened to him, Elizabeth?'

'Fatty? Drowned, I suppose. He was always off swimming in the river, or up the ponds. He had a screw loose, I fancy.'

Will nodded and said, 'There was never any sign of a body, though. We'd have found him if he'd drowned.'

'I s'pose so. Well, I expect he ran off somewhere and got done in.'

'Perhaps he was grieving for his mam,' said Will.

'Oh, I don't think so! She was always drunk. I think he was afraid of being put with the nuns, they'd have made him wash!'

The front door opened and Mervyn came into the room.

'Talking about that Bevan lad who disappeared? I know he's dead and you shouldn't speak ill, but I couldn't stand him. Cocky little git, he was!'

'Tea, Mervyn?'

'Please. Always up to something he was. They reckon it was him who set fire to Dai Full Pelt's bloody—'

Bessie coughed loudly, and blushed.

'Beg pardon. My wife is averse to bad language, but I picked a lot up on the buildings over the years. Started at the bottom. Hard work got me where I am today.'

That and a bit of arm twisting, thought Will.

'Does the other Elizabeth . . . er . . . Iffy, still live round here?'

'No. She disappeared.'

Will felt his heart leap.

'Disappeared?'

'Oh, not like Fatty did. She got a scholarship to a convent down the valley.'

'St Martha's, that was,' said Mervyn. 'I seen her once in her uniform down by the docks in Cardiff. She was talking to a boy. She looked the other way quick and pretended she hadn't seen me. Stuck up little bug— madam! Thought she was better than us with her fancy clothes and her posh school.'

'I lost touch with her after primary school. Our houses were pulled down and we all moved.'

'You must have missed her,' Will said.

'No, not really. She wasn't my type. I made new friends at secondary modern school. It's odd looking back, isn't it? I mean you don't notice things when you're little, but I think Iffy was . . . er . . . was illegitimate.'

Mervyn interrupted. 'Obvious really, wasn't it? She was very dark-skinned.'

'She showed me a picture of her mam, once,' said Bessie. 'A newspaper picture. She said it was the only one she had. She said her nan didn't like her showing it to anyone. Then, years later I saw her mam, recognised her from her photo.'

'I thought she was an orphan,' said Will.

'She was.'

'So where did you see her mam?'

Elizabeth Prosser laughed. There was a nastiness behind the laughter that made Will cringe.

'I saw her in a film at the Limp! It was the same woman in the photograph. I must have been daft! The picture was of Elizabeth Taylor. It was that film with Richard Burton.'

Will sighed.

'So you've never heard from her?'

'No. It was sad about her grancha, though. Her grandparents brought her up. He died in the fire.'

'The fire?'

'In the Big House. The night it went up. About a year after we'd all moved. She was ancient by then, old Mrs Medlicott. She'd gone funny in the head by all accounts. The old man was passing and he went in to try and get her out, but it was too late. It cost him his life trying to save her. And Iffy's nan died not long after. Anyway, I'm afraid I must away to my practice in the chapel.'

Will walked with Elizabeth Tranter down past the Big House.

'It's strange, isn't it?' said Elizabeth. 'When we were kids we used to step right out in the road to avoid the gates. I was terrified of the place and soon I'll be living there.'

'Why were you so afraid?'

'Oh, ghosts and stuff, and Iffy's nan reckoned the old woman wasn't safe around children.'

'Why was that?'

'I don't really know. Mrs Medlicott's husband, the old doctor, drowned himself in the pond and everyone said he haunted the place.'

Will thought of Agnes Medlicott's strong hands and wondered. He paused outside the gates and looked into the gardens. The statue Mervyn had been carrying lay in the grass.

'Those statues are really very beautiful.'

'Ugh! I think they're awful.'

Will pointed. 'That one lying there in the grass looks as if someone has tried to cement the head back on.'

Elizabeth laughed. 'Oh, that was Fatty! I remember now. There was an old woman, a mad old thing, who walked around with a cart. I forget her name, she was a nasty, foul-mouthed old thing. She lived in Dancing Duck Lane. The statue's head was in the cart. There was some story about the old doctor being in love with some girl and chopping her head off. Honestly, it's a wonder we weren't half terrified to death with all the daft stories. Headless ghosts and dancing statues. It was all nonsense.'

'And Fatty stuck the head back on?'

'Yes. He snuck in there in the dark.'

'Why?'

'Goodness only knows, he had this mad idea of giving her her head back. He was always doing daft things. Iffy was as bad as him. She told me once that she'd seen a human skull stuck in the ice the year the river froze over. A skull with two front teeth missing! I remember too, she told me that Fatty had said he'd found a jarful of angels, but she said that after Fatty had disappeared, she swore that she and Billy had seen them. They were both a pair of liars, her and Fatty. Thinking about it p'raps neither of them was right in the head!'

'You didn't believe her?' Will asked.

'That she'd seen a load of angels? No! Fatty just had this way of convincing people to believe him. Iffy always fell for his yarns. Not me, though! I might not have been clever like they were, but I had plenty of common sense! A jarful of angels, my foot!'

'"There are more things in heaven and earth, Horatio, than are dreamed of in our philosophy."'

'I beg your pardon?'

'*Hamlet*.'

'Oh.'

There was a pause.

'As to Fatty's disappearance, he was always saying he was going to run off. He was going to make his fortune and come back for his mam and Iffy! He was sweet on Iffy Meredith. He was always up to some nonsense or other.'

'Does Billy Edwards still live around here?' Will asked.

'No. I'm the only one left of the four of us. Last I heard of Billy, he'd emigrated, gone to Australia, or it might have been

Canada. He married a girl from over the next valley. They had twins, two sets, I think. Excuse me a moment.'

They had reached the gates to Carmel Chapel and Elizabeth opened them with a clang.

'I know you're in there, Lally Tudge! Come on, out of it!'

Will saw a shadowy figure duck behind a grave, then hurry away towards the trees.

'Don't want the likes of her hanging about the place,' Elizabeth said to Will.

'Who is she?'

'Lally Tudge. She's not all there. Wants locking up if you ask me. Wandering about with an old doll wrapped in a blanket like it was a real baby.'

'Why does she do that?'

Elizabeth lowered her voice, 'She's not a very nice type of person, Mr Sloane. She had an illegitimate baby years ago down in the home for bad girls.'

'Poor, poor girl,' said Will sadly.

Elizabeth Prosser stared at him as though he were mad.

Iffy, Fatty, Billy and Bessie were crouched down in the gwli that separated Sebastopol Row from Balaclava Row. Dai was late. The moon rose higher over Blagdon's Tump and the liquorice-black river magicked itself to a twist of silver.

A dog barked far off in one of the tumbledown hill farms. Darkness crept stealthily up the gwli towards them and covered them up one by one, turning them into sinister crouching dwarves.

Behind them in Balaclava Row the gas lamps began to light up the windows of the crooked old houses and black monsters writhed and lurked behind ghostly curtains. The first cold breeze was blowing as summer tipped towards autumn, and Iffy knew with a horrible ache that the lovely days of freedom were coming to an end. She thought of the itchy winter uniform they wore to school, the cold swish of Miss Riley's skirts, the pad of her feet on icy linoleum, and she shivered.

An owl called somewhere up on the Black Band and an army of ghosts tramped up and down Iffy's spine.

'Where the hell has he got to?' Fatty hissed and his voice was strange and savage in the dark.

Dai was always in the lav by nine. They knew his routine by heart.

Iffy began to pray that Dai wouldn't come out to the lav at all. Then they'd have to abandon their plan and slope off home. It wasn't such a good idea. It had sounded great when Fatty had first said it. Most things Fatty said sounded great, like the time he'd had the brilliant idea of cooking tinned tomatoes with a blow torch, only he hadn't take the lid off first.

They would get into terrible trouble for what they were going to do. The coppers would catch them and put hand-cuffs on them. They'd go to prison. Iffy pictured herself in a suit with arrows on it, a ball and chain dragging behind her like the villains she'd seen in comics.

She prayed to God. Gritted her teeth and prayed really hard. Dear God, please don't let Dai come out to the lav tonight. Let him die in his chair before he needs to go.

She prayed to the Virgin. Dear Mary, please make Dai constipated.

She didn't ask God for constipation, he probably got the women saints to answer those sorts of prayers.

Blessed Virgin, please just bung him up a bit.

She prayed to all the saints she could remember. Saint Francis the Cissy, Joan of Fark.

They waited, ears pricked for any sound. No sign of Dai.

Thank you, God. Thank you, Blessed Virgin. Joan of Fark and Francis the Cissy.

'Come on, let's go,' Bessie whispered, but Fatty made no attempt to move.

A mouse squeaked somewhere close by and Bessie pulled her skirts tight around her bum in case it took a flying leap at her privates.

Then there was a noise. The sound of a door creaking open, wood scraping harshly across a stone floor.

Oh God!

Fatty grinned like a demon. Dai was on his way! He was going to step right into the trap!

Bessie poked Iffy hard in the ribs and she jumped and sniggered with nerves.

'Hush up, you two! Don't give the game away!' Fatty hissed.

They shut it. He was the boss.

Iffy screwed up her face and tried to squeeze away the tears of fear that were coming.

Fatty swept his eyes over them like a general over his men.

'Everyone know what they're doing?'

Iffy and Bessie nodded weakly. They knew their jobs. They'd rehearsed them often enough.

Fatty had the scariest job of all. He was in charge of the newspaper, an *Argus* he'd pinched from the letterbox of a posh house up in Georgetown where teachers and shopkeepers and crooks and people who'd won the pools lived.

Bessie was in charge of the bolts. Fatty had greased them with lard earlier so that they wouldn't squeak and give them away.

Iffy was in charge of the box of matches which she'd borrowed from the pantry cupboard.

Fatty was also doing the countdown. Like Americans did for space rockets.

Billy hadn't got a job, he was just there for the ride.

'Keep them matches still, Iffy!' Fatty said.

The matches rattled in her hand and she closed her fist tight to stop them. Billy smiled at Iffy kindly. She smiled back. He had pretty dimples when he smiled.

Fatty didn't have a nervous bone in his body, he was crouched down like the rest of them, but there was no sign of fear about him. He was enjoying every minute of it. Iffy was terrified. So was Bessie.

Fatty breathed slowly, calmly. Just a few more minutes and then that fat bastard would get what was coming to him. He owed him. Oh yes, he owed him.

He bit his lips and tried to put the memory of his mam out of his mind. He'd been coming over the bridge when he'd seen Iffy's grancha. The old man's face was contorted with pain and exertion. He was carrying Fatty's mam as though she was a small child and Fatty'd known by the droop of her head and her wide staring eyes that she was gone from him for ever.

Over at the end of the gwli, the wonky lamp post outside the Old Bake House threw a pool of light onto the road. A lone bat danced through the ballroom of its light. Somewhere a sash window rattled like old bones and then crashed shut.

Iffy sneaked a look at Bessie who was crouched next to her, and then wished she hadn't. Bessie's eyes were on leave from their sockets. At any minute they might pop out, roll down her cheeks and get lost in the darkness of the gwli; sticky eyeballs covered in dirt. Iffy imagined Bessie scrabbling about in the muck to find them, having to rinse them under the tap and pop them back into her empty sockets. She had to look away in the end because Bessie's face made Iffy want to laugh and Fatty would kill her if she did.

Bessie pulled at Iffy's cardie.

'Let's go home,' she whimpered. She was shaking like blancmange, her lips two wriggling grubs, beads of sweat bubbling between her lip and her nose.

On the other side of Iffy, Billy grinned like a fool. Iffy just hoped he could run fast enough when the time came. He was going to need to, they all were.

Dai was out on his step, Fatty could hear his wheezy breath and the bubbling green phlegm in his pipes. The breeze carried his smells of tobacco, stale beer and sweat.

Iffy hoped Dai couldn't smell them. Bessie stank of talcum powder. Billy smelled fragrantly of bread: Swansea batch, cobs and bloomers. Fatty smelled of nettles, bubblegum and horse shit. Iffy wasn't sure what she smelled of.

Dai crossed the bailey and they heard the latch lift on the lav door.

Then he was inside the lav and only the whitewashed wall separated the four of them from him. He was close enough to touch!

They stayed crouching.

Pins and needles burned Iffy's feet and she bounced with terror. She thought that at any moment she might start to bounce faster and faster and not be able to stop. She might bounce away along the gwli, down the hill and into the river.

Iffy imagined Dai's face in the darkness of the lav: the huge great pumpkin head, tumbleweed hair, his sucked gobstopper eyes and wonky nose, nostrils wide as arches with sticky-out hairs, and his awful mouth – the great black dirty hole where one yellow fang hung by a sticky thread. She felt sick with fear.

It was pitch dark now in the gwli and Bessie's hand came out of the blackness and found Iffy's for comfort. Iffy was glad even though she pretended to pull her hand away.

'Got the matches ready?' Fatty whispered, his eyes gleamed with delight.

Iffy nodded dumbly, afraid she wouldn't be able to stop her hands from shaking long enough to get one out of the box, never mind light it.

'Bessie, pull the bolts back when I tell you,' said their general.

Bessie's eyes had gone back into her head. She had her lips bitten back inside her mouth and looked like an old granny with no teeth.

Then came the noise of Dai's braces pinging and the sound of his trousers dropping on the stone floor. The wooden boxseat of the lav creaked under his weight. Any minute now he would light the candle and set it on the little ledge on the wall and he would settle down to read his paper.

They heard him strike the match, and candle light crept through the cracks in the wall.

Dai coughed and settled himself down. He grunted, whinnied like a stallion, grunted again.

Fat pig.

Then he farted. A wet-sounding 'fwarp' that echoed off the walls, loud as a bullet in the silence of the gwli.

They bit back laughter, holding onto their bellies, except for Bessie who looked disgusted and covered her nose with her hanky.

Fatty wiped the silent laughter from his face with the back of his hand and gave them a look to shut it. There was silence again except for the sound of their breathing which seemed deafening.

Billy grinned at Iffy, his teeth very white and beautiful in the dark. Iffy was terrified, but no way could she back out.

Fatty remembered the faces of the drowned puppies. Five dead puppies lying in the grass among the daisies and the buttercups.

Please God, Iffy prayed, let me light the match.

Dai was reading in the lav. Stumbling over his words like a little kid, leaving big gaps between the words. Then it was all quiet again while he looked at the pictures.

The silence wasn't going to last for ever. Any minute now all hell would be let loose.

A lump was growing in Iffy's throat. She tried not to think of the consequences, just to remember to run.

Fatty looked round at everyone and put his fingers up in a victory sign, not the dirty way round which meant shag off.

The lump in Iffy's throat was like a golf ball. She swallowed. It was like swallowing a goose egg.

Fatty began the whispered countdown.

'Ten!'

Somewhere behind them there was an eerie wail. It was all Bessie could do to stay put. She looked fearfully over her shoulder. Two green eyes watched them from a wall in Balaclava.

'It's only a stuffing cat, Bessie!'

Bessie hung on to Iffy. They were clinging together, Siamese twins joined tight at the shoulder. Fatty gave them a warning look.

'Nine!'

Fatty was twisting up the newspaper. Iffy'd never noticed before how slender and soft his hands were.

'Eight!'

Iffy wanted to wee something chronic.

'Seven!'

Her bladder was an out of control balloon.

'Six!'

The first drops of wetness were warm in her knickers.

Bessie crossed herself even though she wasn't a Catholic. Ace on the forehead. Jack on the belly button. Left nipple, king. Right nipple, queen.

'Five!'

Iffy prayed to God, the Blessed Virgin and all the saints. She prayed for Nan to start calling her in. Bessie hoped that someone would come along the gwli so they'd have to abandon the plan and run away home but the gwli stayed silent and empty. Not a soul was in sight.

'Four! Bessie! The bolts!'

Bessie's hand hovered, shaking. Then the bolts on the trap door at the back of the lav drew back without a sound.

'Three!'

The trap door was open a tiny crack.

'Two!'

Fatty's voice was a hiss of steam and his eyes glowed like coals.

'Iffy! The matches!'

Billy had to help her. He held her hand and steadied the matchbox. The wavering match lit, the sulphur smell was strong in the night air. The flame caught at Fatty's rolled-up newspaper. A small yellow flame, growing fast into a bright flaming beacon. It reminded Iffy of the flames of hell. Their faces exploded into orange and red. Flickers of fear bounced off Iffy and Bessie. Fatty looked like the devil himself in the middle of the fires of hell.

'One!'

Hot pee ran down the top of Iffy's leg.

Fatty pushed the burning newspaper through the trap door.

'Blast off!'

The fire disappeared inside the lav on the end of Fatty's arm. Iffy's heart bounced up into her throat like a hot chestnut, roaring filled her ears and a million wings prepared for flight inside her head.

She was transfixed. Her feet seemed bolted to the ground. Her bones wouldn't move, her muscles were on strike, wobbling jelly muscles.

Fatty came back for her. She made it to the end of the gwli, Fatty dragging her roughly by the arm.

Billy and Bessie were there waiting, panting loudly in the shadows.

'Why didn't you run, mun?' said Bessie.

Iffy didn't answer. Her legs were wet and itchy with hot wee. She hoped no one would notice, especially Bessie.

'Right,' Fatty said. 'Quick check to see no one's looking and then we slip down one at a time past the steps. It's too dangerous to hang around.'

There was only one chance of a quick glance as they fled, because doors were opening all along Sebastopol. Light flooded into the bailey.

Just one quick look. A photograph in Iffy's mind that would last for ever of Dai Full Pelt out on the bailey, hopping up and down like a tribal dancer, his shirt-tail flickering with sparks. His bum a giant glow worm!

Ruby Gittins running out of the back door wearing shocking-pink baby-doll pyjamas. Then standing stock still and staring, with her mouth wide open.

Dai bellocking.

Ruby screaming.

Dai roaring, 'Get some water quick, woman! Put it out!'

'Burn, you fuckin' bastard, burn!' said Fatty.

Then the three of them were off down the hill behind Fatty, their hearts bursting.

'Iffy-O!'

'Bessie-O!

The town clock bonged.

Fatty and Billy disappeared into the shadows of the gwli. Iffy and Bessie went hell for leather down the steps to Inkerman.

Marlene poured the tea and handed Will a plate.

'Welsh cake, Will?'

'Thank you.'

'Anything else from the dim and distant past I can help you with?' asked Gladys. 'Oh, before I forget, I must get Marlene to make up that herbal brew for you. One of Carty Annie's old recipes.'

'The old woman from Dancing Duck Lane?' Will asked.

'That's the one. Lived to be well over a hundred.'

'Going back to the past. You said you did quite a bit of trade with the Medlicotts.'

'Yes. There was no shortage of money. The girls were all from very well-to-do Spanish families. We made up a lot of dresses for the young ladies there,' said Gladys.

'I don't suppose they'd be of any interest to you but we've still got records going back to those years,' said Marlene.

'You have?'

'Just hold on a second.'

It took some time before Marlene came back carrying an armful of dusty old red leather books.

'Here you are. Take your pick.'

Will leafed through the books until he came to the year he was looking for.

Marlene looked over his shoulder.

'There, look, that's the last order we ever made up for the young ladies.'

'Now, I can't remember what I had for breakfast but I can remember the very last time they all came in here. There were three of them. Came to have their measurements taken. Such lovely names the Spanish have,' Gladys said.

Will read the names, 'Maria Garcia Martinez, Elena Maria Rigau, Ekaterina Velasco Olivares.'

'They were all from a place called Valencia. They pronounced it Vallentheeya something like that. Now that one there was a beauty,' said Gladys squinting through her glasses, pointing at the page.

Will looked down at the name.

'She was about Marlene's age. She was very pale, peaky-looking, and with a woman's instincts I knew why. Those dark rings under the eyes, a little widening of the hips. About five months gone, I would have said. It was all the talk that it was the doctor's child.'

Marlene laughed.

'You don't think it was the doctor's child?' Will asked.

Marlene said, 'Now the answer to that I do know. There was a chap who lived up in the Three Rows, a bit older than her. He was the father of the baby.'

'Marlene, you never told me at the time.'

'Mam, I was young. There were a million things I didn't tell you when I was that age.'

'Probably just as well I didn't know,' said Gladys.

'I got quite friendly with her. She told me, you see, that she was expecting a baby and that she was going to run away with her young man before anyone found out. Only I think someone had already found out.'

'What makes you say that?'

'Maggie Rafferty and me were seeing a couple of chaps who lived up past the rec. We used to meet up under the old bridge. Used to write our names on the roof. One night we heard a hell of a row. The old doctor shouting and a girl crying and then this fellow, the handsome one, came through the bridge. He was in a right state. His eyes all blacked and his two front teeth knocked clean out!'

'What was his name?'

'I can't for the life of me remember. I never saw him or Kat again.'

'Kat?' Will said.

'Short for Ekaterina,' said Marlene. 'More tea? Or cake?'

Iffy left the bacon untouched until round waxy spots of fat formed on the plate. It was impossible to eat. Her stomach felt as if it was full of wriggling worms. She wondered if Dai was dead. Was Sergeant Rodwell up in Sebastopol taking fingerprints?

Nan was cracking eggs into the old black frying pan at the range. One was a double yoker.

When Grancha killed one of his chickens sometimes there were still eggs inside their guts. It reminded Iffy of those Russian dolls: small, smaller, smallest.

The double yoker sizzled in the pan. The smell of it cooking turned Iffy's stomach.

'Come on, Iffy. Eat up your food. Got to get a bit of meat on them bones. Proper tin ribs you are.'

She couldn't swallow.

When her nan wasn't looking she slipped the bacon to the cat and then pretended to chew.

Winnie Jones came in through the back door.

'Come in, gel. Smelled the tea, did you?'

'Have you heard?' lisped Winnie.

'Heard what?'

Winnie took her false teeth out and put them in the pocket of her pinny.

Iffy heaved, but there was nothing to come up. Her belly was only full of fear.

'Last night, mun, there was all hell up! Morning, Iffy.'

'Morning, Mrs Jones.'

Iffy slunk into the pantry afraid of what Winnie was going to say.

Nan poured tea for herself and Winnie.

'All hell up where?'

'Up in Sebastopol.'

'What happened?'

Winnie took ages to get to the point and for once Iffy was glad.

Her teeth rattled as she stood on the other side of the pantry door.

'The police was up an' all.'

Her knees joined her teeth in the rattle.

'Terrible it was.'

She could hardly breathe.

'What was terrible?'

'Ruined his vest into the bargain.'

'Winnie, what the hell are you going on about?'

'Haven't you heard, gel? Someone set fire to Dai Full Pelt last night.'

Iffy's heart punched at her ribs. Bomp. Bomp. Bomp.

'Ay, set fire to him! Lucky not to have killed him, mun.'

'Who done that then?'

'They don't know. No one saw nothing.'

Thank you, God. Thank you, Saint Francis the Cissy. And Joan of Fark.

'Didn't Dai see who done it?'

'No, he was in the lav.'

'In the lav! You can't fit two people in the lav. How the hell did they set light to him?'

'They opened the door at the back.'

'You've lost me, gel.'

'The little door in the back of the lav. The ones they used to open years ago when they took the pails out for emptying.'

'I still don't get it.'

'Dai was on the lav! Whoever it was pushed burning papers in through the little door at the back.'

'Oh right, I'm with you.'

'Set fire to his arse they did!'

'His arse?'

Nan spat tea, a wide arc of tea that hissed as it hit the flames in the grate. Iffy watched through the crack in the door as Nan dabbed her mouth with her pinny.

'And singed all his doodah into the bargain!'

'Singed it! Oh stop it, Winnie, don't talk daft.'

'Honest to God. Apparently there's not a hair left on him down there.'

Nan screeched.

'Ruby said his clods are like a pair of stewed plums!'

Nan laughed, a cackle and then a roar.

'Don't know what you're laughing for. It's dangerous, mun, people going about doing things like that to innocent people.'

Innocent! Innocent people don't drown little puppies. Or . . . Iffy didn't want to think about what she'd heard under the bridge the night Fatty had stuck the head back on the statue.

Nan spat out more tea and held on to her belly.

'Oh my God. Bill? Come and listen to this!'

Grancha came out of the back parlour and into the kitchen.

'Tell him, Winnie.'

Winnie stiffened up with importance.

'Just telling Nellie about Dai, I was, Mr Meredith.'

Nan was rocking backwards and forwards, her face in her pinny.

'What about him? What's he been up to now?'

'Been injured,' said Nan, snorting.

'Got his fingers caught in the till, did he?'

'Mr Meredith!'

'Bloody old rogue that he is.'

'For Christ's sake, tell him, Winnie.'

'Last night, Mr Meredith, someone set fire to his arse!' said Winnie, shocked that Iffy's nan found it so funny.

'His arse! Did it burn well?'

'Mr Meredith!'

'Should have put paraffin on it first.'

Iffy felt for her eyebrows at the mention of paraffin.

'Mr Meredith! Don't be so wicked.'

'Not a hair left on him!' shrieked Nan.

Grancha was laughing, first a belly wheeze, then a splutter and on to a deafening roar. It was catching.

Behind the pantry door Iffy started to giggle. Nan was purple with laughter, her face wet with tears, her pinny splattered with spat tea.

'Oh God! Not a hair left on him and his clods like stewed plums. Waaaarrrrgg!'

'Who done that then?' said Grancha.

'No one knows. Must be a nut case on the loose.'

'He's got plenty of enemies, mind.'

'Want locking up whoever they are!'

'Kids, I s'pect,' said Grancha.

The pantry grew icy around Iffy.

'Was there much damage done apart from his privates?' Grancha's words creaked with laughter.

'Ay, ruined his vest, scorched to bits it was. He's in a hell of a state by all accounts.'

Iffy snorted into her hand.

'Did they take him up the hospital?'

'Yes. But he wouldn't let none of the nurses look at it. Ruby had to rub lard on it and send to Morrissey for ice from the fridge.'

'Well, well, well,' said Grancha. 'Best laugh I've had for years.'

Iffy struggled to stop laughing behind the pantry door.

'Mind you,' said Winnie, 'Sergeant Rodwell said he'll catch whoever was responsible, and when he does they'll swing.'

Iffy heard the clank of chains, a priest reading the last rites. She felt the hangman's bag come down over her head and the pantry spun, as her head left her body and she slipped into darkness.

Will sat up at the desk in his room in the Firkin, leafing through his old notebooks. He had always been a copious note-taker when he was on a case. He was glad of it now, reading through them he was able to conjure up the scenes from the past.

The boy had had three close friends according to Sergeant Rodwell who had advised Will against visiting Billy Edwards because the boy couldn't speak. He had told him the story of Billy's brother's tragic death. Rodwell had been very cut up about it.

Rodwell had been working over in another valley and had been called out to the scene of the accident. He'd said it had been the worst thing he'd ever had to deal with. The boy had been mangled to death in the wheel. He'd been the one who had to break the news to the mother. To carry the kid's shoes back to the parents.

Will had interviewed the other two friends. Two little girls. Elizabeth Meredith and Bessie Tranter.

They'd both lived a stone's throw away from where the clothes had been found, in Inkerman Terrace.

Chalk and cheese if ever two girls were, Will had thought afterwards.

He'd talked to Elizabeth Meredith first. She lived with her grandparents. Rodwell had filled him in on her background. The girl had no parents: her dad had committed suicide, he'd left a note and his clothes on a beach down on the coast a few days after the child had been born.

'And her mother?' Will had asked.

'Don't know much about her really. Talk is she ran off and left her the day she was born.'

Elizabeth Meredith was sitting outside on the front step when Will had walked along the bailey of Inkerman Terrace.

He was aware of curtains twitching as he passed, doors opening a crack, people coming out of their houses and crossing to the outside lavs as a pretext. He heard the gathering whispers as he walked towards the girl.

'Hello. You must be Elizabeth Meredith.'

'Yep. But everyone calls me Iffy.'

She was a bright, dark-haired, friendly little girl.

She stood up as her grandmother came out onto the step.

'Iffy, what are you doing out there without any shoes on? Get them on now before you catch your death.'

Will had introduced himself to the old woman and asked if he could have a few words with Elizabeth.

Mrs Meredith was also friendly. A warm, homely woman in her early seventies, he'd guessed. She'd made tea and put a plate of cakes on the table and then diplomatically left him alone with Iffy.

He'd sat at the table while Iffy had put on a pair of old daps.

'You know why I'm here . . . er . . . Iffy?'

She'd nodded, tilting her head to one side, the dark curls falling over her forehead.

'Now, could you tell me if you have any ideas where Lawrence Bevan might have gone?'

She'd smiled then, a lovely smile that lit her face with a warm radiance.

'Fatty,' she said. 'We call him Fatty. We never call him Lawrence. He isn't fat though. Just sort of plump, we don't call him Fatty to be nasty, it's just a nickname.'

'Right.'

He noticed the tense she used; she still spoke of him in the present tense. She was too young to have realised the implications of his disappearance, the fact that everything pointed to him being part of the past. Dead. Gone.

'So when did you last see him?'

'Well, I can't remember exactly. I think it was the day before he disappeared.'

He didn't believe her. She didn't seem the type of kid not to remember things clearly.

He'd shown her the clothes and she'd been taken aback. Her face had paled, her blue eyes had welled up with tears.

'Are these Fatty's clothes, Iffy?'

She'd bitten her lip, struggling to hold back the tears and nodded.

'You are sure they're his?'

She'd nodded again.

'Why are you so sure?'

'I just am. Khaki shorts. Blue T-shirt. Nobody else had clothes like that round here.'

'What sort of shoes did he usually wear?'

She looked away again quickly.

'I dunno. I never noticed. Just ordinary old shoes.'

'When you last saw him did he say he might be going somewhere?'

She hesitated for a second. 'No.'

'Do you know where he might have gone?'

'No, but he'll be back.'

'What makes you say that?'

She looked Will in the eye as she spoke, it was a defiant look but he knew that tears weren't far away.

'I just know he will, that's all. He's always doing it, going off for adventures. He's probably camping out somewhere. Once he went for a week.'

She'd said it so matter of factly as though it were quite the normal thing for a ten-year-old boy to disappear for days on end without anyone worrying.

'You're not worried about him then?'

She'd looked away again, but not before he'd seen the glistening tear that had slipped from her eye.

'No. He can look after himself. He's brave. He's not afraid of nothing, Fatty.'

'Just one other thing, Iffy. He always wore a belt, didn't he?'

'I dunno.'

For a second, Will had the feeling that she was again withholding something from him, not telling him the whole truth.

Elizabeth Tranter lived a few doors along the row. Will had banged on the green-painted door and been kept waiting for an age before the bolts had been drawn slowly back and an elderly woman had come to the door.

He had been invited in, but with ill-disguised annoyance.

The house was a shrine to housework. Every surface was polished to a burnished sheen. The smell of bleach and strong disinfectant hung in the air.

Elizabeth Tranter, dressed as though she were going to a party, sat up at the kitchen table reading a book, or at least pretending to read a book.

She was as sickly looking as Iffy had been healthy. She was pale-skinned, her fair hair was styled into a mass of bobbing ringlets. Her chest creaked and groaned in the silence of the room. She was a nervous wreck this one, looking across at her mother all the time for reassurance.

He'd asked her the same questions as he'd asked Iffy but she'd barely spoken, just shaking her head or nodding.

'My daughter, we call her Bessie, won't be able to tell you anything. She didn't bother with the likes of Fatty Bevan,' said the woman.

'How would you describe the likes of Lawrence Bevan, Mrs Tranter?'

'Well, he wasn't from a God-fearing family for a start. He was a rough boy. We wouldn't like to think Bessie had anything to do with him.'

'I understand he was a very scruffy boy, by all accounts, dirty in appearance,' said Will.

Mrs Tranter had nodded and flinched visibly. Will thought she probably found the word 'dirt' extremely offensive.

When he'd shown the clothes to Bessie, Mrs Tranter had looked as though she might faint.

'Are these his clothes, Bessie?'

Bessie had sniffed and nodded.

Then she spoke, 'Except for his cricket belt and shoes.'

'What sort of shoes did he wear, Bessie?'

Without hesitation she'd told him that Fatty always wore scruffy old red sandals that should have been put in the bin years ago.

'That's all she knows,' said Mrs Tranter firmly.

She must have been in her late forties when Bessie had been born. A prim, fussy, over-protective type, and she couldn't wait to get him out of her house.

Will was recalled unwillingly from the past to the present by a knock at the door.

When he opened it he was surprised to see a young man in dungarees standing on the landing. He smiled at Will sheepishly. He was, with some difficulty, holding something large, wrapped carelessly about in green tarpaulin.

'Special delivery, sir. Thought I'd better wrap it up a bit. Didn't want to offend any old grannies. Shall I carry it in for you?'

The young man propped the delivery up against the wall near the window and took his leave.

Will pulled the tarpaulin away and revealed the statue that had lain in the long grass in the garden of the Big House. The head had recently been quite expertly rejoined to the body and the whole thing had been cleaned up. The only flaw in the beautiful thing was a chip across the right foot.

A gift card had been tied to the statue's arm. He pulled it away and read,

Dear Mr Sloane,
    I'm getting rid of all them old statues as a job lot but Elizabeth thought you might like this one.
Best wishes
Mervyn Prosser

Will smiled.
Perhaps he could ask his funeral directors if they'd put this on his grave.

Iffy knew she'd gone straight to Hell. Flames were licking up her nostrils, the inside of her head was on fire. She opened her eyes to redness.

The Devil was leaning over her, his glowing red eyes looking into hers. His whiskers brushed against her burning face. Crimson flames were licking upwards behind him. The screams of tormented souls were all around.

She closed her eyes and felt the sweat prickle on her scorched skin, then dropped into darkness again.

Red and yellow fire. Her grancha was the devil.

'All right, little gel? Gave yourself hell of a crack, mun.'

Hell was the kitchen. The flames in the range flickered red and gold. The kettle screamed and danced on the hob.

The fire in her head came from a little brown bottle that Nan held under her nose.

'Let's get you up to bed, little gel. You had a funny turn. Bit of rest is what you need.'

Grancha carried her through the back parlour. The lid on the biscuit tin lifted, a black hand waved at her. The bleeding heart drip dripped onto the sofa back.

Up the wooden hill she went and soon she floated in the

big rocking bed until the sun went down and Carmel Chapel blazed and the Old Bugger hooted low in the graveyard.

They were going to take Fatty away. Iffy was hiding under the kitchen table when she heard Mrs Bunting telling Nan, and Mrs Bunting had heard from Bridgie Thomas and she had got it straight from the horse's mouth: Father Flaherty. Fatty's father was signing him over to the church and they were going to put him in the children's home. It was for his own good.

As soon as she could escape from under the table, Iffy went looking for Fatty. She found him down by the river.

'Fatty! Fatty! I've got something to tell you, only don't say I told you, but I heard them talking.'

'Calm down, Iffy. Heard who talking about what?'

'They're going to put you in a home!' she said breathlessly.

'Who told you that?'

'Honest injun, Fatty. Mrs Bunting told Nan, and Bridgie heard it from Father Flaherty, so it must be true. They're going to put you in Bethlehem House.'

'Not on your fuckin' nelly,' he said.

'But you can't argue with them,' Iffy said. 'They can make you do anything they want.'

Bethlehem House was an orphanage. It was a tall, ugly red-brick house on the far edge of town down past the park. There were nuns at Bethlehem House. The Sisters of Mercy. Fatty'd always said that they looked like black umbrellas stalking up through the town. They wore long black habits and lace-up shoes that squeaked on the floor and they smelled of incense and strong-smelling soap. They never smiled.

'I can come and visit you, though.'

'I'm not going.'

'I could bring you sweets and comics.'

'No!'

'But, they'll make you, Fatty.'

'No they won't. I don't care what they say. They can piss up their legs and play with the steam for all I bloody care.'

He got up and scrabbled up the bank.

'Fatty, where are you going?' She tried to follow him. 'Wait, Fatty. Please.'

But there was no stopping him, he ran up past the Big House and didn't look back once.

Fatty ran and ran, on past the rec. He leapt over the stile, arms pumping, head spinning. When he could run no further he threw himself down in the long grass and sobbed. He wasn't going to let them take him to the orphanage. If only his mam hadn't died! Everything had been spoiled. He'd always planned on escaping, getting rich and coming back for his mam.

He'd already thought of running away, he hated being at home with his dad, especially now his mam wasn't there. There was no way Father Flaherty was going to cart him off to Bethlehem House. He had to get away! There was nothing worth staying for any more, except for Iffy. He didn't want to leave Iffy Meredith. He couldn't imagine life without her.

Oh God! He needed to think. He needed to make plans, and quickly, before they came for him.

The sun burned behind the windows of Carmel Chapel as Will stepped into the graveyard. Walking quickly between the rows of graves, he found what he was looking for easily.

Grass had grown over the mound of wet earth he had looked down on that summer day long ago.

No one had erected a stone to her memory. The rotting wooden cross tilted towards the earth. Her name had faded but was still just legible.

ELLEN JENNIFER BEVAN

Underneath her name someone had painted on the words:

AND FLIGHTS OF ANGELS SING THEE TO THY REST

Will began to tremble and he had to lean against the wall of the chapel for support. The words hadn't been on the cross when he'd visited the grave just after the boy had disappeared.

He knew now without a doubt that these words had been written by the boy. The small 'e' was identical to the 'e' of Lawrence Bevan's name written on the hump-backed bridge. Identical to the 'e's in the notes written in the encyclopedia.

And that could only mean one thing: the boy had still been alive, still been somewhere around, when Will had been investigating his disappearance!

Will's head ached but things were falling into some semblance of order.

Fatty Bevan had still been alive after his clothes had been discovered down by the river. But where had he been hiding? Why? What had he been wearing?

Rodwell had said that he only had one set of clothes to his name. If he'd wanted to disappear so badly why would he have left the clothes on the river bank and thus ensured their discovery and the subsequent police enquiry?

Unless he'd wanted them to think he'd drowned?

Will knew that Iffy Meredith hadn't been telling him the truth, that she'd been hiding something. There was something else about Iffy that he was trying to recall, something he'd seen that day when he'd spoken to her in her grandparents' house.

Some small detail, apparently insignificant! And yet somehow, if he could only remember what it was, he knew it was important.

There was no sign of Carty Annie. Fatty tip-toed gingerly up to the house and pressed his nose against the filthy window pane. His eyes were sore from crying and his head was thumping but he had to see, to convince himself that he hadn't imagined it. He peered into the kitchen. He could just make out the dresser and a vague outline of the jars. He screwed up his eyes trying to get a better look.

Then he took a deep breath, turned the door handle and slipped silently inside the house.

It took several minutes for his eyes to adjust to the darkness of the kitchen. Then he walked quickly across the room towards the dresser.

He stopped. He felt as though his eyes would pop out of his head. His heart was thumping painfully. He stared at the jars, mesmerised.

Loads of old empty jars.

Except for one.

A jarful of real live angels. They weren't like angels were supposed to be at all. Not like the ones he'd seen in books. Those ones all had soppy smiles, beautiful shining faces and too fucking good to be true.

Fatty grinned.

'Bloody hell,' he said. He couldn't take his eyes off the jar. 'They're beautiful and ugly all at the same time.'

He crept closer still.

There were loads of them in the jar. Tiny little angels, all crushed up tight like them fish in a tin with a key. Their pudgy snouts were all squashed up and their twisted lips stuck like pink slugs to the sides of the jar. Their hot breath filled it with steamy clouds. Their eyes held his gaze; bright, shrewd, crafty eyes glaring at him. His hands were shaking uncontrollably as he reached forward and picked up the jar.

Slowly, breathing noisily, he began to twist the lid. Slowly it loosened and came off.

He put the jar back down on the dresser and held his nose. Jesus! The stink was terrible. The stench of sour sweat and stale wee all mixed up with the reek of pickled onions and vinegar.

Now the lid was off the room filled with their noise. He heard the terrible scratching and squeaking sounds of their fingernails scraping against the murky glass of the jar. The awful grinding and gnashing noises of their sharp pearly teeth and the rubbing friction of their torn and tangled wings. Dreadful noises they were, that made his ears weep and his gums ache.

'Calm down for Christ's sake,' he said.

He steadied the jar with one hand and put his other hand inside it, lifted one angel out and popped it into an empty jar. He screwed on the lid tightly and then he was out of there and legging it down Dancing Duck Lane.

Fatty had made his plans carefully. He'd had it all worked out. He'd made the decision to go and no one was going to stop him. If they thought he was going to live with a bunch of mealy-mouthed old nuns they could think again.

Iffy was the only person he'd told. He hadn't said a word to Billy, even though he'd wanted to. He knew he'd miss Billy, he'd miss his silence. Fatty had been shocked that even though Billy couldn't speak, he had worked it out for himself and somehow knew that Fatty was going away.

He'd brought him a present, an old duffel bag containing a T-shirt, a pair of shorts and even pants and a vest. Fatty'd never had pants before. Best of all, there was a pair of almost new shiny brown sandals that had been recently polished. They had cream-coloured crêpe soles and they still had the price on the bottom. Fourteen shillings and sixpence. Fatty'd tried them on and they fitted a treat! Billy had grinned at Fatty, then he'd run off, stopped further down the road, looked back, put up his thumb and raced away.

The sandals would be perfect for all the walking that he was going to have to do over the next couple of weeks.

Fatty had planned to hide away in the pipe and as soon as it was dark he was going to creep out from his hiding place, leg it away down the river and get as far away down the valley as he could that first night.

He knew a couple of safe places he could stay without being discovered. Then, when he reached the sea . . .

Iffy had promised to get rid of his old clothes. He had no intention of being recognised and brought back. It wasn't likely that anyone would report him missing. The old man was off on a bender with his mam's insurance money. There was no one to know he'd run away except Iffy, and by the time anyone had realised, it would be too late!

He was going to leave tonight. Hiding in the pipe, waiting for darkness to fall he heard the sound of voices. Sergeant Rodwell was down on the river bank talking to another man. A plain clothes copper by the look of him. An important-looking man who was holding up Fatty's shorts and T-shirt. It looked to Fatty as though he was smelling them, like a bloodhound!

Shit! What were his bloody clothes doing down there! What was Iffy playing at? He panicked and crept back into the darkness of the pipe. Just as he stepped into the cover of the bushes in the grounds of the Big House, a strong hand was pushed hard against his mouth and he couldn't scream even if he'd wanted to . . .

*

Will could not sleep. His brain was working overtime and yet to no good purpose. The same old nagging thoughts were rattling around inside his head . . .

He sat up in bed and looked across the room at the statue. The moonlight glistened on the smooth white stone. Agnes Medlicott had certainly been an extremely talented sculptor. She had captured in stone the very essence of carefree youth. The slender limbs had a subtle vibrancy, the playful tilt of the head, the wrinkling of the pretty nose, a young face turned towards the sun. The soft, sweet, wistful smile.

He couldn't remember now whether it was the Eskimos who believed that inside every lump of rock there was a statue already carved. That you merely had to chip away at the superfluous rock until you revealed a beautiful discovery deep inside. It was a lovely idea.

He felt as if this case were the same. Chip away for long enough and eventually you would come up with the answer. Only at the moment there seemed to be more questions than answers.

He imagined the boy creeping across the satin smooth lawns of the Big House in the dead of night to replace the head on this statue. Did he stand back and look at her? Did he see, as Will did now, the soft moonlight shining across her young face, a face full of hope. A girl in love.

He felt a strange sensation realising that he and the boy had both gazed upon this face by the light of the moon.

Then he remembered something that had seemed of no relevance before. It set off a whole train of jumbled thoughts.

Elizabeth Tranter had mentioned that Iffy's nan had said old Mrs Medlicott wasn't safe around children. Yet Agnes Medlicott had talked to him about her own dead child with such sadness. She had spoken too about all her girls. He'd thought that the statues were all her children. He remembered looking at Agnes

Medlicott's hands . . . hard, strong, sinewy hands.

Not safe around children.

No one had found the boy's cricket belt.

Elizabeth Tranter had said that Iffy had seen a skull stuck in the ice. A skull with two teeth missing. What was so significant about that?

Jesus! Gladys Baker had told him they'd found a headless corpse.

Gladys Baker's friend Esther somebody or other had spent a night fighting off Dr Medlicott in the air-raid shelter.

Sergeant Rodwell had told him there was no point speaking to little Billy Edwards because he was dumb. He'd told him the horrific story of Billy's older brother's death. About the brown paper bags and the sandals. The new brown sandals with the price still on the bottom!

Dear God, he'd been a fool. It was staring him in the face!

He threw back the bed covers, dressed quickly and slipped silently down the stairs and out into the moonlit night.

Iffy lay in the big bed. The gas mantle popped and the light grew dim, then bright. She closed her eyes against the dripping shadows of bats.

Outside the town clock bonged twelve o'clock. Midnight. Soon ghosts would start to walk the dark gwlis. Lunatics would come out on the prowl. The moon would rise above the mountain and turn the river to a trickle of silver.

Down in Carmel graveyard the Old Bugger hooted low and long. Branches tapped against the window and she thought of Blind Pugh, his eyes pale in the moonlight, tap tapping his way towards her window. She thought of Fatty out there somewhere in the dark night, roaming the hillsides or swimming naked in the deep ponds where wild boys and drunk men had drowned and never been found.

She'd betrayed him! He would never speak to her again.

Oh, why had she done it! Fatty had asked her to meet him down by the river. He'd called out to her from where he was hiding in the long grass. She'd jumped when she'd seen him because he was wearing different clothes and she'd never seen him in anything other than the faded T-shirt and the enormous shorts. He'd said that he was going to run away and made her swear not to tell. He'd given her his old clothes and told her to get rid of them. He said he needed time to get away. He couldn't wear his own clothes because he'd be recognised.

But Iffy hadn't got rid of them. She'd taken them home, crept into her bedroom and tried them on. Then she'd taken them off, held them to her nose and breathed in his smells, the gloriously splendid smells of bubblegum, horse shit and freedom.

Then she'd panicked. Rolled the clothes up, wrapped them in one of Nan's old aprons and hidden them in the pantry, stuffed deep down behind the mangle by the Fairy soap.

Then, when she couldn't bear the thought of losing him she'd betrayed him.

In the early evening she'd slipped back down to the river and left the clothes in a neat pile in the grass, but she hadn't been able to part with the cricket belt or the battered old sandals.

She just couldn't.

She wanted them to think he'd drowned so that they'd start a search, catch him and bring him back. She couldn't stand to think of him going away from her for ever. She would rather he be taken to Bethlehem House, at least she'd be able to visit him.

Afterwards, she'd felt really bad and gone back to get the clothes, but when she'd looked over the bridge Sergeant Rodwell was there with a man in a suit.

Then the man she'd seen with Sergeant Rodwell had come to the house to ask her questions. He'd been quite nice. She'd told him that Fatty'd be back and that he could look after himself. But he'd given her a funny look and she knew he hadn't believed her. And then, when he'd gone, she had cried because she knew how badly she'd let Fatty down. If they caught him and brought him back it would be all her fault and he'd never forgive her.

She buried her head in the pillows and wept.

Will reached the bridge and stood resting against the parapet waiting for his breathing to slow down. The sun was beginning to rise. Carmel Chapel was washed with a soft pink light. Birds began to sing in the grounds of the Big House.

He slipped in through the gates. Mervyn Prosser had already begun his work. The thick jungle of grass had been hacked away. The statues were all gone. The ground beneath where they had lain for so many years was bare in contrast to the verdant green grass. A concrete mixer stood close to the boarded-up French windows.

He walked swiftly across the garden, his heart beating fast, hoping that Mervyn hadn't uncovered it first. He knew now that while he'd sat in this garden one hot afternoon drinking tea with Agnes Medlicott, not ten yards away the boy had been hidden.

He found the privet hedge. He guessed it had been planted sometime after the war, to hide the door, and the rockery had been built to cover the unsightly corrugated iron of the air-raid shelter.

He had to breathe in to squeeze behind the privet hedge. His heart beat painfully and he stood and looked at the door for a long time, unsure now whether he wanted to know what he would find on the other side of the door.

Then, he took the bunch of keys from his pocket. He'd kept

them from his days on the force; skeleton keys that had never failed to open a multitude of locks. He tried three of them in the rusty lock with no luck. The fourth key turned stiffly and the lock clicked.

He tried unsuccessfully to steady his breathing.

The door opened with the minimum of force. He took a deep breath of cool air before he stepped into the blackness of the shelter.

The air inside was fetid. He covered his nose with his hand. For a few moments he allowed his eyes time to adjust to the darkness which was almost absolute, only a weak shaft of daylight penetrated a foot or so in front of him. With faltering hands he took out his torch and switched it on.

The shelter was filled with cobwebs, curtains of cobwebs from ceiling to floor. He pulled them away in handfuls. The torchlight picked out the bright eyes of a rat. The rat surveyed him for a second and then scurried away.

In one corner lay the rusty frame of a camp bed, the canvas rotted away. A few scattered tins lay in a pile, corroded with rust. A heap of pop bottles. Two rusty candlesticks.

This was where Lawrence Bevan had spent his last hours. Dear God! And he had sat not ten feet away drinking tea with Agnes Medlicott!

There was no sign, as he'd imagined and dreaded of the remains of Lawrence Bevan. No small skeleton among the dusty debris in the shelter.

Then he saw the box. A small metal box covered in a thick layer of dust and cobwebs. He stooped forward, picked it up and stepped back out into the fresh morning air, locked the door and crossed the gardens. Gardens lit now with a watery light. A magpie eyed him malevolently and screeched from the chimney top of the house and a cold wind brought a salty whiff of the faraway sea.

*

As soon as the town came to life he hurried out into the town and bought a tape measure. Coming back to his room at the Firkin, he noticed the sunlight, which slanted through the window and fell in a pool of light at the statue's feet.

Ekaterina Velasco Olivares

He looked at the left foot of the statue. It was whole. The right one had been chipped at some time. He pulled out the tape measure and measured the left foot across the base of the toes. Eleven centimetres.

He measured the right foot. Eleven centimetres to where it was chipped. It still had five toes, the sixth toe had been broken away.

Ekaterina Velasco Olivares had six toes on her right foot!

He found one of his old notebooks and turned the pages carefully.

There!

Thus ... successive generations of human beings may have an excessive number ... or a deficiency of fingers and toes.

Fatty Bevan had underlined the words carefully and in the margin he had written: MeASURe BOTH CATS FeeT.

Now he knew what had been troubling him. He remembered Iffy Meredith stepping into her daps in the kitchen of the old house in Inkerman Terrace. Her bare brown feet on the linoleum, and one extra toe on her right foot!

The boy had known the truth, had uncovered a closely guarded secret.

Other thoughts raced through Will's mind: the old Italian reading the book behind the counter of the café; Laurie Lee's journey down through Spain.

Fatty Bevan had worked it out for himself but had someone wanted to stop him from letting the secret out? Someone who had kept him, against his will, locked in an old air-raid shelter. And then what had happened? He couldn't bear to contemplate it.

Ideas were coming fast and Will hardly dared pause for fear of losing the train of his thoughts. He scribbled down a few notes, then he visited the town library where he took down the *Yellow Pages* directory from the reference section and flipped through it.

Please God, let it still exist. His heart leapt when he saw the name in black print. He wrote down the address and telephone number, and then rang a cab from the telephone booth in the entrance lobby.

Will walked up the gravel driveway, and stood before the enormous oak door and tugged the bell pull.

A grille in the door opened and dark eyes scrutinised him.

'Will Sloane,' he said.

'Ah. Sister Immaculata is expecting you.'

Sister Immaculata, an ancient-looking nun, sat behind a large table in a bare room, the white wall behind her punctuated only by a stark crucifix, as black as gangrene.

'How may I help you, Mr Sloane?'

'Perhaps you can't, Sister. I'm trying to trace an ex-pupil of yours, but she was here a very long time ago.'

'Well, the only good thing about old age, Mr Sloane, is the improvement of long-term memory. Try me.'

Will could barely contain his impatience as Sister Immaculata turned the pages of a huge black book the size of an old family Bible.

'Here we are,' she said and beamed up at Will.

He closed his eyes as she spoke.

'Elizabeth Gwendoline Meredith. She won a place here

because she was the most outstanding student in her primary school.'

Will's heart began to race.

'So she was a pupil here?'

'No,' said the old nun.

'But you said—'

'She was due to start here. She was an orphan, and was going to come here full time. Some of our pupils stay here all the time, we make special provision during the holidays. Her grandparents, who had brought her up, had both recently died.'

'So what happened?'

'She'd been fitted out with the uniform but she never arrived.'

'What?'

'Don't look so alarmed.'

'But she didn't arrive. Did she have an accident?'

'No. It says here that there was a last-minute telephone call from someone, a foreign relative of hers. There was a change of plan. She went abroad to live. Her suitcase had already arrived, but we never actually met Elizabeth Meredith.'

Will's head swam.

Mervyn Prosser had seen Iffy Meredith in her uniform down by the docks talking to a boy. Someone had rung the school to say there was a change of plan! This school was miles from the docks.

'Thank you, Sister,' he said.

'Mr Sloane, do you feel all right? You've gone very pale. Can I get you something?'

'No, really. Thank you for the information.'

'There's just one more thing, Mr Sloane, that might be of help.'

Sister Immaculata rang a small brass handbell that was on her desk and, as though by magic, a young nun appeared in the doorway almost immediately. Sister Immaculata stood up and spoke quietly to her and the young sister scurried away.

Rain had begun to fall as the enormous oak door of St Martha's Convent closed quietly behind Will Sloane.

'May God bless you, Mr Sloane,' Sister Immaculata called out through the grille.

'He just did, Sister.'

He walked slowly away down the drive. Beneath his feet the gravel crunched as though he was treading on ancient bones. Clutched tightly to his hammering chest was the battered suitcase that Sister Immaculata had given him.

There was no sign of Fatty. Days passed. The ponds were dragged. Weeks passed. Posters were nailed up all over the town. The policeman who had spoken to Iffy went away.

Iffy stood outside the Limp and looked at a poster pinned to a tree. Fatty's face stared out at her. She swallowed the lump in her throat at the sight of his tousled curls, the cheeky tilt of his head. It was a black and white photograph which didn't show the blue and black of his eyes, the silky dark eyelashes, his skin the colour of toasted tea cakes.

Iffy was coming up past the hump-backed bridge when she heard the whistle. 'Wee ooh wit!'

She stood quite still and listened. Her heart bumped wildly against her blazer badge.

'Wee oo wi i i it!'

She'd know that sound anywhere. It was Fatty's whistle.

'Iffy! Under the bridge.'

She looked around fearfully, but the road was deserted. It was dark under the bridge, the slippery walls were dappled with moving shadows and all around her was the glug and slippery suck of the river.

'Fatty?' she whispered into the darkness.

'Over here.'

Fatty stepped out of the shadows.

He was dirtier that she'd ever seen him. Stinking, rotten dirty.

'What are you wearin'?'

'Recognise it?'

She peered at him, looking him up and down. It was Bessie's Sunday school frock. It still had frog blood on it.

'I got it out of the ash tip, thought it might come in useful. Shut your eyes a minute.'

She shut them tight.

'You can open them now.'

Iffy squealed.

'Hush up, Iffy! Someone'll hear you.'

Iffy put her hand over her mouth.

Fatty's syrupy-coloured hair was gone. In its place were thick black curls.

'I can see the join,' she said.

'Take Bessie down to Morrissey's tomorrow for sweets. She won't want to marry him when she sees he's bald. He's got a head like a baby's arse.'

'Fatty, how did you get it?'

He tapped the side of his nose. She hated it when he did that.

'They'll catch you if you go running round wearing a girl's frock and a wig!'

'I've got some new clothes too. Iffy, how come they realised I was missing so quick?'

And, swallowing hard, she told him the truth.

'What the bloody hell did you do that for?'

'I just didn't want you to go.'

'Look, Iffy, I've got to go, but I'll be back one day.'

'Promise?'

'Cross my heart and hope to die.'

'But the police are looking for you. They've got posters of you up all over town. Where've you been hiding?'

'Can't tell you that. But they won't catch me. I'm going away, Iffy.'

'You can't just go away.'

'There's things I've got to do. Remember what Bridgie said that day about secrets? Well, she was right, there are secrets in this town.'

'But Bridgie Thomas is nuts!'

'Remember the wishes we made?' he said.

She nodded.

'Well, mine came true. I said I wanted to be an orphan.' There were tears in his eyes as he spoke. 'That night under the bridge when we heard . . .'

Iffy took his hand.

'He's not my dad! That was the best part of the wish. I know that that fat spiteful bastard isn't my dad and I'm glad about that.'

'Where will you go?'

'Abroad.'

'Abroad!'

'I've got a map, I've got some money. I've got something really special too. Look!'

He took out the jar and showed her. Iffy stared at it.

'What's so special about that?'

It was grimy old jar with a few holes punched in the tin lid. She looked closer, just an empty, steamed-up jar.

Iffy stared at Fatty as though he'd lost his marbles.

'It's just an empty jar, Fatty.'

He sighed, put the jar down very carefully, and smiled sadly.

'I'm going to follow the river down to the sea.'

'But you can't!'

It had been a plan of theirs. They'd always said that one day they were going to follow the river down to the sea. They were going to wear wellies and take sandwiches and fishing nets and sleep under the bridges at night. For a month at least. They were just waiting for the right day.

And now Fatty was going all by himself.

'What will you do when you get to the sea?'

'Get on a boat and hide away.'

He was the bravest boy she knew. The bravest boy in Wales and probably in the whole wide world.

'But Fatty . . .'

'Don't worry.'

'When are you going?'

'Tonight. About nine. I've got to go and see someone first. Can you meet me here? Promise me, though, not a word to anybody mind. I've got to trust you this time, Iffy.'

She felt her cheeks go red with shame.

'Okay,' she said quietly.

She left him then, and ran up the hill towards home. Darkness crept up the river like smoke. The windows of Carmel Chapel blazed with the last glow of the sun and turned black.

A light burned in an upstairs window of the Big House. She felt the eyes of the old woman upon her, but she was no longer afraid. She stopped beneath the lamp post by the Dentist's Stone. She turned around slowly and waved. The old woman waved back, and then the light went out.

The gaslights began to light up the windows of Inkerman. Somewhere a mouse squeaked.

Iffy slipped out of the back door just as the town clock chimed the first stroke of nine. The breeze was cold and she shivered. A dog howled somewhere in the darkness.

'Wee ooh wit!'

She legged it down the hill, over the slippery bank and under the dark archway of the bridge.

Fatty's face leapt at her from the shadows, glowing in the torchlight.

'I brought you some sandwiches,' she said. 'I made them myself. Bread and butter and sugar. Your favourite.'

'Thanks, Iffy.'

She swallowed the lump in her throat. Goosegog size.

'Please don't go.'

'Listen, I've got to go, but I promise I'll be back for you.'

She didn't believe him.

'Remember the wish you made that night, Iffy?'

'You don't know what I wished.'

He smiled.

'I'm gonna try and make it come true for you.'

'But you can't.'

'You'll understand sometime, Iffy. I've got to go.'

His eyes gleamed in the torchlight and she knew that she would always love him.

He blew her a kiss. A steamy kiss that wafted from his warm fingers. That kiss was fragrant with the beautiful smell of bubblegum and horse shit and a million other things.

She tried to smile, but the emptiness of a world without him was too awful to bear. She rubbed the tears from her eyes with the back of her freezing fists and swallowed the lump in her throat, the size of a plum.

Fatty plonked a smacker right on her lips.

Then he was gone. She touched her lips. They buzzed with the heat of him. She watched as he sloped off into the moonlight. Watched as he walked away down the river, past all the farms that she didn't yet know the name of, all the way down the valley that led to the sea that she had never seen.

The moon was full. Agnes Medlicott stood behind the curtains of the upstairs window of the Big House looking down into the darkness below. The statues in the garden gleamed in the silvery light which dripped through the wavering trees. The water in the fishpond reflected the stars.

She knew now that she had been right to come back. She thought that she'd probably always known the truth, but hadn't wanted to admit to it. It was one thing to be married to a philanderer, but her husband had been much more wicked than that.

It had happened while she'd been away for a few days. When she came back he'd told her about Kat, only he hadn't told her the whole truth. He'd said Kat had been pregnant and had given birth early. The midwife, Mrs Bevan had helped him with the delivery, but the baby girl had been born dead.

Agnes Medlicott had thought at first it was his baby, but now she knew that it wasn't. She had never seen Kat again. He'd said it was imperative to get Kat away, save her from scandal and she had gone away. The baby had been buried beneath the lilac bush and no one had known except Ellen Bevan and he'd paid her handsomely for her trouble. But Agnes knew now! She'd dug up the lilac bush and uncovered the box. It had held no remnants of a dead baby only a pile of old love letters.

Ekaterina had been sent back to Spain having been told that the baby had died! That poor, poor girl. Agnes knew what it was like to lose a child. How could he have been so cruel. No doubt he'd taken great pleasure in telling Kat of her lover's suicide.

And then that night she had seen the child with her own eyes, the very spit of her mother. Dear God! Looking at Iffy through the gate was like looking at Kat all over again!

And the boy. That beautiful, brave boy. That day when he'd crept through the pipe, she hadn't meant to scare him so. She'd kept him safe. She'd lied to the Inspector. He was a nice man, a good man and she'd felt bad about it, but she'd respected the boy's wishes to keep silent.

She saw the movement down by the bridge.

She had said goodbye to Fatty earlier, had given him plenty of money, a map, Ekaterina's last known address in Valencia and then she'd locked the door to the air-raid shelter for the last time.

Moonlight fell on the boy's face as he turned to wave back at the bridge. The light picked out his eyes, a glistening blue-black blur. She knew that he was crying. Then he turned and walked away down the river bank into the night.

It was the last time she would ever set eyes on him. She waved from the darkness of the window knowing he couldn't see her. She waved until her arm grew numb and the numbness spread through all her body.

December 1963

It was winter. The snow lay thick on the Sirhowy Road, puddles of ice gleamed in the pale winter sunlight and the river was a twist of frosted glass. As they passed the gates to the Big House Mr Sandicock stepped out in front of them.

'Here,' he said gruffly to Iffy. 'Mrs Medlicott has saved you some more of those postcards with the foreign stamps you collect.'

'Thanks, Mr Sandicock,' said Iffy, and she took the brown paper bag containing the postcards that he held out to her and put them quickly in the pocket of her gabardine mac.

She had loads of them now. She had memorised all the post marks.

Santander
Bilbao
Calahorra
Logrono
Zaragoza
Teruel

She loved the sound of the foreign names and just saying them made her shiver with pleasure.

She looked up at the upstairs window in the Big House. She and Billy waved every time they passed, but the old woman was too weak to wave back. Iffy knew that something unseen passed between her and Mrs Medlicott, a silent message of hope.

She sat there for hours every day in her bath chair staring down the valley. She was very ill and the doctor called every day and sometimes the figure of a nurse could be seen standing behind her chair. Iffy'd heard Mrs Bunting tell Nan that Mrs Medlicott had had a stroke and could no longer speak, or do anything for herself, couldn't even understand what was going on around her.

But they were wrong.

Each time a postcard arrived Mrs Medlicott knew that Fatty was a step closer to his destination. When old Sandicock handed them over to Iffy she knew too. It was their secret: that the bravest boy in Wales and probably the whole wide world had nearly made it.

Iffy and Billy passed the rec, climbed the stile and struggled through the drifts of snow in Dancing Duck Lane. They pressed their small noses up against the dirt-streaked windows of Carty Annie's lopsided house. Their hot breath made rivulets in the grime on the cracked panes as they strained to see inside.

It was dark inside the gloomy kitchen. Ice hung on the

cobwebbed curtains. Sunlight slipped into the kitchen and the cobwebs dripped with silver light. Iffy held her breath and clasped Billy's hand tight.

The large pickling jar stood on the dresser between filthy cracked cups and the leery-eyed Toby jugs.

Holding tightly to one another Iffy and Billy saw with their own wide eyes what Fatty had seen. There, on the dresser, inside the misty jar, the tiny bodies of captive angels writhed and danced an agitated dance. The small, angry faces stared out at them. Their eyes were bright and wild in their pale faces, their sharp, pearly teeth glinted in the sunlight.

'Fuckin' Ada!' said Billy.

Iffy turned and stared at him.

His words echoed all around.

Iffy's wild laughter rang out on the crisp cold air. As she hugged Billy she felt the spirit of Fatty all around her.

And then they ran, flying away down the lane as the snow began to fall thick and fast.

The town clock chimed. The moon was high and full. A milky white moon spinning over the mountains. Somewhere on a hill farm a dog barked.

Will pulled on his jacket and put a torch into his pocket. As he was going downstairs his landlady appeared.

'Mr Sloane!'

He turned around in alarm.

'This letter came for you. Marlene Baker handed it over the bar and asked me to make sure you got it. They've rushed her mother into hospital, so she couldn't wait to see you.'

'Is she all right?'

'Apparently she's had a massive heart attack. There's not much hope I'm afraid.'

Will took the bulky envelope from her and slipped it into his pocket.

'Thank you.'

He walked up through the deserted town, past the darkened windows of Gladys's Gowns and on past Zeraldo's café. He stepped into the archway of the bridge and stood there in the moving blackness. Then he shone his torch over the roof of the bridge.

GEORGE LOVES BRIDGET
CM LOVES EVO
EVO LOVES CM
LB 4 eGM
MERVYN PROSSER IS A FAT BASTARD

Ekaterina Velasco Olivares loves Charlie Meredith.

Will knew that Charlie Meredith had died at the hands of Dr Medlicott. He guessed that the suicide note would have been cobbled together from the letters that Charlie had sent Ekaterina. He had found the letters in the box in the shelter and had read them in his room. They were heart-breaking. He'd found out enough about Charlie Meredith from reading them to know that he had truly loved Ekaterina. He knew the plans they'd been making to run away and make a life for themselves and their baby. Ekaterina would not have left her baby behind.

Something must have happened.

He had also looked through the battered old suitcase that Sister Immaculata had unearthed for him from the convent attic and had held in his hands the mildewed pile of regulation convent cotton drawers and vests, the grey school socks, aertex shirts and flannel games shorts.

Beneath the sensible viyella nightdresses he had found an odd assortment of articles. Reminders of Iffy's home in Inkerman Terrace: a green glass bottle of holy water from Lourdes and an empty wooden biscuit barrel. And, last of all, wrapped in tissue paper that disintegrated at his touch, a pair of ruined red sandals and a twisted red and white cricket belt.

He'd always known that Iffy Meredith had lied to him.

What was it that Bessie Tranter had said? That Fatty was always talking about running away and making his fortune and coming back for Iffy. She'd said he was sweet on Iffy.

And he had come back for her! Mervyn Prosser had seen her down by the docks talking to a boy.

Will's one unsolved case was resolved. And yet, instead of euphoria, he felt an awful sense of deflation. His last great challenge was over and all he had left to contemplate was death.

Will turned off the torch and left the dark shadow of the bridge.

Somewhere in the grounds of the Big House an owl hooted as he walked on past the padlocked gates. He passed the rec where the roundabout turned slowly in the moonlight. For a moment he thought he heard the sound of children's voices. A cool wind blew up the valley from the faraway sea.

He climbed over the rotting stile and stopped in alarm. He thought he saw the shadow of a body hanging from the gnarled old tree, but it was just a trick of the moonlight. He walked on down the silent lane. Dancing Duck Lane.

He turned on his torch. Only the rubble remained of an old house.

He stood there in the moonlight for a long time, then felt in his pocket for the envelope and shone the torch onto the crumpled paper.

Dear Will,

My time is coming to an end. All potions have their sell-by dates. I think you may, by now, be nearing the end of your search. I have enclosed a photograph for you. Somehow I felt it was important. Ellen Bevan, she was Ophelia, you know. And a very beautiful one.

304

Will held the photograph in his trembling hand. A yellowing photograph cut from an old theatre programme.

He looked with astonishment at the woman in the photograph and felt his throat constrict with emotion.

He read on.

Sir, in my heart there was a kind of fighting, that would not let me sleep . . . There's a divinity that shapes our ends, rough hew them how we will . . .

A quotation from *Hamlet*.

Will, she gave you a little love and comfort in your time of need. You gave some back and then, out of guilt, you steeped yourself in grief. Forgive yourself now.

Look at her face and remember. Look at her face and know.

He had betrayed his wife. He had taken another woman in his arms. He'd met her on a routine call at the home for bad girls. They'd arranged to meet for a drink. Jenny she'd said her name was, he'd never known her second name. It hadn't been love but it had been comfort of a sort. Afterwards he'd felt suffused with shame and guilt.

With a heavy heart he read the last lines of the letter.

When I first saw you, you reminded me of someone. Now I know without a doubt who that someone is. I pray, Will, with all my heart that you have time enough left . . .

Tears clouded his eyes, the writing on the page wobbled and blurred. He wiped his eyes and tried to focus. His hands shook uncontrollably, his heartbeat was erratic.

I pray, Will, with all my heart that you have time enough left to find him, because Will, your son, Lawrence Bevan, is out there somewhere.

They were Gladys Baker's last words to him.

The moonlight was growing brighter. Dandelion clocks, stinging nettles and yellow poppies grew in wild profusion. He took out a bottle from the envelope and turned it over in his hands. Gladys Baker had asked Marlene to make him up a bottle of Carty Annie's herbal brew.

He unscrewed the top, put the bottle to his lips and drank. He only hoped it would work and he would have enough time left to find the boy.

The long lost boy.

His son.

All those achingly long years of loneliness after his wife had died. All those years he'd punished himself. And yet . . .

The emptiness that had filled him up for so long evaporated now in the moonlight.

His heart beat steadily for the first time in many years. He felt the warm blood pumping through his veins.

Dear God. Out there, out there somewhere at the end of all this darkness was his son.

My son.

My son.

My own flesh and blood.

Not a boy any more now. He must be at least . . . No, it didn't matter how old he was. He was his very own boy.

Will looked up at the moon. A huge spinning moon in a dark starless sky. And as he looked he thought for a moment that a red kite crossed it. One bright star splintered the darkness way above the moon. Then another, until there were four stars in the night sky. Stars as bright as ice, hot as molten silver.

The red kite slashed the moon.

One star wobbled and left the sky. The space where it had been glowed brightly for a few seconds. The star fell towards the spinning earth.

He dropped down onto his knees, ran his fingers through the damp soil and let it trickle through his fingers. There in the coal-black earth he found the splintered remnants of tiny bones and the fragments of a hundred broken jars. Jars that once held so terrible and marvellous a secret.

He stood up slowly.

Tomorrow he would follow the river down towards the faraway sea to search out his own miracle.

Glossary

Alley Bompers: shiny silver marbles
Bailey: backyard, but often, as in the iron workers' cottages, a communal yard that ran the length of the terraces
Belloching: roaring or shouting
Black Pats: the local name for cockroaches
Bosh: kitchen sink
Churros: popular snack in Spain, loops of deep-fried batter usually in a spiral shape
Cop: name for the local co-operative society
The Corn Shop: shop that sold all types of chicken feed, horse feed, etc
Cwtching: cuddle
Daps: local word for plimsolls
Doubler: working a double shift
Duw: God
Fausty: damp-smelling, dirty
Fussell's Milk: a thick white condensed type of tinned milk
Grandfather chair: high-backed chair, often called a Captain's chair
Gwli: the gwlis were the back lanes or alleyways that divided the rows of houses
Had her/his hair off: (Bessie had her hair off) Bessie was in a temper

Haisht: hush, ssshh!
Half-soaked: not all there, dopey
Jackie Long-Legs: Daddy Long-Legs
Kidney beans: runner beans
Peed the bed leaking: wet the bed in a big way
Pwp: shit
Spanish: liquorice
Tamping down: (as in tamping down with rain) raining very heavily
Toc H lamp: (She was as dull as a Toc H lamp) used to describe someone dopey. Badges worn by members of Toc H had an oil lamp on them (oil lamps burn with a very dim light)
Tom Pepper: liar
Tump: hill/hillock
Twp: dopey, not all there
Wetted: as in wetted the tea (brewed, mashed)
Wimberries: another name for bilberries or huckleberries
Yellow poppies: the Welsh poppy. *Meconopsis Cambrica* (Latin)